# A Taste for Love

# A Taste for Love

JENNIFER YEN

RAZORBILL

# RAZORBILL

An imprint of Penguin Random House LLC, New York

First published in the United States of America by Razorbill,
an imprint of Penguin Random House LLC, 2021

Copyright © 2021 by Jennifer Yen

Penguin supports copyright. Copyright fuels creativity, encourages diverse voices,
promotes free speech, and creates a vibrant culture. Thank you for buying an authorized
edition of this book and for complying with copyright laws by not reproducing, scanning,
or distributing any part of it in any form without permission. You are supporting writers
and allowing Penguin to continue to publish books for every reader.

Razorbill & colophon are registered trademarks of Penguin Random House LLC.

Visit us online at penguinrandomhouse.com.

LIBRARY OF CONGRESS CATALOGING-IN-PUBLICATION DATA
Names: Yen, Jennifer, author.
Title: A taste for love / Jennifer Yen.
Description: New York : Razorbill, 2021. | Audience: Ages 12+. |
Summary: Both high school senior Liza Yang and her mother share a love and talent
for baking but disagree on the subject of dating, especially when Mrs. Yang turns her
annual baking contest into a matchmaking scheme.
Identifiers: LCCN 2020049702 | ISBN 9780593117521 (hardcover) |
ISBN 9780593117545 (trade paperback) | ISBN 9780593117538 (ebook)
Subjects: CYAC: Dating (Social customs)—Fiction. | Baking—Fiction. |
Taiwanese Americans—Fiction. | Asian Americans—Fiction.
Classification: LCC PZ7.1.Y48 Tas 2021 | DDC [Fic]—dc23
LC record available at https://lccn.loc.gov/2020049702

Printed in the United States of America

1 3 5 7 9 10 8 6 4 2

Design by Dana Li
Text set in ITC Legacy Serif

For those who still dream in secret.
It's never too late to be brave.

# A
# Taste
# for
# Love

# Chapter 1

"It is a truth universally acknowledged, that a mother in possession of great wisdom, must be in want—nay, in need—of a daughter who will listen."

The neon letters mock me from the plaque's smooth black surface. Surely, Mom hasn't twisted the words of one of my favorite authors. My jaw swings open, but the curse never quite leaves my lips. Instead, I squeeze my eyes shut and wish for the words hanging over my desk to disappear. I pry one eyelid open.

Nope. It hasn't changed.

*Jane Austen, give me strength.*

The corner of Mom's mouth twitches as I swivel to look at her.

"So, what do you think? Sharon was running a sale, and I thought this would be the perfect addition to your room."

Of course it came off Etsy. I wish I'd never introduced her to that hell site. It's like Pinterest for people with insomnia and money.

"It's clever, right? I came up with the quote myself," she continues, eyes glinting. "By the way, I don't know why you love that story so much. If I were Mrs. Bennet, those girls would have been married off in half the time."

I cringe. If fictional characters aren't safe from her meddling, what chance do I have? I can't even remember a time when Mom wasn't bossing me around. I'm pretty sure Jeannie and I were barely out of diapers when she taught us the two most important things to have in life:

1. A useful college degree, so we can take care of her when she's old.
2. A good husband, so he can take care of us.

Not one to leave things to chance, the minute we hit puberty, Mom also gave us her cardinal rules for dating:

1. No dating while you're in school.
2. Only Asian boys allowed. The more traditional, the better.
2.5. The best type of Asian to date is Taiwanese, then Chinese. There are no others.
3. He must be tall. At least three inches more than you.
4. He has to be smart and choose a stable career like doctor or engineer.
5. He must be Asian (this point is so important, it's stressed *twice*).

Jeannie, my older sister, is the poster child for obedient Asian daughters. She followed all but the first rule to the letter, something Mom easily forgave. To make matters worse, everyone loves her.

"She's so graceful and well spoken!"

"Jeannie is the nicest person! She's always smiling."

"I love her style. I'm always stalking her Insta to see what she's wearing!"

Jeannie's so pretty a modeling scout chased after her for weeks to sign her. In fact, we have one of her first pictures sitting on the mantel. Whenever we have guests, Dad always jokes it's the one that came in the frame.

As for me?

I'm the rebel—or if you ask Mom, the troublemaker.

"Watch where you're going, Liza! I can't believe you just walked into a parked car."

"Why did you have to say that in front of Mrs. Zhou? I'm so embarrassed!"

"Stop slouching. It looks lazy."

And let's not forget one of Mom's favorites:

"You act too smart. Boys don't like girls who are smarter than them."

She had a million of these—advice for how to make a boy like me. Not any boy, mind you. Only the ones who fit her list of rules. It didn't take long for me to realize what she really wanted was for me not to be . . . me.

Like that was going to happen.

So I broke her rules. Not to annoy her, though it was an added bonus. I just didn't see the point. Why make myself something I wasn't just to convince a boy to date me? Especially when there were guys out there who already wanted to.

I hid it from her, of course. I didn't have a death wish.

The first time Mom caught me, I was at the movie theater with my first real boyfriend, Jeremy. We met shortly after he moved from Ohio with his family. He had sea-green eyes and a mop of chestnut curls, and I was convinced we'd be together forever. My cousin Mary spotted us two rows ahead of her. By the time I got home, Mom was livid. A two-hour lecture on boys and the only thing they all want followed. I also got a bonus lecture on why all non-Asian boys should be avoided.

Three hours of my life I'll never get back. I still have nightmares about it.

After six straight months of house arrest, Mom decided I'd been punished enough. So long as I followed her rules, I could hang out with my friends again.

Did I turn into a law-abiding citizen?

Not even close.

She still wanted me to date only Asian boys. I was going to give her everything but. Jeremy was just the first. He turned out to be a total weeb, by the way. We broke up when he found out I wasn't Japanese. Mario, I met in gym class, but it didn't last long. He got tired of how clumsy I was. After Isaiah, who dumped me because I hated sports, there was Mason, who obsessed over being shorter than me.

Eventually, Mom changed tactics. Suddenly, I was subjected to a never-ending string of matchmaking attempts. Some were blatantly obvious, like the time I came home and found a complete stranger sitting at our kitchen table.

"Liza! I want you to meet Zhang Wei! He'll be staying with us for the next two months as our new foreign exchange student!"

Mom put him in our guest bedroom. Every morning, he paraded past my door in nothing but tighty-whities and a grin. He couldn't leave fast enough.

Then there was Wang Yong. He was her coworker's nephew. We ran into him at the pharmacy where he was shadowing for the summer. Mom had smiled innocently as she pointed in his direction.

"Go ask him where the tampons are."

"But we could just check the aisles . . ."

"Go. Now!"

It was the most cringeworthy convo *ever*. I left with burning cheeks and the determination to never go back.

Other times, it was a crime of opportunity. Like Tony, the delivery boy who worked at our family's restaurant.

"He was studying chemistry, Liza. He's probably going to be a doctor one day."

Let's not forget the son of Mom's best customers, who happened to attend my school—Li Qiang.

"Doesn't his name remind you of that captain in *Mulan*? You like him, don't you?"

Yeah, well, Li Shang was hot. Li Qiang reminded me of a dumpy tree frog. Hard pass.

It's been two years, and Mom hasn't let up. It's become like a game between us. She sets me up with a snobby jerk or fobby nerd. I dodge them with an excuse or two. I've leveled up so much, I could take on the big boss.

At least, I hope so.

Recently, Mom's found other things to focus on. She's pressured me about college, which is fine with me. Scholarship deadlines and class rankings are ideal distractions to keep her from finding out about Brody. We've been dating for two months, but my heart still pounds every time I see him. Tall, blond, and with the whitest teeth I've ever seen, Brody is the definition of all-American. He's the captain of the basketball team and has a full scholarship to play for UT–Austin next year. He's also everything Mom hates about the guys I date. If I can make it to graduation without another one of her well-meaning matches, I'll be set.

Now Mom clears her throat, drawing me out of my thoughts.

"Just remember. Life is the sum of your choices." She glances pointedly at the plaque. "And it's my job to teach you how to make good ones."

With that, she walks off toward the kitchen. I go back to staring at the abomination on my wall.

That's not a reminder.

It's a declaration of war.

# Chapter 2

Whoever said "The way to a man's heart is through his stomach" was obviously thinking of Mom's famous buns. Her steamed buns, that is. Every time our customers bite into the soft, white dough, their mouths sing her praise. Some like the savory ones filled with Chinese barbecue or vegetables and vermicelli. Others prefer the sweetness of red bean or custard cream. Even I can't resist. I'm always getting caught sneaking a fresh bun off the oven tray.

Like today.

"*Aiya!* How many times have I told you not to touch them when they're hot?"

I can't answer Mom. My mouth is already stuffed with red bean and dough, the flavor unmatched even by the buns from the bakery we used to live down the street from back in Taipei. It takes a second for my tongue to register the heat, and I'm forced to puff out my cheeks like a chipmunk until it stops burning.

She cocks an eyebrow. "I told you."

"Sorry, Mom," I mumble automatically. "I'll remember next time."

"I'll believe it when I see it, Liza. Now go help Tina out front."

I stay in the back until the last bite of the bun makes its way down to join the others in my stomach. Then I wash my hands before stepping out to greet the customers.

I kind of wish I hadn't promised to help out today. It's Saturday morning, and we've already got a line out the door. When I woke up earlier, the moon was still flirting with the horizon. Two hours and endless batches of pastries later, the bakery brims with activity. Mom's bustling about, answering this question and that while restocking the perpetually empty shelves. At least a dozen people browse the display cases, their shopping trays weighed down with buns and bread. Tina, our neighbor and two years younger than me, is busy bagging the latest batch of *bo luo* bread in cellophane sheets.

I walk over to the cash register and wait for the first purchase of the day. Soon, a woman in her forties steps up to the counter holding a tray laden with breakfast items.

I smile politely. "Are you ready to check out?"

She glances at the case of neatly decorated cakes and points to the chocolate cake with strawberry filling. Each slice is topped with a single berry, delicately carved so it fans out atop the airy brown frosting.

"Are the strawberries fresh?" she asks in Mandarin.

"Yes, they are," I answer immediately.

"Then I'll take one, please."

I wrap it in a square paper box, the flaps on top twisting together to form a paper bow.

"Anything else?"

She shakes her head. I ring up each of her items and hand over the bag with her receipt.

"Thank you. We hope to see you back soon."

The line for the register continues nonstop until lunch. By then, we've sold hundreds of dollars' worth of pastries, and I'm ready to take a nap right there on the counter.

This is a far cry from when our family first immigrated to the States twelve years ago. Mom spoke very little English, so she'd sell her buns to our neighbors for spare cash. Word spread about how good they were, and soon, she had enough orders to start her own baking business. Right before my freshman year, Mom and Dad decided to open the bakery along with the restaurant. They found a spot tucked in the corner of a giant shopping plaza in Chinatown. It was half hidden behind a pillar holding up the second floor. You'd think that would make it easy to overlook, but her talent has kept our little shop constantly packed with hungry customers.

Mom taps me on the shoulder. "Liza, why don't you go ask Dad to make us something to eat?"

"Okay."

I remove my apron and walk into the Chinese restaurant connected to the bakery. Each has its own storefront, so customers are often startled to walk in and find one big room. Only our regulars know the truth. The two are actually halves of a whole, with Dad running the restaurant while Mom bakes.

My favorite part about the family business is the name—Yin and Yang Restaurant and Bakery. It sounds like a marketing gimmick, but it's not. Mom bakes using secret Yin recipes passed down from her mother and grandmother. Dad, the oldest of the Yang clan, has never met a dish he can't replicate and often puts his own spin on it. Therefore, Yin and Yang.

"That's how I knew your father was the one," Mom likes to joke. "Although I suppose I could have just married another Yang."

The dining area is filled with wooden tables of various sizes and shapes, and the clamor of customers and plates fills my ears. I bypass the front counter as Danny takes down a phone order. A junior at Bellaire High School, he started working for Dad last summer. I nod hello and head toward the cloth curtain separating the kitchen from the front.

I duck through just as Dad tosses some sliced eggplant into the wok. Garlic perfumes the air as he throws a pinch of it into the mix. I take a deep breath and smile before moving over to stand quietly beside him. He works the fire like a bullfighter, the wok bobbing and weaving over the flames with each flick of his wrist. Dad then moves on to an order of pepper steak, followed by salt and pepper shrimp and mapo tofu. By the time he pours the last dish onto a plate, I'm drooling.

He pauses to look at me. "Is it lunchtime already?"

I nod. "It's almost two o'clock."

"You want anything special?"

My eyes drift over to the eggplant.

He laughs. "All right. One fried eggplant with chili salt for you, and one stir-fried with no salt for Mom. Anything else?"

I purse my lips. "Sesame chicken?"

"That's too much fried food, Liza. I'll make you some chicken with brown sauce instead."

I sigh. Why ask me if he's going to veto it anyway? I head back out to our usual table. Tina is already waiting, and she pats the seat beside her. The dining room has emptied out quite a bit, save for a table of businessmen having a late lunch. A few minutes later, Danny stops by to drop off the first of our dishes.

"I'll be back," he says.

An errant lock of black hair tumbles across his brow as he smiles at Tina. She flushes pink, her eyes never leaving him as he heads back inside. I suppress a grin. Mom better not catch her staring, though. She tried setting Danny up with me a few weeks ago after running out of the usual candidates. Thankfully, since I warned him this could happen, he lied and said he had a girlfriend.

Once he's done cooking, Dad joins us in the dining room. He and Mom eat quickly, always with one eye pinned on the doors. Barely fifteen minutes later, they've scurried back to their respective kitchens. Tina, Danny, and I can take our time, as long as we tend to any customers who walk in.

As luck would have it, today's stragglers all belong to the bakery, which means I'm the last one to finish and get stuck with cleaning duty. Not that it surprises me, of course. Dad's cooking definitely packs a room, but it's Mom's savories and sweets that keep them coming back time after time. Those tempted away by the shiny new bakeries in Chinatown invariably return with their heads hung low. Some of our customers even swear her treats changed their lives.

"My children wouldn't eat any vegetables until I brought your steamed veggie *baozi* home. One taste, and they were hooked. Now they eat everything!"

"Your egg tarts saved my marriage! My husband and I have never been happier!"

"Those multigrain *mantou* cured my stomach pain."

"I brought your taro cream buns to my boss at work and got a raise the next day. You're a miracle worker, Mrs. Yang!"

Yeah, right. I've eaten her buns for years, and I can say with complete certainty there's nothing magical about them—unless you want a bigger butt. For her part, Mom just thanks them and offers up a taste of whatever recipe she's working on.

With lunch finished, I tackle the huge to-do list Mom gave me this morning. I want to finish with time to get ready for Sarah's birthday party, especially since Mom agreed to extend my curfew by two hours. That hasn't happened since she forgot to spring the clocks forward for daylight saving, so I'm totally making the most of it.

I'm in the middle of printing fresh labels for the shelves when the bell connected to our front door jingles. I glance up and freeze. I know that face. It's on the front page of our local Chinese newspaper.

"What is *she* doing here?"

There's unbridled animosity in Mom's voice, and it surprises me. This woman isn't the first competitor to walk through the door, though she *is* the most well-known. One by one, our customers pause to stare at the local celebrity in their midst. They whisper among themselves, but it's not hard to guess what they're saying.

"Is that her? Teresa Lee?"

"*The* Teresa Lee?"

Her face is unmistakable. Ever since Mrs. Lee announced plans to open the latest branch of her award-winning bakeries in Houston, every Chinese media outlet has been putting out stories about her. Even the American news channels did a feature on the owner of Mama Lee's Bakery, including an interview with Mr. Lee and a tour of their headquarters. After all, she chose our city over Dallas, Los Angeles, and Seattle.

Mrs. Lee's hair curls softly around her face, the strands so black they glint blue under the fluorescent lights. Her eyes are framed with dark, winged liner, and her signature red lips play off her porcelain skin perfectly. I don't know much about fashion, but everything she's wearing oozes designer and expensive.

Though she likes to be neat, Mom's never been overly concerned about her appearance. Today, graying strands of her shoulder-length hair have come loose from the hairnet she wears when baking. Her face is bare, and she's dressed in one of the T-shirts I outgrew and a long linen skirt.

I catch Mom checking her reflection in the nearest display case. She surreptitiously fixes her hair and removes her apron as one of our customers approaches Mrs. Lee, speaking in a timid voice.

"Mrs. Lee, it's a pleasure to meet you! You're even more beautiful in person."

"Thank you!" She presses a hand to her chest. "It means so much to me."

Another customer steps forward. "How is Mr. Lee? Is your family well?"

"Everyone's great. It's so lovely of you to ask," she answers.

An older man steps forward, his phone in his shaking hand.

"Mrs. Lee. May I take a picture with you?"

The request is followed by many more. The delights of our bakery are forgotten as everyone lines up for a selfie. Mom growls, the sound low in her throat as she glares at Mrs. Lee. I nudge her with my elbow. She shakes off what I suspect are rather murderous thoughts and arranges her lips into a welcoming smile. Mom then steps out from behind the counter.

"Mrs. Lee! What a pleasant surprise!" she greets, hand extended. "I had no idea you were going to grace us with your presence."

Mrs. Lee smiles, but the gesture is strangely menacing. Maybe it's the way her lips are pulled tight across her unnaturally white teeth. As the two women size each other up, I settle in for some entertainment.

"Ah, Mrs. . . . . Yang, is it?"

*(Translation: I think I've heard your name somewhere.)*

"Yes," Mom says, mimicking Mrs. Lee and pressing a hand to her chest. "I'm honored you know who I am."

*(Of course you know who I am. Everyone knows.)*

Mrs. Lee gestures around the room. "It's quite a cute shop you have here."

*(Unlike my incredibly stylish, museum-quality stores.)*

"Well, thankfully my many customers don't mind that it's a bit small," Mom answers with a dismissive wave. "They really come for the pastries."

*(Flash won't make up for subpar baking, lady.)*

"I'll be thrilled if my new branch is half as successful as what you have here."

*(I'm going to drive over you with a truck filled with my famous breads.)*

"Then I must make a trip out to see it."

*(More like criticize how your buns are bland and your breads are hard.)*

Mrs. Lee flutters her lashes. "A little birdie told me you also run quite the local baking contest every year."

*(I'd never heard of it, so obviously it's not that big a deal.)*

"Yes, we're heading into our fifth one. It grows bigger every year, especially since we offer a scholarship to the winner," Mom replies, patting her hair. "It's a lot to do by yourself, but there's nothing more rewarding."

*(Unlike you, the face of an assembly line. I'll bet you don't even bake.)*

I snicker at the last bit. Suddenly, they both turn my way. Mrs. Lee walks over and looks at me from head to toe. She peers over her shoulder at Mom.

"Is this your daughter?"

Mom moves to stand beside me and puts a hand on my arm.

"This is my youngest, Liza. She'll be graduating high school in a couple of weeks."

"How lovely." Mrs. Lee meets my eye. "You're as cute as this shop."

I grit my teeth. Forget Mom; I'm going to kill her.

"My older daughter, Jeannie, is in New York." Mom can't resist boasting. "She's a very successful runway model."

Thanks. That makes me feel so much better.

"Is that right? Well, I hope I'll have a chance to meet her too," Mrs. Lee comments, baring her teeth again.

"You must be too busy to have a family of your own, I imagine," Mom counters. "Juggling all these locations."

Mrs. Lee rears back as if slapped. She's quick to resume looking unaffected.

"Actually, my husband and I have a wonderful son together. He's my little prince, although I suppose he's not so little anymore. He is, however, handsome, smart, and very popular."

I bet Prince Lee is just as conceited as she is. At least Mom won't set me up with this particular Asian boy, a small but important victory.

"Is he in town?" Mom asks.

Or will she?

Mrs. Lee straightens. "Actually, he's been busy with college and work, but I'm sure he'll come down and visit once summer starts."

She pans a smile across the shop to grace everyone inside. Even the dining room has fallen quiet, the restaurant customers listening closely to the exchange. They recognize good gossip when they hear it.

"Well, you'll have to excuse me, Mrs. Yang. There's still so much to do before the grand opening." Mrs. Lee peers down her nose at Mom. "Be grateful you don't have to deal with all those pesky permits and regulations. Ah, well. It's all part of running such a big company."

She pivots like a dancer, smirking right before giving Mom her back. With a practiced laugh, Mrs. Lee pauses for a few more selfies before sweeping out of the shop. Some of the customers follow her out, even though they came in to buy something. It's the last straw for Mom. She stomps through the curtain into the back, cursing in Mandarin all the way.

# Chapter 3

A couple of hours later, I cross the last thing off my list and get ready to head out. There's just one more thing I need to do. With a deep breath, I poke my head into the back.

"Mom, would you mind if I use the kitchen after closing?"

She glances up from wrapping chicken and vegetable buns, but before she can offer a reply, the words tumble out of my mouth.

"It's just for a few days, and I'll clean everything up before I leave."

In middle school, I helped out at the shop every weekend. I was obsessed with the magic of rising dough and the alchemy of blending flavors. Mom taught me so much during that time—the different kinds of flour she used, the techniques for making various pastries, and how to balance the bread-to-filling ratio. It was the one thing we could do together without getting into a screaming match.

Mom even encouraged me to enter several children's baking competitions. She never looked prouder than when I took home first place. It wasn't long before I had a shelf of trophies in my room to rival Jeannie's many ribbons and awards. As I got older, I started experimenting with my own recipes. Some were unmitigated disasters, but others impressed Mom so much she added them to the bakery's menu. The notebook I wrote them in still sits on a shelf in my room.

Mom arches a brow. "Why the sudden interest again?"

"I don't know. I've just been thinking about it lately."

It's only half a lie. I never stopped thinking about it. Baking is such a part of me I'm positive cream runs in my veins. As soon as I hit high school, I even asked Mom and Dad if I could attend culinary school instead of college. I figured with both of them in the industry, they would understand. Instead, it went over about as well as a slap in the face.

"Why would you want to do that?" Mom demanded. "We didn't sacrifice for this many years so you can pay someone else to learn what we can teach you at home."

Dad nodded. "Mom's right. Get a college degree first. Something useful. Don't waste our money on English or communications. Then we'll see."

"But I'm really good—"

"So is everyone else," he continued smoothly. "How about a degree in accounting? We need help working the numbers at Yin and Yang. It's taking up too much of our time, and I need someone good with a computer."

I tried several times to reason with them, but they refused to hear me out. It was decided last year that I'd attend Rice, close to home, next fall. I stopped baking soon after. What was the point? It was now a cruel reminder that my parents would only ever support Jeannie's dreams. I never told Mom and Dad the reason I quit, no matter how many times they asked.

It's only recently that my fingers started yearning for the feel of dough again. Maybe it's because I've spent the last two weekends binge-watching every baking show on Netflix. There's nothing quite like the high of a successful bake, after all.

"I do remember how much you used to love baking."

Mom's voice drags me back into the present. She inhales as if planning to say more but stops herself. I recognize the look in her eyes.

*You used to love baking with me.*

Again with the guilt. Still, I can't deny we had a lot of fun together.

I smile. "It's been a while since you added anything new to the menu. Maybe I can work on a few things while I'm here."

"That's not a bad idea," she answers after stacking the last wrapped bun on a tray. "I've been thinking the same thing. I wouldn't mind hearing your thoughts."

"Really?"

"Why not? Some of our customers' favorite buns are your creations."

My smile broadens. I'm glad she remembers. Maybe there's hope for my dreams yet.

"Okay! Um, I'll start working on some recipes."

"Good, and don't forget I want you home by ten," she reminds me with a pointed look. "You promised to help out again tomorrow, remember?"

No, I didn't remember, but I'm not about to risk her saying no to the party now.

I nod. "Yes, Mom."

I skip out of the bakery with a smile and head to my car. As I slide into the driver's seat, my phone buzzes, and I pull it out of my pocket. My heart sinks a little; it's just Grace saying she'll be a few minutes late. Brody still hasn't replied to my text from this morning.

I send him another message and drive out of the parking lot.

On my way to Sarah's party, cotton candy clouds dot the summer sky, playing hide-and-seek through the trees. I drive past dark redbrick and white stucco houses before parking in her circular driveway. Sarah's house is a blend of neutral-colored brick and tan exterior walls. The second-floor patio extends out over the garage, framed by three arches and a wrought-iron railing. I ring the bell.

"I'm coming! I'm coming!" I hear Sarah shout.

Footsteps race toward me from the other side of the door. A second later, Sarah swings it open. Her auburn curls are pulled back into a ponytail, and she's dressed in a cute floral pajama set. A smattering of freckles across her nose and cheeks stands out against her creamy skin.

"Liza!"

She throws her arms around me before tugging me inside. "Where are your pajamas?"

I groan. "I totally forgot about that."

There's a glimmer of disappointment in her green eyes, but she blinks it away.

"It's okay!" She waves a hand dismissively. "I'm just glad you're here."

I kick off my shoes as Sarah shuts the door behind us.

"Oh, you don't have to do that!"

"It's okay," I say, setting them neatly by the wall. "I don't mind."

I follow her past the curved staircase and into the house. Soft yellow walls are covered in family photos and oil paintings. Tucked between a pair of floor-to-ceiling windows clad in heavy drapery, there's a canvas print of Sarah from one of her local opera performances. In the living room, a flat-screen TV three times the size of ours at home hangs over the fireplace.

On the other end is a massive kitchen, where stainless steel appliances contrast with dark wood cabinets. Crystal bowls and pristine white plates sit laden with chips, wrapped candy, and various dips on the island. My mouth waters at the sight of all the forbidden food. Sarah hands me a plate.

"Mom said we could order whatever we wanted," she says matter-of-factly. "I was going to get some pizza, unless you want something else."

A chip freezes halfway to my mouth. "Is your mom not home?"

"Nope. She and Dad went out of town on vacation. They won't be back until tomorrow night."

Okay, definitely something Mom does not need to know.

The doorbell rings, and Sarah sprints to the door.

"Becca! Tiff!"

I poke my head out from around the corner. I don't recognize either of the girls. They must be part of the same music program at school. Sarah inhales opera like I do baking. Becca and Tiff take turns staring at me while we exchange awkward greetings. As they grab their plates, I swear I hear one of them say Brody's name. With no polite way to ask if they're talking about my boyfriend, I shove another chip into the salsa.

Over the next hour, more and more guests arrive, until the once-spacious area feels uncomfortably cramped. Caught between the rise and fall of voices, I suddenly realize I'm the token Asian in the group. I snap a pic to text Grace, my best friend.

**Please tell me you're on your way.**

A second later, my phone pings.

**Sorry. Was looking for some cute PJs.**

Of course she was. Grace never leaves the house without looking runway ready. It's no surprise people always assumed she was Jeannie's sister when we'd hang out together. I quickly tap on Brody's name in my messages—still nothing. I sigh and tuck my phone back into my pocket just as Sarah waves me over.

I endure fifteen minutes of well-intentioned introductions and fake smiles. Thankfully, Grace arrives right before the pizza, and the tension in the room evaporates. After all, nothing bonds people together like cheese and bread—especially if you're on team no-pineapple-on-pizza.

By the time we reach face mask heaven, I've nearly figured out which of the three Jennifers is which. That's when the alarm on my phone blares. Seriously? It can't be almost curfew. I squeeze my eyes shut and pray for some timey-wimey stuff to happen.

Sadly, the clock still reads nine thirty. I pick my way past the limbs spread across the floor. Sarah's making a TikTok in her panda face mask, and she calls out to me.

"Do this one with me, Liza!"

"I can't," I groan. "I have to go home."

Her face falls. "What? Why? The party's just getting started!"

*Because life isn't about having fun. It's about hard work and long hours and studying until you die.*

"I promised to help my mom at the bakery tomorrow," I say out loud.

Sarah pouts. "You really can't stay?"

"I wish I could. Maybe next time," I say, shoving my phone into my pocket. "Thanks for inviting me."

She starts to get up to walk me out, but one of the Jennifers grabs her and pulls her onto the couch for a selfie. I head to the front to put my shoes back on.

Grace plops down next to me. "I'll probably leave soon too. It's kind of boring. They're arguing over which celebrity Chris is the hottest."

"Hemsworth, obviously," I answer instantly.

She grins. "See? You're not missing anything."

She tugs me in for a quick hug before I open the door. Sarah pops her head up from a mound of pajama-clad girls like a gopher.

"Bye, Liza!"

I shut the door behind me and get in the car. With a final glance in my rearview, I drive off.

• • • • •

By the time I wake up the next morning, Mom's already left for the bakery. I turn off the alarm on my phone and check the texts Grace sent me overnight. Ice cream, pedicures, a rom-com, and . . . karaoke?! No! I missed out on karaoke. What did I do to deserve this? I toss the phone onto my bed and trudge into the bathroom to get ready. Too bad I can't scrub FOMO off my brain.

I arrive just as the sun crests over the skyline. From the outside, the shop looks empty, but I spy the thin sliver of light seeping past the drawn curtains. I relock the door after walking in and head straight to the kitchen. Mom's standing by the stainless steel table nearest to the ovens. She never lifts her head to acknowledge me, focused on the list of bakes for today as she checks something in the leather-bound book beside her. It's her most prized possession, containing all the recipes she's created over the years. She misplaced it once for about thirty seconds, and I thought she was going to spontaneously combust.

As soon as I throw on an apron and roll up my sleeves, Mom starts calling out ingredients for me to pull from various drawers. Then, Mom removes some dough from the fridge and plops the giant ball in front of me.

"Red bean buns."

It's been years since I've stood beside her, but my hands instinctively know the rhythm. It isn't long before I'm slicing the dough into smaller pieces to roll into balls. I place them on a baking tray and repeat this until there's enough to cover with plastic wrap and proof a second time. After fifteen minutes, I set the oven to preheat and bring them back out to stuff. Each ball is flattened in my palm before receiving a scoop of red bean paste in its center. It then gets wrapped and returned to the tray. A final egg wash later, they're ready for baking.

Meanwhile, Mom mixes flour, yeast, and sugar together before combining it with eggs, milk, and water for a second batch of dough. Cutting the whole thing into smaller, more manageable pieces, she begins to knead. This has always been one of my favorite things to do, and I slide one over to my area. I slam the mixture down onto the table.

*This is for my ten o'clock curfew.*

Dough strikes steel with a resounding thwack.

*And this is for having to leave the party early.*

I smash the innocent dough into submission.

*And karaoke. I still can't believe I missed karaoke!*

The table trembles from the force of the smack, and Mom narrows her eyes.

I smile sheepishly. "Sorry. I got carried away."

I resume pounding, though with more care than before. After about ten minutes, I stretch it out in the air to check for gluten. Satisfied, I add it to the fresh dough Mom's prepared.

"What's next?" I ask.

She goes to the fridge and pulls out two bowls of meat, one minced with chopped vegetables and one dark red and diced.

"Pork buns and *char siu bao.*"

She takes charge of the pork buns, while I try my hand at the char siu bao. The trickiest part is folding the buns correctly. I wiggle my fingers. Come on, muscle memory. My first one turns out too tight. Filling gushes out from the side before it makes it onto the tray. My second is too loose and leaves a big hole at the top. If I bake it like this, the meat will dry out. Mom side-eyes my efforts.

"Mistakes in the kitchen . . ."

"Perfection on the shelves," I finish.

Some things never change. I put my practice buns aside to steam later. They'll still taste good, even if they're not pretty enough to go on a shelf. When my next bao comes out perfect, I raise it to the sky, triumphant. If only I had a dramatic sunrise and an African choir to serenade me . . .

"Stop fooling around, Liza," Mom chides. "We've got more to do."

The bao finds a spot on the tray beneath her withering gaze. I continue wrapping until I run out of filling, something that never fails to happen despite years of practice. One of these days, I'm going to figure out Mom's secret. For now, the extra dough is wrapped in plastic and set aside while I grab a stack of steam baskets off the shelf. I bring them back to the table and line the bottoms of the baos with paper.

Within minutes, carefully arranged baos are ready for their steam bath, spaced in the baskets so they don't stick. Mom has finished her pork buns and moved on to the brioche. The sweet aroma of red bean alerts me that the buns are ready even before the timer goes off. I pull the first batch out and place them on our metal cooling rack. Another set of trays goes into the oven before the golden-brown buns are ready for their clear plastic wrappers.

We continue baking like this for the next two hours, until the air is laden with delicious temptation. As I stock the shelves, I check out the line already forming outside. I remove my apron, dust the flour off my face, and unlock the door. Customers flood into every corner of the bakery to jockey for their personal favorites. Empty shelves and happy sighs are the only things left in their wake.

I start to upload a pic for the bakery's Instagram, but pause when I see a comment on my post about Sarah's party. It's from Brody.

Next time save me some pizza. Pineapple free.

I grin and slip my phone back into my apron. I really should stop worrying over nothing. He's just bad at texting.

Mom and I man the store for an hour. Then Tina arrives and takes over the wrapping and restocking. The day flies by, and before I know it, we're ushering the last customer of the day out the door and turning off our neon OPEN sign. I duck into the back and find Mom taking a quick break on a nearby chair. The day has been so hectic we haven't had time to properly clean. I rinse off the dirty trays and utensils before loading the dishwasher. As I wipe down the tables, she shoots me a grateful smile.

"So, tell me what you're thinking about for summer."

I drop the towel into the laundry bag and lean against a nearby counter. "What about some of the snacks I've been telling you about? The ones all the teahouses are making."

"I don't know," she replies. "I'm not a fan of trends. I'd rather have something we could add permanently to the menu if it does well."

I take a deep breath. "I get that, but some of this stuff's been around for years and is still popular. Like those Hong Kong egg waffles. My friends are obsessed with them."

"You and your trendy foods," Mom playfully chides. "I still remember how you always knew where the animal waffle cake was at the day market."

For a second, I'm distracted by the memory of the noisy market in Taiwan Mom would take me to for the week's groceries.

Without fail, I'd always go in search of the soft, puffy pastries amid the throngs of impatient customers and stalls bursting with vegetables, fruits, and meats. Then there was the old man who made the most delicious fried chicken—

"Don't they require special equipment?" Mom continues, interrupting my thoughts. "Plus, I'm shorthanded. And we have the junior baker contest to worry about when summer starts."

"I bet you can rent those irons. And it's easy enough to create a recipe for the batter," I say, doing a quick search on my phone. "I could probably come up with something in a few hours."

The words leave my mouth before I realize what I've done. How did I not see this coming? Baking for fun is one thing, but slaving away in a hot kitchen for free is another.

Mom, expectedly, grins like a Cheshire cat. "Okay. I'll give these waffles a shot, but if they don't sell, we stop. Got it?"

That's it. I'm stuck. If I back out now, she'll never let me forget it.

"All right, but I can't start until finals. Plus, I have that trip to New York to see Jeannie after graduation."

"Of course. School is the most important thing," she says. "But you should start working on that recipe. We need to have it ready for summer."

She won this round. I demand a rematch.

# Chapter 4

Six words. Six words are all it takes to turn my life upside down.

"You should date nice Chinese boy."

We've all gathered at Yin and Yang for Sunday brunch, our family tradition for the past ten years. Dad shuts down the restaurant one Sunday afternoon each month and invites close friends to join us for a five-course meal. It's his chance to have fun and cook dishes you'll never find on the menu. Usually, he makes some sort of big speech beforehand, but today, he flashed me a strange look before disappearing behind the curtain.

Too bad I just figured out it was a warning.

Auntie Chen—no actual relation—leans forward. Probably in her sixties or seventies, she has dark, tattooed brows and a powdered face that make her a dead ringer for a Kabuki mask. Even the bright red lipstick adds to the effect, the color cracking as she smiles brightly.

"I help find you good one."

My jaw hits the table. "Excuse me?"

"Your mama say you date American boy."

If looks could kill, I'd be behind bars for the one I send Mom. Instead, she plucks a steamed pork dumpling off the plate and carefully balances it on her chopsticks. Could she know about Brody? I sneak a longer look at her. No, she's far too relaxed. I turn back to Auntie Chen, lips pressed together in the semblance of a smile.

"That was almost a year ago, *āyí*. I'm focusing on graduating now."

Auntie Chen shakes her head, and my hope for an end to the conversation evaporates faster than the steam off the bamboo baskets in front of me.

"American boy not good. Chinese boy good. They have respect for elder."

I glance at Dad for support. He's gulping his way through the corn and crab soup as if it's the most delicious thing he's ever eaten. No one else at the table is of any help either. Both Mom and Uncle Chen are busy pretending not to listen with rapt attention.

"Ready for your next course?"

Our waitress freezes as all eyes land on her. Grateful for her interruption, I grin winningly.

"Yes! I'm starving!"

The rest of lunch passes like any other meal. Dad's experimental dishes go over spectacularly, and by the time we reach the third course, I'm nearly stuffed. That doesn't mean I've let down my guard, though. Auntie Chen is a notorious schemer. When she sets her mind to something, all anyone can do is get out of her way. Sure enough, she starts waving enthusiastically at a family of three who arrived just before Dad closed up for the day.

"*Mèimei!* You here today too? Come, come! Come sit with us. Plenty of room."

The couple looks to be around my parents' age, and they're with a boy I recognize from school. I realize what's about to go down the minute our eyes meet.

It's a setup, and a very public one.

I should have figured this out sooner. The minute she arrived, Auntie Chen insisted we sit at a larger table than usual. Not to mention Mom fussed over my outfit before we left the house. The woman eagerly tugs her mortified son toward our table and shoves him into a free seat. She and her husband settle into the other two before the former dips her head slightly.

"Thank you for being kind enough to include us, *dàjiě*."

"What a lovely surprise running into you, Mrs. Lim," Mom greets warmly.

"Yes. Good surprise," Auntie Chen chimes in. "With your husband and son too."

Mrs. Lim starts. "Oh, how rude of me! Let me introduce my husband, Mr. Lim, and my son, Reuben."

"You've already met my husband, Mr. Yang," Mom replies, and gestures toward me. "And this is my younger daughter, Liza. Liza, say hello."

"Hello, Lim āyí, Lim *shūshu*," I offer automatically.

I'm rewarded for my obedience with a jab to the ribs. I scowl at Mom, whose eyes shoot daggers while her lips stay curved.

"You forgot to say hi to Reuben."

I drag my gaze over to my fellow victim with a blithe smile.

"Hello, Reuben."

His face reddens. "Hi."

Oh, he doesn't stand a chance. Lucky for him, I've got no intention of being roped into this. I slip my phone out of my purse and text Grace. Then I prepare to play the game.

When the next course arrives, Reuben's hand grabs hold of the rice pot before anyone else can react. He dumps a big scoop into his bowl, and then proceeds to use his own chopsticks to pick through the other dishes. It's hard to say who's more appalled—Mrs. Lim or Mom.

The corner of Dad's lips twitch as our eyes meet across the table.

Mrs. Lim transfers some vegetables into Reuben's bowl. "*Bǎobèi*, you need to eat more vegetables."

He promptly picks them out and—to everyone's horror—puts them back on the communal plate.

"I don't like vegetables. I only eat meat."

She tries again. "It's important to eat a balanced diet. That's what Dr. Dang said, remember?"

He pushes his bowl away. "Screw him. He said I was fat."

"Reuben, language!" She smiles apologetically at us. "And Dr. Dang didn't call you fat. He only said you should watch your weight."

He glowers. "Same thing."

I've decided Reuben would be the first to go in a zombie apocalypse. He'd probably demand they leave him alone because he's too important to die. The thought makes me giggle, but I swallow it when Mom glares in my direction. The table falls silent. That is, except for Reuben, who spends the next ten minutes chewing with his mouth open. I should feel bad for Mrs. Lim, but it's too much fun watching Mom's matchmaking going up in flames. Others at the table, however, are not so quick to give up.

"So, Reuben. Your mama say you go to school with Liza," Auntie Chen says.

He shrugs. "Uh, I guess so. It's a big school."

Wrong answer. A second later, Reuben lets out a yelp and rubs his arm.

Mrs. Lim clears her throat. "What he means is he doesn't have any classes with Liza."

"That's too bad," Mom jumps in. "I hear Reuben's an excellent student. All As and plays the viola. So much discipline. Liza could learn a thing or two from him."

I grit my teeth. She knows perfectly well I'm a straight-A student . . . *and* I eat all my vegetables.

"Thank you, but Reuben spends too much time playing video games," Mrs. Lim insists. "In fact, I've been trying to teach him how to cook some basic dishes."

Auntie Chen claps her hands together. "Maybe Mr. Yang teach Reuben about cooking. This restaurant most popular in Chinatown."

Dad ducks his head to hide the look of chagrin on his face as he answers.

"You're too generous, Mrs. Chen. We are just lucky to have loyal customers such as yourself."

"To be honest, Reuben's more of a sweets person," Mrs. Lim admits with a small smile. "He loves his desserts. Every time I bring something home from your bakery, Mrs. Yang, it's gone in one night!"

"I'm so happy to hear that, Mrs. Lim," Mom murmurs demurely.

"Will you be running the baking contest again?" Mrs. Lim asks. "I heard it was very successful in past years."

Mom originally came up with the idea for the contest after we watched a season of *The Great British Baking Show* a few years ago. She was searching for a way to give back to the local Asian American community while promoting Yin and Yang. The competition includes ten bakers from local high schools. Mom keeps the recipes fairly easy to follow and re-create, and the contestants have five days between baking challenges. The winner gets featured in the Chinese newspaper and on a local cable talk show.

"Thank you for saying so! Actually, I've got some very exciting things planned for this year's competition," Mom stage-whispers.

"And is there a prize for the winner?"

Mom nods. "First prize is a five-thousand-dollar scholarship."

"Oh, well, isn't that lovely, Rueben?" Mrs. Lim's eyes take on an unsettling glint. "Too bad you don't know how to bake."

I cringe. Here it comes.

"Liza's a wonderful baker. In fact, she's even won several contests in the past." Mom peers at me. "I'm sure she'd be happy to give Reuben some lessons. Wouldn't you?"

I'd be happier dropping dead first, but I bite my tongue. Reuben, on the other hand, doesn't hold back.

"Baking is for girls," he tells everyone with a scowl. "Besides, why would I waste time trying to make something I can just buy?"

Oh, this is almost too easy. I prop my chin on my hand, injecting a hint of saccharin into my voice.

"I think all guys should know how to bake. It takes a lot of patience and attention to detail."

I slide my eyes over to Mom, expecting her to disapprove. Instead, she's wearing an odd little smile that makes me sit up straight. Meanwhile, Reuben's eyes are pinned to his lap. Mrs. Lim fumes beside him.

"Reuben," she hisses. "Your attention should be on the table, not on that phone!"

As if on cue, my cell starts to ring. I hide my grin as I answer it. "Hello?"

"911 at your service," Grace chirps. "What excuse are we using today?"

"Hey! I thought we were meeting tomorrow at lunch," I say loudly.

"Ah, the last-minute project. Got it."

She raises her voice while I pull my ear away from my phone just enough for Mom to eavesdrop.

"Where are you? We're all here at Boba Life waiting for you!"

"I don't know if I'll make it on time," I answer tightly. "I'm at lunch with my family right now."

Dad's head pops out from behind Mom's shoulder. "What's going on, Liza?"

"I was supposed to meet up with a group to work on our final world history project." I grimace. "I thought it was tomorrow, not today. I must have mixed up the time."

"This is why I keep telling you to write things down," Mom mutters with a sigh. "What time do you have to be there?"

I speak into the phone. "What time was I supposed to be there?"

"One thirty," Grace fibs.

Dad gasps. "But it's almost two o'clock already!"

I glance at my watch, eyes widening with mock dismay.

"You're right! Oh, but . . . we're not done with lunch, and I don't want to be rude."

"School comes first," he answers predictably. "Go. We'll pack this up and you can eat it for dinner."

Grace, who's been listening in on the whole conversation, seals the deal with her parting words.

"Great! We're waiting for you to start, so get here as soon as you can!"

I hang up, biting my lip so I don't burst out laughing. Mom and Dad left early this morning to open the restaurant and bakery, so I'd taken my car to meet everyone here. The Four Horsemen couldn't have planned this better. I politely excuse myself and practically sprint out of there. Once I'm safely in the car, I dial Grace.

"Girl, that was the best! You should have seen the look on Auntie Chen's face. I think there was legit steam coming out of her ears."

"Glad I could help."

"So where are you now?" I ask, turning the engine on.

"At Boba Life. Duh."

"Wait, you were serious?"

She chuckles. "Why are you surprised? Don't you need a tea fix?"

"This is why we're best friends," I reply, grinning. "I'll be there in a few."

# Chapter 5

I pull out of the parking lot and drive down Bellaire, the main road that cuts through Chinatown. Four blocks down, I arrive at my destination. Situated at the junction of an L-shaped plaza, Boba Life is almost always packed on weekends. Like most teahouses, a row of flat-screen TVs above the counter displays the menu. The walls are painted black and covered with chalk murals by local artists. The exposed dark wood beams give the shop the illusion of having high ceilings. Tracks of pod lights illuminate the otherwise dim space, and a mix of K-pop and *Billboard* Hot 100 plays from the surround sound speakers. A long mahogany table sits in the middle of the front room, and smaller square or round tables line the walls.

I make my way past the groups of people chatting and a few working on their laptops. Grace is sipping casually on a taro cream tea at our usual table in the back room. As I plop down next to her, she points at the other drink on the table.

"I got your usual."

I unwrap the straw and jab the pointed end into the plastic covering. It gives with a loud pop. One sip later, I'm happily chewing on the squishy dark brown balls I love so much.

Grace cocks her head. "So, who was it this time?"

"Some guy named Reuben. Reuben Lim."

"Wait. I think I know him," she says, her brown eyes lighting up. "Is he kinda short, with a bad bowl cut, and looks constipated all the time?"

I think back to my brief encounter and nod. "Yep. Sounds just like him."

Grace leans back into her chair with a long sigh. She twirls a strand of hair around her finger. The ends are still blond, but her natural black color has taken back most of her head in the past year. Her makeup is flawless as usual, so natural you can only spot it up close. Even though we're both wearing maxi dresses, she looks like she's stepped out of a magazine, while I just look . . . comfortable.

"My mom set me up with him last year. As you can imagine, it was a total disaster."

I take another sip of my tea. "Are you telling me you *actually* went on a date with the guy?"

"It was the only way to get her off my back," Grace says with a shrug. "It was a small price to pay for Mom-free bliss."

I make a face. "Well, I don't have that option. It would only encourage my mom."

We share a laugh and another round, this time on me. It's a while before I notice Grace is overly quiet, fidgeting with her straw instead of drinking her tea. I reach across the table and touch her lightly on the arm.

"What's wrong?"

Grace starts. "Huh? Oh, nothing's wrong."

"Of course there is. You haven't said a word in ten whole minutes. It's like some sort of record."

Her eyes drop to the table, and she chews on her lower lip.

"Okay, yeah. There is something," Grace says.

My stomach knots instinctively. "Grace, what is it?"

"I think, um . . . I think Brody's cheating on you," she finally blurts out.

For a second, the world around me tilts violently. My fingers tighten around my cup, and tea spurts out from the straw. I barely notice the sticky residue as it drips down the back of my hand.

"How . . . how did you find out?" I whisper.

Grace slides some napkins across the table, but I'm frozen to the spot. She dries off my limp fingers before answering.

"Sarah told me. She overheard one of her friends talking about it at the party after you left."

I probably shouldn't have ignored the fact that Brody recently forgot my birthday and made it up with vending machine candy, or that he's been canceling plans and leaving my texts on read. He told me he was just busy with finals, but now . . .

"When did this happen?" I gulp. "And with who?"

"Apparently, they've caught him holding hands with and kissing Melissa Nguyen," she tells me, playing with the napkin still in her hand. "But they didn't say how long it's been going on."

Of course he's cheating on me with the captain of the school's dance team. It's so predictable, it's nauseating.

"I wanted to tell you right away, but we wanted to make sure we had proof," she adds. "So we followed him around school the other day, and, well . . ."

Grace hesitates for a second but ultimately pulls up a video on her phone and presses play. It's shaky, but I can make out Brody in his basketball jersey standing over Melissa in the hallway outside of class. Her thick black hair is pulled into a high ponytail, the glittering uniform they wear practically painted onto her. She giggles at something he says, and he wraps his arms around her waist and kisses her. I wrench my eyes off the screen.

Grace grabs my hand. "Liza, I'm so sorry."

I should've known things with Brody were too good to be true. To my utter mortification, I feel my eyes tear up. Grace tucks me into the crook of her neck until I pull myself together.

"What are you going to do?" Grace asks gently.

"I . . . I don't know. I know I need to break up with him, but I . . ."

Her grip tightens around my shoulders. "Well, you don't have to do it right now. Take as much time as you need. Sarah and I are both here for you, even if it's to help hide his body."

I laugh despite myself. We stay for one last round of tea (minus the boba), though I suspect it's more to distract me than anything else. We leave together, and Grace walks me to my car. As I unlock the door, she hands me a sheet of paper.

"What's this?"

"Last week's project outline. Figured you might need proof."

I give her a quick squeeze. "You're the best, you know that?"

"Of course I do. You'd be in matchmaking hell without me," she jokes back.

"One of these days, I'm gonna be the one saving your ass."

Grace rolls her eyes. "If you say so. Until then, you're paying for all our teas."

"Sounds fair to me," I answer. "You've got a deal."

"See you tomorrow."

I fold the outline and tuck it into my pocket, and we go our separate ways. I drive home without bursting into tears again, but I still take a few minutes to compose myself in the car. Mom's sitting in the living room when I walk in, and she doesn't waste a second interrogating me.

"Were you really with Grace?"

I nod, grateful for the alibi. "Yes, Mom. We were at Boba Life, working on our project."

Her eyes narrow. "You weren't out with a boy again?"

"No. We were working on the project, just like I told you," I answer.

"Then show me what you did."

She's both surprised and annoyed when I unfold the paper for her to examine.

"Put that in your backpack so you don't forget to turn it in."

Satisfied, Mom turns back to the book she was reading. I head to my room, closing the door behind me. I'm quiet during dinner, but Mom doesn't mention it. Afterward, I retreat to my room and listen to my Spotify GOT7 playlist on repeat, hoping to distract myself. When Brody texts me out of the blue, I don't answer, even when my phone goes off several more times. I cry for a little bit before reminding myself he's not worth my tears. I've just dried my eyes when someone knocks on the door. Mom pokes her head in.

"By the way, I invited Reuben to come by the house for dinner on Friday. You should get to know him better."

I balk and sit up in bed. "Seriously? After the way he acted at lunch?"

"Don't be so judgmental, Liza. Most people think baking is for girls. He's still a nice boy."

*You mean a nice* Chinese *boy.*

I pretend to check my phone calendar. "That's the day my group's going to meet after school to work on the project. It's our last chance before it's due, so I might be getting home pretty late."

"You can't skip dinner, Liza. That's not healthy."

The set of her jaw makes it clear she thinks she's won, but I've still got a card to play.

"We're going to be ordering some pizza. Besides, it won't look good if I'm the only one not staying for the entire thing."

She huffs. "Fine. I'll tell him to come Saturday instead."

"I can't do this Saturday. Grace and I are . . . studying for a math test," I fib.

The corner of her right eye twitches. Uh-oh. That's not a good sign. It only does that when she's about to blow. I flash back to the conversation we had just a couple of weeks ago at the dinner table.

*"Why won't you give these boys a chance?" Mom asked. "They come from respectable families and are good students. Some of them even have fun hobbies!"*

*"Maybe because I don't want the guy I date to sound like a walking college application."*

*"Liza! There's nothing wrong with a smart, successful boy. What about John Wu? You attend school with his sister Mona. He's already been offered jobs with four of the biggest engineering firms in California. It's a pity he's three years older than you. If he were younger, he'd be perfect."*

*Mona Wu looks like she took a frying pan to the face. Nope. Not a chance.*

*"He's not my type," I insisted firmly. "Even if he was my age, he still wouldn't be."*

*"Then who is? American boys?" Mom scoffed. "American boys don't know how to work hard. They just want to party and do drugs."*

*"Not everyone is like your reality TV shows, Mom! There are plenty of nice guys out there."*

*"You only say that because you like them." She shook her head. "Aiya, Liza, all flowers wilt. Don't be fooled by a pretty face."*

*"So . . . I should date a tree?" I couldn't resist saying. "I've never really thought of a sequoia that way, but I suppose—"*

That comment earned me three days in Mom's special level of hell—no Wi-Fi. I wouldn't wish it on anyone. I need to play this right. My freedom hangs in the balance.

"Next Friday, then."

Mom's voice is firm, inviting no further argument.

I lower my eyes. "Okay, yeah. I guess that works."

Satisfied she's gotten her way, she shuts the door and leaves. Finally alone, I smile to myself.

*Checkmate.*

• • • • •

Most of the time, school is my escape from obedient daughter duties. The campus of Salvis Private Academy encompasses five large buildings wrapped around a triangular central courtyard. A forest of oak and pine, with a bayou abutting one side, surrounds the whole school. Behind the main building is the athletics field, though I honestly have no idea what it looks like. I try never to end up there intentionally.

Salvis also boasts a ninety-nine percent college acceptance rate, with nearly every top-ten student landing at an Ivy League school. It's the only reason why Dad pays the equivalent of in-state college tuition for me to attend. Jeannie might be the star student in the family—valedictorian of her class, president of student council—but I hold my own. My teachers love me, and the grades come pretty easily. The only challenge these days is getting through my intense senioritis. It came in like a wrecking ball, and it takes everything in me not to slack off like some of my friends.

For the next four days, however, school is my own personal hell. I avoid Brody and ignore all his calls and texts. Either Grace or Sarah walks me to every class. Their scathing glares could level armies, much less a cheating jock. By Thursday night, I've weathered enough of the storm—though battered and bruised—to break up with him. I do it over text because, well, I'm not *that* sure of myself. When he doesn't reply, I binge-watch the latest season of *Queer Eye* and pretend my tears are happy ones.

The next morning, exhausted and bleary-eyed, I pull into the school parking lot. As I get out of the car, Brody catches me off guard and steps into my path.

"Okay, babe, you need to tell me what's going on. What's with this text? Is this your idea of a joke?"

I balk at him. This from the guy who left me on read all night?

"You mean like how you've treated this whole relationship?"

"What are you talking about?"

I push past him, but he steps in front of me again. I narrow my eyes.

"Get out of my way."

"Not until you tell me why you're trying to break up with me," he demands. "What the hell is that about?"

Fine. He wants to act innocent? I've got receipts.

"How about the fact that you've been cheating on me, Brody? And don't deny it. I have a video of you with Melissa."

He looks at me as though I've stepped on a puppy. "You were spying on me? How dare you, Liza?"

"How dare I?" I clench my fists. "How dare *you* cheat on me?!"

Brody pales. "I don't know what video you're talking about, but you're wrong. It wasn't me."

I plant my feet and cross my arms over my chest. "Maybe next time you're going to cheat in public and lie about it, don't wear a basketball jersey with your last name on the back."

As we argue, the pressure in my chest forces my voice higher and higher. Some of the other students eye us with open curiosity as they stroll past. Brody grins sheepishly at them before leaning in with a hiss.

"Stop yelling, Liza. You're embarrassing me."

"Embarrassing you?!" I say, incredulous. "You know what's really embarrassing? Me wasting all this time on you!"

I take a step forward, intending to storm off, but he suddenly shifts to block my way. I stumble back against my car as Brody leans in close.

"Nobody dumps me, Liza," he says in a low voice. "I'm Brody Smith. I do the dumping."

"Hey! Why don't you leave her alone?"

The voice draws closer with every word, but I can't make out who's speaking.

Brody's face deepens in color. "This is between me and my girl-friend, so back off."

My would-be hero comes to a stop next to us, and I finally get a good look at him. Despite the tension, my brain registers that he's really tall for an Asian guy. Brody is five foot eleven—he claims six feet—and this guy has at least two inches on him. His black hair brushes across his strong eyebrows, a slight wave giving it the volume mine lacks. His brown eyes are serious, and his skin enviably clear. As he talks, I catch the tiniest hint of a single dimple cupping the left corner of his mouth.

"I'm pretty sure I heard her say she was breaking up with you."

"She doesn't know what she's talking about," Brody insists.

"Yes, I do," I contradict softly. "We're done, Brody."

The guy arches a single, unperturbed brow. "How about now?"

A teacher passes by, and I take the opportunity to duck under Brody's arm. He sneers at me.

"Whatever. I was getting tired of you anyway. You never want to do anything. Melissa knows how to be a real girlfriend."

In a daze, I stare at his retreating back. It takes a long minute to realize my rescuer is still standing next to me. As mortified as I am, I force myself to look up at him.

"Um, thanks for your help. I didn't expect him to act like that."

He doesn't reply, instead watching Brody stomp up the front steps into Building A. Maybe he didn't hear me. I square my shoulders and stick my hand out.

"I'm Liza. What's your name?"

His eyes rake across my features, his expression bored.

"Next time, try dating someone who's less of an asshole."

My eyebrows shoot up, and the words slip out before I can stop myself.

"That rules you out."

He frowns. "What did you say?"

The morning bell rings, the sound piercing the air around us. I give him a sickly sweet smile.

"Oh, just that I'm lucky you were here to help."

"Uh, sure," he mumbles. "Better get to class."

My mystery man pivots on his heel and walks toward the school without another word.

"What the hell just happened?" I say to no one.

The one-minute warning bell rings. I sprint along the same path, veering toward Building C. I glance back when I've reached the doors.

He's gone.

# Chapter 6

I try my best to get through the rest of the day, but I'm as good at dodging gossip as Tom Holland is with spoilers. It doesn't help that friends keep texting to ask if I'm okay. Still, they're nothing compared to the smug grins of the girls in the hallway. When the last bell rings, I make a break for the sanctuary of my car. Since Mom set the Do Not Disturb while Driving on my phone, I don't notice the two new messages until I've pulled into the driveway.

**Someone said they saw you with some hottie this morning**, Sarah sent. **I stan, btw.**

**Where'd you go?** the one from Grace says. **You're supposed to meet me, remember? Fake project?**

Shit. I totally forgot. Luckily, Mom's working at the bakery until seven—the one good thing going for me today. I drive over to Boba Life and find a spot right in front of the shop. My hand is on the door when I hear my name.

"Liza! Liza!"

I glance to my left and see Sarah jogging toward me.

"Sarah! What are you doing here?"

I give her a quick hug. She puts a hand over her brow and peers into the teahouse.

"Grace told me you two were meeting up here. Figured I'd come hang out with you guys."

Sarah pulls open the door, but I step through first and lead her to the back room, where she hugs an equally surprised Grace at our booth.

"I didn't know you were coming," she says to Sarah.

My eyebrows shoot up. "I . . . thought you invited her."

"Neither of you did," Sarah interrupts with an exaggerated pout, "but both of you should have. I'm hurt."

"Sorry," Grace and I murmur at the same time.

Sarah brightens in the blink of an eye and glances around the room.

"This place is so cute! Is this like an Asian Starbucks?"

"Starbucks serves coffee, Sarah, not tea," Grace corrects.

"Starbucks serves tea too."

Grace prepares to launch into a speech, but I shake my head. There's a reason we don't invite Sarah to Chinatown. Her family moved from a tiny town in central Texas a year ago. While she's super chill and fun to be around, ignorant things tend to come out of her mouth at the worst possible moments.

"It's kind of like a Starbucks," I explain, "but better. They don't just serve tea. They also do smoothies, ice blends, and coffee too. Oh, and there's the sinkers. They're the best part."

"What's a sinker?"

I wave at the row of multicolored jellies, puddings, and boba lined up behind the glass case next to the register.

"Those are sinkers." I point at a freshly made milk tea on the counter. "We like the boba. You can get them at the bottom of your drink and suck them through a big straw. It's fun."

Sarah scrunches her nose. I spot Grace stiffen in my periphery and grab Sarah's hand.

"Come on, I think you're gonna love it."

Grace stays behind to hold our table, which is just as well. After her trip to Taiwan last summer, she's been hyped up on national pride. I can't count the number of times she's corrected people when they call her Chinese. I don't mind, though. She's introduced me to Jay Chou and Jolin Tsai, not to mention the black hole of T-dramas on Netflix.

We get in line, and I show Sarah how the ordering is done. She reluctantly agrees to try a sample of boba, and I bite back a laugh at the faces she makes while chewing. She bursts into a grin.

"Okay, I take it all back. I love this stuff! It's like a gummy bear I can put in my drink! I can't believe you guys didn't bring me here sooner! I'm going to try all the flavors and sinkers!"

"I'd . . . just avoid the durian," I warn her half-jokingly as we sit back down at the table.

"Why?"

Grace laughs, choking on her tea. I pat her on the back before offering Sarah an explanation.

"It's an acquired taste," I say. "It's common in Asian countries, but not everyone likes it. I'm personally not a huge fan."

"Me neither. It smells horrid," Grace adds, far less tactful. "And tastes even worse."

Sarah blanches. "Got it. Scratching it off the list."

We lapse into silence, sipping on our tea and watching people come and go. I notice Grace tapping her nails on the table, but the two of them have the decency to let me drink some of my tea before peppering me with questions.

"Okay, I have to know," Sarah blurts. "Who was the guy?"

"What did Brody say when he found out?" Grace asks simultaneously.

"I heard he was, like, *super* hot," Sarah says.

JENNIFER YEN

"I heard Brody punched him in the face," Grace whispers, smirking.

I roll my eyes. "Okay, first of all, nobody punched anybody."

I recount what happened this morning, a twenty-minute ordeal because I keep getting interrupted with questions. Finally, the two of them sit back in their chairs.

Grace frowns. "Are you telling me this random guy defended you and then . . . insulted you?"

"Yep."

"I don't get it. He sounds so hot," Sarah murmurs with a mouthful of boba.

"Exactly. He's hot. He's probably never had to be nice to anyone in his life," Grace asserts, planting one elbow on the table and resting her chin on her hand. "I wouldn't be surprised if he thought Liza was going to faint dead at his feet."

I chuckle. "I think you've been reading too many romance novels."

"And whose fault is that?" she counters.

"Whatever. We both know your life is better with the Bridgertons in it."

Grace crosses her arms in front of her. "Fine, but my point stands. The hot ones only care about themselves."

I catch the tiniest quiver in her voice as our eyes meet. She's thinking about Eric again. It's been three years, but you never forget the first time a guy breaks your heart.

"Mmm. Fair enough," Sarah utters, unaware. "But would you go out with him if he asked you?"

"Totally, because I haven't dated enough jerks for a lifetime," I answer with a playful shove. "Of course not. I don't even know his name, and I've never seen him around school."

"Maybe he just doesn't do first impressions well. I think you should give him a chance."

"Says the girl who hasn't gone on a date with anyone the whole time we've known her," Grace teases.

"Hey! I can't help it if I have standards." Sarah twirls her hair around a finger. "Besides, if I want to be as successful as Jessica Pratt, I need to practice day and night. Getting into SMU is just the first step."

I don't have a clue who Jessica Pratt is, but it's easy enough to guess she's one of Sarah's idols.

"Oh, that reminds me. I've gotta go. Voice lesson," Sarah tells us after a glance at her watch. "But you'd better text me if Mystery Guy shows up again, Liza."

"It's a deal."

We exchange hugs before she leaves. I go up and order two more teas before sitting back down with Grace.

"What did your parents say when you told them you wanted to take a gap year?"

She plays with her straw. "They weren't super into it at first, but I told them I could spend it interning in Taiwan. We have a family friend who works for one of the big TV networks, and she offered me a spot with them."

"Really? That's amazing!"

"Yeah, I guess so," she replies. "Especially since I'm still not sure what I want to do just yet."

I prop my chin on one hand. "And your parents don't mind that you don't know?"

"Not really. I mean, they want me to be happy with whatever I decide. As long as I graduate, they'll be okay."

I shove aside the jealousy that pops up immediately. Grace is an

ABC—American-born Chinese—and so is her dad. Her mom's family immigrated when she was ten. As a result, her parents keep a lot of the same traditions, but they're also way chiller.

A kid at the next table stabs a fried squid ball with a toothpick, and my stomach calls out to it.

I nudge Grace. "You want to grab something to eat? I told my mom I'd be out late so she wouldn't invite Reuben over."

"She's still at it?" she asks. "My mom gave up a long time ago."

"That's because you date the right kind of boy now," I tell her. "Not like me."

Her stomach joins mine in a symphony of gurgles.

Grace grins sheepishly. "Yeah, dinner sounds great."

We grab our empty cups and toss them in the trash. Outside, neon signs of all colors and sizes fight for our attention in the shopping plaza. I peer over at her.

"What're you in the mood for, Grace?"

She shrugs. "You pick."

"I feel like Korean barbecue is the only acceptable choice given the day I've had."

"Agreed. Let's go."

I lead us away from Boba Life and down the row of shops until we reach the building at the end. All our senses are bombarded as we step through the door of Tofu City. To the right of the hostess stand is a glass case of *sampuru*, plastic models of their most popular dishes. K-pop plays over speakers tucked into wood-slatted walls while a TV plays the accompanying music video. Steam rises above the many grill tables to the melody of sizzling meat.

The place is packed, so after putting our names down, we stand off to the side and wait. It doesn't take long for our clothes to absorb the smell of the food. It's a badge of honor, really. The mark of those who have met the challenge of fire and conquered it. I turn to say something to Grace, but she's smiling at someone past my shoulder.

"Who are you looking at?"

"No, don't—"

Oh, wow. No wonder she's distracted. The guy sitting with his back to the far wall is so pretty, it's intimidating. His black hair is parted slightly off center, the ends gracing the peaks of his brows. His face is annoyingly symmetrical, and when he smiles, I feel the sudden urge to giggle. Only Grace could date a guy like him and not look like a troll. I nudge her with my elbow.

"I thought the hot ones weren't worth your time."

She glances at me. "I never said that."

Her eyes drift back to the hot guy, and I swallow a laugh.

"Right. I guess I misunderstood."

Our hostess calls my name. We follow her over to a table along the back wall. Before she can put the menus down, Grace gestures at the empty one right next to Pretty Boy.

"Actually, I like that table better."

The middle-aged woman doesn't hide her scowl but moves us over anyway. Grace makes me sit on the same side as Pretty Boy so she has the perfect view. After a few minutes, our waitress, a stout girl with large brown eyes, comes by with two glasses of ice water.

"You know what you want?"

"Can you give us another minute?" Grace asks.

The waitress huffs and walks off. I always get the same thing, so I wait for her to look over the menu. Unfortunately for me, she's too busy checking out what's next door to order. When the waitress swings by a second time, I nudge her with my shoe.

"Grace, I'm starving, and she's waiting on us to order."

"You pick something for me," Grace mutters.

I sigh. "Um, one barbecue combo and one bibimbap combo, both with mushroom tofu soup."

"How spicy?" the waitress asks, pointing at the flame scale.

"Number one spicy for me."

Grace's eyes are still pinned on her prize. The hangry part of my brain demands justice, so I give in to the prank.

"And number three for her."

The girl leaves to put in our order, and I take the opportunity to take a closer look at Pretty Boy. He's sitting by himself, but there are two settings on his table. He also hasn't ordered anything. While Grace bats her eyelashes at him, he's focused on the front door. Every time a guy walks through, he straightens and then slumps back into his chair.

Since I want an actual conversation with dinner, I twist in my chair and stick my hand out.

"Hi. I'm Liza, and this is my friend Grace."

His easy grin stuns me for a moment. "Hey! I'm Ben. Nice to meet you both."

Grace giggles when he turns to flash her a smile. I bite back a groan. Most of the time, she's a warrior queen and my voice of reason. Today is not one of those times.

"Are you eating by yourself?" she practically purrs.

"Actually, I'm waiting on my cousin to get here. He texted me to say he was parking."

"Good luck to him," I quip, waving toward the door. "Chinatown on a Friday night is like a BTS concert."

Ben laughs, a soft, gentle sound that fills me with warmth. If he wasn't sitting right there, you wouldn't be able to convince me he's real. Only book boyfriends are that perfect.

"Oh, there he is!"

He waves at someone by the door. As his cousin steps into view, my heart sinks.

It's him. Broody hero guy.

"I saved you a seat, James."

So that's his name. It's far too nice for someone like him.

I turn to tell Grace he's the guy from the parking lot, but she's too busy flirting to notice my attempts at getting her attention. James weaves between tables and waiters with enviable grace, sliding into his chair with one smooth motion. Unbidden, my eyes search for his secret dimple.

*No, Liza, stop it. Remember. He was a total jerk to you.*

*But he came to your rescue this morning*, a traitorous little voice chirps in my head.

I squash it like a cockroach beneath my shoe.

"Why are you looking at me like that?"

Mr. Broody is staring directly at me, his expression quizzical.

I stammer. "What?"

"I said, why are you looking at me like that?"

"Like what?" I echo stupidly.

"Like you want to step on my head."

A strange giggle bursts from my chest. It ends as a squawk as I slap a hand over my mouth. Grace hides her smile behind her hand, while Ben chuckles lightly.

"You always know how to make an impression, James," he says. "Two minutes, and she's already pissed at you."

"I'm not pissed at him," I practically shout. "I . . . I have a stomachache."

James recoils as if the very air around him is contaminated, while Ben leans in with a frown.

"Has it been happening for a while?"

"Er . . . not really. It only just started," I hedge, playing with an earring.

"Well, you haven't eaten anything yet, so it's probably not a stomach virus," Ben surmises with a purse of his lips. "Maybe you waited too long to eat today. Did you have lunch?"

I start to answer, but James interrupts.

"Or it could just be a stomachache, Ben," he says, glancing up from his menu. "Not everything has to be a disorder."

Grace glances between us. "Did I miss something?"

"James is just teasing me, Grace," Ben answers, cheeks tinged pink. "Because I want to be a doctor one day."

"A doctor?"

Grace repeats the magic word. At least five Asian moms turn toward our side of the room, their heads popping up like meerkats in a nature documentary. Ben doesn't seem to notice, his eyes drawn to her.

"Yes. A future one, hopefully."

Even our waitress is summoned by his choice of career. She appears at their table with a fresh coat of mascara and coral lip gloss. Her hair, which had been in a messy bun, is now brushed and pulled back into a ponytail.

"Are you ready to order?"

She licks her lips, her eyes shifting between the two cousins like she's trying to decide which one is tastier. I bite my lip to keep from laughing. The waitress eventually settles on James and hovers over his shoulder with a hopeful smile. He's busy staring at the menu, so she clears her throat.

"What would you—"

"I'll have the barbecue rib combo," James interjects brusquely. "With mushroom tofu soup, level two."

He raises his eyes only to make sure she's written down his order. He then pulls out his phone and starts fiddling with it while our waitress deflates. Ben makes up for his cousin's rudeness with a bright grin.

"I'd like the bibimbap with seafood tofu soup, please."

She blinks furiously, her pen frozen over the pad. I think he broke her. James finally glances in her direction.

"Did you hear what he said?"

She jumps. "Oh, yes, bibimbap with seafood tofu. Got it."

Our waitress skitters off. A second later, she returns and bows her head at Ben.

"I'm sorry. What level of spice do you want for your seafood tofu soup?"

"Oh. Um, number two, please."

She makes a hasty exit. Ben stares at James reproachfully.

"What?"

"You didn't have to be rude, James."

"What are you talking about?"

"The waitress?" Ben tips his chin in her direction. "You could have given her a minute to catch my order. I think you hurt her feelings."

"It's her job to write down orders quickly so her customers don't go hungry," James answers matter-of-factly. "I thought she didn't hear what you told her. That's all."

"Still . . ."

He arches one brow. "Let me guess. You want me to apologize?"

Ben nods. Secretly, I expect James to shake him off. Five minutes in his presence was enough to know he's not the type to say he's sorry.

His face softens, and he sighs. "Fine. When she comes back, I'll apologize."

What did he just say? Someone please come pick my jaw up off the floor.

Ben grins triumphantly. "Thank you."

I peer at Grace. She's normally the first to call this stuff out, but her lips are sealed tonight. Ben shifts in his seat so he's facing her.

"So, do you guys go to school nearby?"

Grace brightens. "We're seniors at Salvis Academy."

"Me too! But I've only been enrolled since spring break," Ben says.

"Wait, really? But I haven't seen you around school."

He squirms in his chair, glancing over at James.

"Well, uh, I'm not on campus much. Since it was so late in the year, my mom talked the school into letting me take my classes online. I only needed a couple to graduate, but she thought it would be good for me to come down before I start college in the fall."

That's a first. The teachers at Salvis are sticklers for attending classes. Ben's family must be super important if Principal Miller made an exception for him. I frown as something else occurs to me and I turn to James.

"Is that why I ran into you in the parking lot this morning? You're also doing online classes at Salvis?"

All three heads swivel my way. Grace's eyes widen, and I give her a quick nod.

James sits back and crosses his arms over his chest. "No. I graduated early."

"So you were what . . . feeling nostalgic?" I retort.

Grace kicks me under the table. I bite back a moan as she cocks her head.

"I left my wallet at his house," Ben explains. "I asked him to bring it to me."

"What have you been up to since graduation then, James?" Grace asks.

"I've been working at my dad's consulting firm."

"James has always been the smarter of the two of us," Ben teases. "Though I'm way more charming."

A dumpster full of rotten eggs would be more appealing than James, but I keep that to myself.

"Well, it's nice to officially meet you," I say instead. "Now that I know your name."

James shrugs. "It didn't come up before."

"Really?" My eyes narrow into slits. "Because I remember specifically asking—"

Grace aims a warning glance at me before turning to give Ben a melting smile. "I hope to see you on campus sometime."

"You will," he answers, winking. "Salvis seems quite nice."

James snorts. "It's not nearly as well-maintained as Superbia. The campus is small, and they're only the tenth best academy in Texas."

"What's Superbia?" Grace asks.

"Oh! Superbia Preparatory in Manhattan. That's the school James and I went to."

"Really?" Grace gestures at me. "Liza's sister, Jeannie, lives there. Liza's going to visit her for a few days after graduation."

Ben leans forward. "You have a sister?"

"Oh, um, yeah. She's finishing up her sophomore year at NYU," I answer.

"She's also a model," Grace volunteers. "A really successful one."

I suppress a groan. Did she really have to say that? People always act so shocked—as if the thought of me being related to someone hot blows their mind. James looks over at me in that moment. His steady stare is unnerving, his blank expression making it hard to tell what he's thinking. Thankfully, the server rolls our meals over on a metal tray. He arranges the small side dishes in the center of the table before transferring our individual plates.

"*Sopa* is coming," he tells us in a mix of English and Spanish.

"Gracias," I reply with a polite smile.

"You speak Spanish?" Ben asks.

"Only a little. I took it for a couple of years back in elementary school. It was my parents' idea."

The same server comes by to deliver their dishes. My head jerks over to James when he starts conversing with him in Spanish. All I catch are a few words, but it's enough to tell he's fluent. The man's eyes light up, and they chat for several minutes before the server excuses himself. James turns back to face us, and Ben laughs.

"Show-off."

I have another word for it. Grace kicks me a second time under the table and shakes her head imperceptibly. She knows me too well. I shove a bite of seaweed into my open mouth to keep it busy. It isn't until Grace nearly spits out the first sip of her soup that I remember my prank. She glowers at me.

"Sorry," I mouth.

Grace pushes it aside and moves to her entree. Little of it gets eaten, because she and Ben keep up steady conversation. As for me, I'm happy to focus on the delicious flavors of my meal. James appears equally content with picking at his plate. When the checks arrive, Ben swipes ours off our table and insists on paying.

"No, I can't let you do that," I protest, trying to grab it. "We barely know each other."

"Then I guess we'll have to change that," he says, looking directly at Grace.

She turns about eight shades of red. James, on the other hand, is a bit green in the face. I can't say I disagree with him on this one. The idea of spending more time in his presence turns my stomach.

Since I have yet to fully master arguing over a check, I allow Ben to pay on one condition.

"You have to let us treat you next time."

Ben looks at James for help, but he tips his head to the side.

"She's got a point. We both know you've been taken advantage of in the past."

I'm tempted to punch him in the face for the implication, but his words convince Ben to grudgingly agree.

"Fine, but it can't be more than what I paid today. That wouldn't be fair."

I square my shoulders. "Deal."

James, Grace, and I head toward the door while Ben pays at the counter. Once he's done, we walk out together. Ben gestures at the parking lot.

"Where are you two parked?"

"I'm in the garage," Grace tells him.

I point toward Boba Life. "I'm just down that way."

"Then we'll walk you both," he asserts, offering Grace his elbow.

James opens his mouth, presumably to complain, but one look from his cousin and he snaps his jaw shut. Ben's lips arch into another stunning smile.

"Lead the way."

# Chapter 7

Mom's been trying to "fix" me since day one. According to her, it's Dad's fault I'm stubborn and strong-willed. If he weren't so permissive, I wouldn't be so *wild*. Meanwhile, I hate the fact she's nice to everyone but me. In public, she's the perfect mother—kind, patient, and encouraging. At home, she's strict to a fault and more opinionated than a top food critic.

Her words roll off my back now, but it was harder when I was little. I still remember the loud conversation she had with our neighbor when we went to buy my first bra. I begged her to stop, cheeks aflame, but she just tipped her head in my direction with a smirk.

"See? So moody and she's barely twelve. She's such a handful."

The news of my plain white underwear traveled like wildfire though Chinatown, and by the following weekend, people I'd never met were congratulating me. I tried complaining to Jeannie, but she only chided me.

"You know Mom didn't mean anything by it. She's just proud of how mature you're becoming."

At fourteen, I hated everything about myself. I dreamed of being petite and delicate like the rest of my friends, but I was a raccoon in a panda cub world. Mom was no help then either, peering at me over her glasses as she complained about my weight.

"You need to stop eating all that rice, Liza. You don't have Jeannie's metabolism."

Other kids played sports and went to the beach. She wanted me to do none of that.

"Your skin should be as pale as the moon," she would remind me, "and your hair black as night. This is how husbands want their wives."

So I curled up in my favorite chair and read book after book. Sometimes, I was swept away to the fantastical worlds of Marie Lu and Sabaa Tahir. Other times, I squealed over the sweet ships from Sandhya Menon and Jenny Han. Anything to forget my real life for a little while.

By the time I was sixteen, I did everything to avoid going straight home after school—clubs, volunteering, even a sport or two (indoor, of course). Jeannie had moved to New York to attend college and model for one of the major agencies there. She was so excited about walking in Fashion Week. Dad and I still got along great, but he was rarely home. He didn't trust anyone else to do the cooking and was always at the restaurant.

That meant Mom and I spent a lot of time at home alone. I hated her daily ritual of finding something wrong with how I looked, how I acted, or what I said. I tried to prove I was a good daughter. I even got a part-time job for a while to buy my own clothes and pay for stuff with friends. I'd come home before curfew and never got anything less than an A in school. None of this mattered, though, as long as I refused to date the guys she picked for me.

That's why I'm not surprised to overhear Mom on the phone with Mrs. Lim when I walk in the door on Monday. Despite my hope of the contrary, she's determined to have Reuben over for dinner. There's a hint of desperation in her voice as she speaks.

"Yes, yes, of course. I'll make sure to avoid cooking anything with garlic that day," she says, bobbing her head up and down. "I wouldn't want him to end up in the hospital because of an allergic reaction."

Note to self: Buy a garlic necklace. A big one. Maybe two.

Mrs. Lim says something in return, and Mom cackles before they hang up. Part of me wants to "forget" we have dinner plans, but there's no way I'd get away with it without paying a heavier price. I try to back out of the kitchen quietly, but she catches sight of me.

"Liza! Come here for a minute."

Damn it.

I slap a blank look on my face. "Is everything okay?"

"Yes, yes, everything's fine," Mom says, moving over to the stove to start dinner. "I just wanted you to know Reuben will be coming over on Friday, so make sure you're home right after school so you can get ready."

"Get ready?"

"He's going to be our guest. I don't want you to look like you normally do."

I glance down at my *Star Wars* T-shirt and skinny jeans.

"What's wrong with the way I dress?"

She eyes me up and down. "I want you to wear a dress like a proper lady. And put on some makeup."

"I *am* wearing makeup!"

Mom steps uncomfortably close to examine my skin with squinted eyes.

She sighs. "I guess you are. Well, then, wear more."

I roll my eyes. "Or he can like me the way I am. Isn't that what he's supposed to do?"

"Don't tell me you're still reading those ridiculous romance novels." She opens one of the kitchen cabinets and pulls out a pot. "That's not how love works in real life."

First she calls me picky. Now she's dragging my taste in reading. Good thing she hasn't found the pile of historical romances on the top shelf of my closet. I'm pretty sure she'd have an aneurysm at the number of Julia Quinn and Eloisa James books I've hoarded. Fed up, I twirl around to make a dramatic exit. I hear her call my name again.

"There's one more thing. I need you to start helping me out at the bakery more regularly. Milly is going on maternity leave," she informs me, one hand on the refrigerator door.

I suppress a groan. I wouldn't mind being at the bakery if she'd stop nagging me while I'm there.

"Why can't you just hire someone else?"

She pulls out some Chinese spinach and shuts the door.

"We put out an ad, but it's going to take time for us to find someone good."

I start to protest, but she puts up a hand.

"Liza Yang, the money Dad and I make pays for the roof over your head, the car, your food, and those clothes you like so much."

I'm instantly wracked with guilt. Mom and Dad are often gone before I wake up and get home long after it gets dark.

My eyes drop to the floor. "Okay, fine. But this is temporary, okay? You know I've got finals coming up."

"Your exams are weeks away," she remarks. "That'll be plenty of time for me to hire someone new."

I lean a hip against the kitchen counter. "When do you need me?"

"Starting this Saturday."

I clench my fists. Why doesn't she ever give me any advance notice?

"I could've had plans, you know. What if I'd already promised to hang out with Grace or Sarah?"

"First of all, you know you have to run that by me," Mom reminds me as she turns the burner on. "Second, is helping your parents really less important to you than spending time with your friends?"

She sounds genuinely hurt. I quickly backtrack.

"Sorry, Mom. Of course not."

"Good."

I start to walk away but pause to look at her. "Anything else?"

"Nope. That was it."

As I walk away, I swear I hear her whisper:

"For now."

• • • • •

On Friday, the dreaded dinner with Reuben arrives. I drag Grace to Boba Life and hide there until Mom starts blowing up my phone. As I walk through the front door, I'm surrounded by a hurricane of activity. Water meets oil in a sizzling dance as Dad juggles multiple dishes on the stove. Mom buzzes around the room, never stopping as she cleans this counter and rearranges that shelf. Faint lines mark where carpet powder was removed by a vacuum, and the smell of fake flowers surrounds me.

In the formal dining room, our normally barren dining table has been covered with a fancy plastic cloth, and four settings await their guests. The laundry rack Mom hangs her delicates on has disappeared, tucked away in a closet for now. Though we're eating in there, the kitchen cabinets are shinier than I've ever seen them. The mess of bills and newspapers normally strewn across our breakfast table has been cleared away, and a small vase of fresh wildflowers adorns the center. The calendar on the wall has also finally made it to May after months of declaring it's still January.

I step fully into the kitchen, and Mom scrunches her nose at me.

"Why are you home so late? I told you Reuben was coming over tonight."

"Sorry. I had to meet Grace to grab some stuff for school."

"You shouldn't rely on Grace so much," she scolds, wiping the counter one last time. "You need to be more organized. Learn to take better notes. Put reminders in your phone."

I say nothing. I've learned the hard way that interrupting Mom only earns me a longer lecture. Thankfully, she runs out of steam quickly and shoos me out of the room.

"Go get ready, and do it fast! He'll be here any minute. I put an outfit for you on your bed."

I shudder at the memories of the horrid outfits she used to put me in for picture day. Thankfully, there's no photographic evidence, because my parents were too cheap to order the prints.

"Mom—" I start to protest, but she cuts me off.

"What are you waiting for? And put on some makeup, for crying out loud!"

I grit my teeth and stomp off to my room. I'm assaulted by the sight of the over-the-top dress the moment I walk in. It reminds me of a wedding cake, with flowers protruding from every inch of the blinding white fabric. With a high neck and hemmed below my knee, it sends a very clear message.

*I'm a delicate, innocent flower. Look, but don't touch.*

I want to take it into the backyard and set it on fire. Instead, I shrug out of my jeans and step into the monstrosity with the utmost reluctance. Maybe the dress will look better on. As I start to zip it, the flowers gather around my chest like puffy homing beacons, while the areas around my hips bunch and crease. I give the zipper a yank when it snags on my lower back. It doesn't go anywhere.

*It's too small. It's too small!*

I quickly abandon the dress and return to my old outfit. Mom's face turns scarlet when I walk back into the kitchen.

"Why aren't you changed? I told you—"

The phone rings, interrupting her. Dad picks it up and glances at Mom.

"It's Mrs. Lim."

She takes it from him with a frown. I can't make out what's being said, but she's definitely not happy. A few seconds later, Mom hangs up.

"I'm afraid Reuben can't make it tonight," she informs us, dejected. "He's sick."

I'd bet money it's a serious case of I-don't-want-to-itis. Dad clears his throat.

"Well, since we're not waiting for anyone, let's sit down and eat."

Mom shakes her head. "I'm not really hungry. You two go ahead."

She walks out. He spares me a wink and leaves to go after her. The corridor between the rooms carries their conversation to me with perfect clarity as I sit down to eat.

"It's just a dinner, *lǎo pó*. It's not anyone's fault the boy got sick."

"We can't lose this opportunity," she tells him. "I'll have to set something up with Mrs. Lim when he's feeling better."

"Why are you so insistent on matching Liza up? She's not even done with high school."

Mom tuts. "Liza doesn't have as many options as Jeannie. She's got too big a mouth and doesn't listen. If we don't start now, she'll end up alone for the rest of her life. Don't you want her to be taken care of when we're gone?"

"Don't worry so much, lǎo pó. I'm not planning on keeling over anytime soon, and Liza's a good girl. She'll find someone when the time is right. Just let her be."

"If I do that, she'll bring home some American boy with divorced parents and tattoos everywhere."

I choke on a sip of water. Why is Mom like this? I show her a picture of Ed Sheeran *one time*, and now she thinks I'm running off with someone like him. Meanwhile, she's never said a word about my cousin Diana, who has roses tattooed on her rib cage.

Their footsteps are heading my way, so I grab my dirty dishes and put them in the sink. Mom insists the dishwasher doesn't do a clean enough job, so we hand wash everything first. I rinse as Dad shovels a few bites in his mouth and packs the leftovers. He brings the other dishes over, and they get washed and carefully stacked in the racks too.

Mom immediately rearranges them. "If you put them like that, they won't be completely clean. Next time, make sure to do it like this."

I bite the inside of my cheek to keep from reminding her I've already washed them once. Instead, I finish up and have a seat on the living room couch while they head back to their room to watch their favorite Chinese soap opera. I promised Grace I'd call her after dinner, but since my bedroom shares a wall with theirs, I don't want Mom eavesdropping. She picks up on the third ring.

"Spill the tea, girl."

I recount the premature end to dinner. Grace bursts out laughing.

"I can't believe he didn't even bother showing up!"

"Believe it. This is exactly why I don't date Asian guys," I confide in a low voice. "They're all like this."

"That's not true! I've dated plenty who are super nice."

"That's because you have options, Grace. All the guys want to date you," I tell her, twirling the hoop on my ear. "So do all the girls. You're perfect, unlike me."

"Don't say that, Liza. You're gorgeous, smart, and super sweet," she says firmly. "Guys are just dumb."

"That's not what my mom thinks."

"I'm sorry," she tells me. "I don't know why your mom says those things to you. They're totally not true."

I shrug even though she can't see me. "It's just how she is. I've gotten used to it."

"Do you think she'll quit setting you up now?"

"I doubt it. She's harder to shake than Lebron. It's only a matter of time before she's at it again."

"What are you going to do when she does?" Grace asks.

"I don't know. I'll figure it out. I have to." I sigh, standing up and heading to the kitchen for a cup of tea. "Change the subject, will you?"

"Okay. Remember Ben from the Korean restaurant?"

"Yeah, why?"

"So, he asked for my number, and we've been texting every night this week. Sometimes during the day too."

She pauses. I hear an intake of breath, but nothing follows.

My hand freezes on my favorite mug. "What's wrong?"

"It's just . . . I don't know if he likes me as much as I like him."

There's a softness, a tinge of anxiety, in her voice I haven't heard in a long time. Ever since Eric cheated on her, Grace hasn't let anyone get close to her. She inevitably breaks things off with whomever she's dating as soon as she starts to catch major feels.

"Why would you think that?" I finally ask. "You just told me he's been texting you constantly."

"I know, but he hasn't technically asked me out yet. We just talk about random stuff and where our families are from."

I pour water into the kettle and turn the burner on.

"It sounds like he's trying to get to know you better."

She sighs heavily. "But what if he just wants to be friends? I really, really like him, Liza."

I think back to Tofu City. Ben was getting plenty of attention while we were at dinner, but he spent nearly all his time talking to her.

"Grace, I have yet to meet a living, breathing human who doesn't have a crush on you."

"You didn't," she teases. "And you've been living and breathing around me since sixth grade."

"I didn't want to risk our friendship."

"Yeah, yeah, you're all talk. I'm too good for you anyway," Grace drawls.

"I'm not going to argue that."

We both giggle. The kettle starts to whistle, and I pull it off the burner before it wakes Mom and Dad. After pouring the hot water into my mug, I clear my throat.

"Maybe Ben's just shy. Remember when you thought Christina didn't like you? Three months later, you guys were dating. Give it some time. He'll ask you out."

"You really think so?"

"I'd bet you a summer's worth of boba," I assert, steeping the tea leaves. "That's how sure I am."

I hear something go off on her end of the phone. She squeals.

"He's texting me now!"

"See?" I cut her off before she can offer an apology. "Go make him fall in love with you."

After we hang up, I tiptoe back into my room and grab my laptop before plopping onto my bed. I forgo the overhead light and leave only the delicate fairy strands hanging above my head. They cast a soft, golden glow over the wall of books across from me. Their spines form a rainbow, arranged by genre and author.

I place my laptop on the lap desk and pull up *Ashes of Love* on Netflix. The Chinese actors talk too fast for me to keep up, so I turn on the English subtitles. It started out kind of slow, but between the gorgeous costumes and epic romance, I'm completely hooked on this C-drama. It doesn't hurt that Deng Lun and Luo Yunxi are ridiculously hot in period clothes.

Who needs a date when I have them?

# Chapter 8

The next night, I pick Grace up from her house and head to Dumpling Dynasty. With tan tile floors and cheap wooden tables, the most impressive part about the place is the framed pieces on the wall from the students attending the Art Institute of Houston.

Scratch that. The food is by far the best thing.

I drop her off at the front door to grab a table while I find a parking space. A few minutes later, I head inside. I'm dressed in my favorite T-shirt, featuring a picture of Stitch cosplaying Toothless. My hair is up in my customary ponytail, though strands have already escaped their binding to graze my jaw.

"Liza! Over here!"

I turn toward her with a ready grin. It freezes on my face when I realize who's seated across from her in the booth. Dressed in a black-and-white-striped tee and ripped jeans, Ben's all twinkling eyes and white teeth. James, to his right, swivels his head slightly to give me the once-over. His eyebrows rise slightly as he takes in Stitch in all his winged glory. I can't tell if he's impressed or embarrassed to be seen with me, but I'm fairly certain it's the latter.

I drag myself over and slide in next to Grace. She's wearing one of her favorite ballet-pink sundresses, with a halter neckline and flouncy skirt.

"You didn't tell me anyone else was coming," I mutter under my breath.

"I didn't?"

She presses a hand to her chest like a Southern belle. I grit my teeth.

*You don't fool me, Grace Chiu. You're going to pay for this.*

"Oh, we didn't realize we were crashing your dinner," Ben says with a worried look.

"No!" Grace practically shouts. "I mean . . . you don't mind, right, Liza?"

*Do I mind that you're forcing me to babysit your crush's irritating cousin? No, not at all.*

I force myself to relax against my chair. "Of course not. The portions here are huge. You'll be doing us a favor."

James, who has been wordlessly staring at the menu, regards me intently.

"Have you eaten here before? Is the food any good?"

"It's great," Grace answers first. "I love the pan-fried dumplings. Super flavorful."

He glances over at her. "Most people add too much oil. I don't like greasy dumplings."

"Then don't order it," I deadpan without looking up from my menu.

That earns me a jab in the ribs. Ben snickers. I stretch my lips like Pennywise, and James's eyes widen slightly.

"What I mean to say is there are many other dishes you can order here."

He gulps. "What would you recommend?"

I consider another snide retort but think better of it. I turn my menu upside down and point at my favorite dishes.

"If I'm in the mood for dumplings, I order the leek ones. They're just as good as the ones I've had in Taiwan," I say. "If not, then I get the bean sauce noodles. Theirs is the best I've tried other than my Dad's."

"That's right!" Ben glances up at me. "Grace was telling me your family owns Yin and Yang Restaurant and Bakery down the street. I hear it's really popular."

"It's definitely one of the best places to go for Taiwanese food. Not that I'm biased or anything."

He chuckles. "Even so, I'd love to eat there sometime. What do you think, James?"

I lean forward onto my forearms, issuing a silent challenge.

*Go ahead. Say something bad about Dad's place.*

"Don't worry, Liza," Ben asserts. "James pretends he's a food critic, but I saw him eat three-day-old pizza firsthand."

"That was one time!" he instantly defends, coloring slightly. He turns to Grace and me. "There was a snowstorm in New York, and I would have frozen to death if I went outside."

I cock an eyebrow. "So it was a matter of life and death, then?"

"If you're referring to my stomach after eating it, then yes," he says.

Ben and Grace crack up. Even I let out a laugh, but James remains impassive. Honestly, I'm not sure if he realizes he made a joke.

"Are you kids ready to order?"

We pause our conversation to pick what we want, and our waitress quickly jots down the orders. While we wait, Grace and Ben send looks at each other, while James takes in the casual decor in the restaurant.

"So, Ben, are your parents going to move down with you?" I ask.

Ben averts his gaze, a tense smile on his lips. "Uh . . . they're not sure yet. My dad is the CEO of Eastern Sun Bank. They do have a branch here, but he travels a lot for work. We're staying with my mom's family in River Oaks for now."

If Mom were here, she'd have his birthday, blood type, and favorite foods in less than five minutes flat. Since it's just me, I leave it at that.

"Does that mean you'll be in town all summer?" Grace asks, her eyes wide and hopeful.

"Probably. We might go up to the Hamptons at some point."

The staff interrupts to drop off the pan-fried and cabbage dumplings. Both guys eye Grace's plate with interest.

"You're welcome to try some," she offers. "I can't eat them all myself."

Ben's answering smile sets even my heart aflutter. He plucks a pot sticker off the plate and dips it into a small pool of soy sauce.

"This is so good," Ben says around the bite in his mouth. "James, you've got to try this."

James pops one in his mouth. "Not bad."

This is probably high praise from someone like him. Our two orders of leek dumplings arrive shortly after, and I dig in right away. My eyes meet James's briefly, and a small smile touches his lips. I chide myself for noticing his dimple while Grace makes another attempt at conversation.

"So James, how are you liking it in Houston?"

He glances out the window before answering. "It's okay. The traffic reminds me of New York."

"Maybe Liza and I can show you guys around one of these days."

He and I shift uncomfortably in our seats. Ben, on the other hand, is thrilled.

"I'd love that! We've been so busy with our families it's been tough to figure out where everything is. Houston is so spread out."

Once we finish our meals, I turn to Ben. "Okay, we're paying this time. Just like we agreed."

He grins. "Too late. I already paid."

I swallow a groan. I should have known he didn't really have to go to the bathroom a few minutes ago. Classic distraction technique. Undeterred, I slide the money across the table at him.

He shakes his head adamantly. "No, I won't take it."

"Ben, come on. I don't feel right about this. We're just friends having dinner."

"Well, maybe I'm hoping things will change soon," he says, glancing at Grace.

She blinks furiously, color rising up her neck. Ever unobservant, James interrupts the moment.

"We should get going, Ben. My mom's waiting on us to help her set up the computers."

"Is it that time already?" He glances down at his watch. "Oh, wow. Time flies."

"Speaking of which"—Grace turns to me—"can you give me a ride home?"

We walk out to the parking lot as a group. It's only May, but the air is already balmy. Fluorescent streetlamps spotlight the flock of midnight-colored crows perched on the roofs of nearly every car. They scatter as we walk toward where we're parked but protest our intrusion with harsh cries.

Since it's clear Grace and Ben want some time alone, I'm stuck distracting James. She's going to owe me her firstborn at this rate.

"Uh, so . . . will you be here long?" I ask.

The soles of James's black leather oxfords scrape on the gravel as he pivots to face me. He fiddles with the buttons on the sleeve of his steel-blue shirt.

"What do you mean?"

"Well, I know Ben mentioned college, but you're just working for your dad's firm, right?"

"Yes."

I take a deep breath and exhale. "Then . . . you're just visiting?"

"No."

My hands fist at my sides. Could he make this any more difficult?

"You're just a fountain of information, aren't you?"

He jerks back. "I'm sorry?"

"Never mind."

"Our grandparents live in Sugar Land," James suddenly blurts out. "And like Ben said earlier, I'm working with my dad's firm, but I might stay for college. Rice offered me a full scholarship."

"That's where I'm going," I say, ignoring the familiar pang in my chest when I think about my future plans—the ones Mom and Dad chose for me. "I would have guessed you'd be going somewhere Ivy League."

"Why?"

"I don't know," I answer, rocking back on my heels. "You just seem like the type who'd care about that sort of thing."

"Oh. I didn't realize."

Was that a tiny hint of hurt in his voice? My eyes skim over James's features but find no clues.

"It was nice having dinner with you guys," I force out.

"Really?" He blinks. "I kind of thought you hated it."

*You weren't supposed to notice, damn it.*

Guilt gnaws at my stomach, so I soften my tone.

"Really. I hope you liked the food."

He slides his hands into his pockets. "Surprisingly, I did. The leek dumplings do remind me of the ones from Taiwan. Thanks for the recommendation."

"Uh, you're welcome?"

James smiles faintly. I glance over at Grace, but she's busy giggling at something Ben said.

*Think, Liza. What else can you talk about?*

"My parents go back to Taiwan every year," I finally say. "To find new recipes for Yin and Yang."

"Do you go with them?" he asks.

I shake my head. "They normally go during the school year because flights are cheaper. Last year, they went on a tour of Japan too. I wish I could have gone with them then."

"Japan is one of my favorite places to visit," James tells me. "Especially during the cherry blossom festival. Ben and I went to Yoshino to see them last year. There's a whole mountain of *sakura* trees there."

My eyes flutter closed as I try to imagine it. "I bet it's beautiful."

"It's one of the most beautiful things you'll ever see," he agrees. "You should definitely go if you get the chance."

"Meanwhile, all my parents got me was was a lousy T-shirt."

For a second, he just stares at me. Then he does something completely unexpected.

He laughs.

The sound is foreign to my ears, but I find myself smiling even as I wonder what to make of this side of him. Thankfully, I don't have to figure it out, because Ben and Grace finally make their way back to us. Their hands are joined, and they're wearing identical sappy grins. James, on the other hand, scowls. So much for civility.

"I'm sorry I have to go." Ben apologizes more to Grace than me. "We'll have to get together again soon."

"Yes, let's do that! Right, Liza?"

Her eyes plead with me to agree. I take a deep breath and smile.

"Sure."

"Then it's all settled," Ben says brightly. "We'll figure out a time."

We say our goodbyes and split up to head to our respective cars. After I start the engine, Grace turns to me with a devilish smirk.

"So . . . you and James, huh?"

*"Excuse me?"*

She pokes me in the arm. "I saw the way he was looking at you. He *likes* you."

"Um, no. You need to get your eyes checked, Grace."

"Why would you say that?"

"For one, the guy could barely stand talking to me, and the feeling's mutual," I say, eyes on Ben's car as it leaves the parking lot.

Grace frowns. "Do you really not like him? He kind of reminds me of Darcy, with that whole awkward silent thing he does."

"I'm offended on Darcy's behalf that you would even say that," I answer. "James is nothing like him."

Grace tips her head toward me. "Okay, fine, but you have to admit, he's total bae material."

"Did my mom put you up to this?"

"Stop it," she scolds, "and don't change the subject. Tell me you don't think he's hot, and I'll leave you alone."

James's full lips and strong jaw flash through my mind.

"I don't think he's hot," I say with flaming cheeks.

Grace laughs. "You're such a liar!"

"No, I'm not!"

My denial sounds empty to my ears too.

I feign a casual shrug. "Fine. James is nice to look at, but he's got the personality of a honey badger."

"Maybe he's just *shy*."

I roll my eyes. "You don't know what you're talking about."

She cackles. "Hmm. Lady doth protest too much, methinks."

"Glad to see you were paying attention during English class, but you're still totally off base," I tell her as I tug at my seat belt.

"I'll bet you an entire *year's* worth of boba you two are gonna hook up."

I jut my hand out. "I'll take that bet."

She gives it a firm shake.

I smirk as I head out of the parking lot. "You better start saving."

# Chapter 9

On graduation day, I wake up before my alarm and throw on the dress Mom bought me. I can't get away with saying it doesn't fit this time because she double- and triple-checked the size before buying it. Thankfully, I was able to skip giving the salutatorian speech since we ended up with two valedictorians this year, so no one will have to see the obnoxiously loud floral pattern peeking out from beneath my robe.

The ceremony is held in our school auditorium. I'm shocked when Principal Miller introduces Mrs. Lee as our commencement speaker. We were expecting Mayor Turner, but he must have canceled. Mrs. Lee is dressed in a well-tailored, dove-white pantsuit, and her hair is pulled up in a chic chignon. Eye-popping diamond studs hang heavily on both earlobes, and a diamond-encrusted three-leaf clover, identical to the one in the Van Cleef & Arpels ad I saw in *Cosmo* earlier this month, hangs around her neck.

I don't remember much of her speech, save for one thing. As she stands tall at the podium, her eyes seem to bore into mine.

"Find your passion. Figure out not just what you're good at, but what you really love to do. What's something you would give up your free time or sleep for?"

My eyes flutter closed. The smell of fresh pastries fills my nose, and the open oven door blankets me in heat. I give myself a shake.

*Give it up, Liza. It's never going to happen.*

My hands clench in my lap as Mrs. Lee continues.

"Do what you love. If you do that, it'll all work out."

Afterward, Mom and Dad head back to Yin and Yang for the rest of the day, while I meet up with Grace and her family at Ramen Time. Then we head to Sarah's graduation party at Boba Life. She's been obsessed with boba ever since we introduced her to it.

We're there until almost ten o'clock. I would stay longer, but I forgot to ask Mom to extend my curfew. She's ready with a lecture when I step in the door, so I end up packing for New York while she paces around my room complaining about how irresponsible Mrs. Lee's advice was. It takes until almost one in the morning before I finish, and it's almost one thirty when I finally pass out.

The next morning, I wake up with a tea hangover. Dad pokes his head into my room. His shoulders relax at seeing me already awake.

"We're leaving in fifteen minutes, so get ready."

After one final check to make sure I have everything, I drag my suitcase out of the room. Both Mom and Dad are waiting at the breakfast table.

"You need to have some breakfast before you leave," Mom says.

I groan. "It's too early to eat. I'm not hungry."

"By the time you get to the airport, you will be, and airport food is too expensive," she insists. "Eat something now."

I grumble but plop down into the chair to make a breakfast bun. I split a mantou down the middle and add shredded pork and strips of egg. I chase it down with a glass of soy milk and move to put on my shoes.

Mom stops me. "Wait a minute."

She leaves the room and returns with a light jacket. "It gets cold on the plane. I don't want you to get sick."

I accept it without protest. "Thanks, Mom."

"Do you have your plane ticket? Did you print it out like I told you to last night?"

"It's on my phone, Mom. They have an app for that."

"You should have a printed copy just in case." She points toward our study. "Go print one."

"Mom . . ."

"If we don't leave now, Liza will be late," Dad interjects. "I'll make sure she prints one from the airline kiosk. She'll be fine."

I smile gratefully at him. I stiffen when Mom abruptly wraps her arms around me.

"Text me when you get there. Promise me."

"I promise."

I didn't expect the idea of me flying alone for the first time to worry her so much. My arms tighten around her for a brief moment before letting go.

I fall asleep almost immediately in the car and startle awake when we pull to a stop in front of the departure gate. Dad gets out and helps me grab my luggage from the trunk. We stare at each other for an extraordinarily long second. Then he steps forward and pats me firmly on the shoulders.

"Don't forget to print your boarding pass."

I smile. "I'll remember."

An hour later, I walk down the ramp onto the airplane. My Kindle, headphones, and phone are tucked tightly under one arm. Once I stick my bag in the overhead bin, I settle into my seat and send Mom and Dad a text.

**Boarded plane. Waiting for takeoff.**

Almost immediately, Dad's reply pops up.

**Good. Text us when you land.**

On a whim, I type out three words and hit send.

**I love you.**

Three dots blink for almost a minute before Mom's reply pops up.

**Be safe.**

I sigh. With my phone tucked into my pocket, I lean back and close my eyes.

● ● ● ● ●

"Liza! Liza!"

When I finally step into the main terminal of LaGuardia, I spot Jeannie waving frantically at me from her spot by the doors. Between college and modeling, she hasn't had a chance to come home for almost a year. I've missed having my sister around. No one else understands what it's like to deal with Mom all the time. As luck would have it, though, she'll be coming back to Houston for a bit during the summer, and I can't wait to have her home again.

I want to launch myself toward her, but hesitate when I grow near. She's always been thin, but the pallor and dark circles are new. When she hugs me, I'm afraid I'll break her.

She takes a step back to look at me. "Oh my goodness, Liza. You're so tall now."

"Don't worry, I still need you to reach the high shelves," I joke.

When Jeannie smiles, her face lights up like it always has, so I trade my concern for a grin. We walk out of the terminal and toward the ride share area together. Jeannie requests a car before guiding us to the numbered spot to wait. I pull out my own phone to text Mom and Dad before I forget. As soon as I do, it rings.

"Hello?"

"Is Jeannie with you? Put her on the phone," Mom demands.

I sigh. *How was your flight, Liza? I miss you already. I hope you have a good time.*

Jeannie bumps her shoulder against mine. I shrug and pass the phone over.

She takes a deep breath. "Hi, Mom."

"Jeannie! Why haven't you called us? It's been almost a month since we talked to you. Are you okay? Is there something wrong?"

"I'm fine, Mom. I told you. I'm just super busy with school and modeling."

Our car arrives, and Jeannie waves the driver over. The middle-aged woman pops the trunk and helps me get my bag inside. Jeannie slides in behind the driver's seat, while I settle into the other side. She keeps the phone to her ear while confirming her address with the driver. As we pull away from the curb, Mom shouts into the phone.

"Are you listening, Jeannie?"

Jeannie cringes. "Yes, yes, Mom. I was just talking to our driver."

She finishes the conversation as I stare out the window. As the Manhattan skyline appears in the distance, Jeannie squeezes my hand.

"This is going to be so much fun," she squeals. "Oh, Mom says she misses you already."

I chortle. "No, she didn't."

"How do you know?"

"The same way you do," I remind her, turning my attention back to the window. "She's Mom."

"So maybe she didn't say it out loud, but I know she does," Jeannie insists.

No matter what I say, she'll never accept that Mom doesn't treat us the same. So I change the subject.

"Is the traffic always this bad?"

Our driver's been squeezing herself into spots barely big enough for her car, and every last-second swerve sets my teeth on edge. Jeannie is unfazed.

"This is actually pretty good for the city. It's even worse when it's rush hour."

I'm ready to call it quits and walk the rest of the way when we finally bank around Columbus Circle. Jeannie suddenly leans forward and points at a building in the distance.

"Right there," she instructs the driver. "You can drop us off after this intersection."

I heave a sigh of relief once my feet hit the pavement. With my luggage in tow, I follow Jeannie across the street to where a row of brick and stone buildings stand sentry over Central Park. We stop in front of a pair of glass doors, and I admire the intricate, swirling design of the metal overlay. Jeannie pulls out her keys, and we step inside. The elevator takes us up to the fifteenth floor, where she unlocks her door and lets me in.

My jaw drops immediately. "This looks expensive."

Jeannie laughs. "It belongs to one of Dad's friends. Remember Uncle Tam, the real estate guy? He needed someone to watch the place while he's out of the country."

Heavy black curtains have been tugged aside to reveal large picture windows overlooking the lush green trees of Central Park. Sunlight softens the edges of the industrial furniture spread throughout. The condo is unmistakably masculine, yet somehow Jeannie's made it her own. Plants line the windowsills, potted in colorful ceramics that offset the navy painted walls. A collection of her old animal figurines lines the shelves and side tables nearby.

I make my way down to Jeannie's room. Just like mine back home, fairy lights hang above her bed. Books on positive thinking and building self-confidence are stacked on her bedside table, including one she gifted me a copy of last Christmas. A small vanity holds all her makeup and jewelry; exposed bulbs ensure she has the best lighting. Down the hall are the full bath and a guest bedroom.

She opens the door. "This will be yours while you're here."

I throw myself onto the mattress and wrap myself in the plush white down comforter.

"I can't believe I get my own room," I say, my voice muffled beneath the blanket.

"What did you think was going to happen?" Jeannie asks, plopping down next to me and swinging her legs up onto the bed.

"I don't know. I thought all New York apartments were supposed to be overpriced closets."

Jeannie scrunches her nose. "You really think Mom and Dad would let me move here if that were the case?"

"Fair point." I stretch my arms out and make a bed angel. "So, what're we doing today?"

"*You* can take a nap or watch TV for now. I have a casting call this afternoon."

My stomach grumbles loudly. "What about lunch?"

I give her my best puppy look. Jeannie doesn't give in, instead hopping up and motioning toward the kitchen on her way out of the room.

"There's food in the fridge. We can go out for dinner when I get back."

"Ugh, fine," I mutter, trailing behind her.

Back in her room, Jeannie touches up her makeup. I marvel at her ability to make it look like she has nothing on. She changes into a plain white T-shirt and skinny jeans and throws her hair up in a messy bun. I walk her to the door.

She pulls me in for a hug. "Okay, I'm off. See you in a bit."

"Bye."

She waves as the elevator arrives, and I head back inside and lock the door. I drag myself to my room and pull the curtains closed with a yawn. My clothes come off, and an oversized T-shirt and sweatpants take their place. Then I slip between the covers and close my eyes.

# Chapter 10

*What was that?*

My eyes pop open. I sit straight up in bed and listen for the sound that startled me awake. For a moment, there's only silence, but then I catch a faint rustling noise. I slip out of bed and pad softly down the hallway. With one eye on the now jiggling lock, I grab hold of the only thing in the kitchen that might inflict damage—a meat tenderizer. I sneak over to the door just as it swings open.

I jump out and swing the meat tenderizer blindly. "Take that!"

"Hey, watch it!"

My first strike met air, so I cock my arm for a second blow. The man puts his hands up and backs out of reach.

"Wait! Jeannie, it's me! It's me!"

I freeze. He knows Jeannie? My hands start to sweat as he peers through his fingers at me.

I level my most menacing glare. "Who are you?"

"My name's Nathan," he says, hands still in the air.

"How do you know Jeannie?"

"She's my friend. Call her if you want. I swear I'm not lying."

I pat my pocket with my free hand. Damn it. It's on the nightstand.

I jut my chin out. "Jeannie said she doesn't have a spare key."

"That's because she lent it to me," Nathan answers slowly. "I was bringing it back to her. And what about you? How do I know *you're* not the intruder?"

"Because I'm her sister."

"Her sister?" His hazel eyes skim across my features. "Oh! Liza, right? Jeannie talks about you all the time. I hear you're an amazing baker."

He flashes me a brilliant smile and points at my makeshift weapon.

"Any chance you'd be willing to put that down?"

I reluctantly put the tenderizer down and step aside to let him in.

"Sorry about that. I guess I've seen one too many crime shows."

"Actually, it was good thinking on your part. If I were a real intruder, I'd be running with my tail between my legs."

He plucks the tenderizer off the table and replaces it in the drawer I pulled it out of. He pulls a pitcher out of the fridge and pours himself a glass of water. I sneak a closer look at him as he drops down onto the sofa. Nathan is exactly the kind of guy Jeannie always goes for—great hair, gorgeous face, tall, and confident. With his thick jet-black hair and hazel eyes, Nathan would get Mom's approval, even from two thousand miles away. I'm surprised they're not already dating. They must be close if Jeannie's lending him her keys. I sit in the armchair across from him and fold my legs onto the seat.

"So how do you know Jeannie?" I finally ask.

He runs a hand through his hair. "We met at a fashion show."

"You're a model too?"

"I am, but don't judge me for it," he replies with a wink.

For a minute, my mind goes blank. I clear my throat.

"So are you from New York originally?"

"I've been all over the place. My dad works in international business, so we moved every few years when I was a kid." He plays with the stitching on one of the cushions. "When my parents got divorced a few years back, my mom and I stayed here."

"Oh, I'm sorry. I didn't mean to pry."

"It's okay. He's not a bad guy. He just wasn't very good at being loyal to my mom. I still see him when he's in town."

"Are you close with your mom?" I ask.

Nathan shrugs. "Usually, but things are kinda tense right now. She wants me to take college more seriously, but I don't see why I can't do whatever I want as long as I take a class here and there." He straightens, the playful glint back in his eyes. "FYI, some colleges offer credit in wine appreciation."

I giggle. Nathan looks me over then, and I clasp my hands in my lap so I don't fidget. He grins.

"Were you asleep before I came in?"

I bite back a groan. "That obvious, huh?"

"I've done some marathon sleeping in my time," he answers, leaning against the back of the couch. "I recognize the signs. I'm sorry I scared you like that."

He props his feet up on the coffee table but immediately removes them when he sees the look on my face.

"Sorry," Nathan says with a sheepish grin. "That was rude of me. Please don't tell Jeannie."

I see why she likes him. He's charming almost to a fault. As I stare at him, something clicks.

"Were you really just wanting to return her key? Because you could have just texted her."

Nathan flushes and rubs the back of his neck. "Ah . . . well, I came by to see if she wanted to grab some dinner. But obviously she'll be busy hanging out with you."

I suppress a smile. "I'll tell her you came by."

*And interrogate her about why she hasn't locked you down yet.*

"Thanks. I guess I should head out."

He takes the glass to the sink and rinses it out. I walk him over to the door.

"It's nice to meet you, Liza Yang," Nathan says, sticking his hand out. "Hopefully, when we see each other again, you won't feel compelled to attack me."

I give his hand a firm shake. "Well, next time, announce yourself first."

"Touché."

He steps out into the hallway. When he reaches the elevator, I hear myself calling out to him.

"I'll ask Jeannie what she's got planned for tomorrow. Maybe we can all have dinner then."

Nathan smiles crookedly. "Promise you'll leave the tenderizer at home?"

"It's a deal."

• • • • •

I tell Jeannie what happened as soon as she gets home. We're sitting together on the couch, and emotions flit across her face as she listens to the story. When I get to the part about attacking Nathan with the meat tenderizer, she gapes at me.

"You did what?!"

"Well, I thought he was an intruder, so I swung and—" I pause, and our eyes lock. "I missed."

We burst into laughter at the same time, and Jeannie giggles until she cries.

"I can't believe you seriously tried to hit him!"

I put on my sternest face. "At least now he knows not to mess with us Yang girls."

"I hope you don't plan on tenderizing all my friends."

"Only the rude ones."

"I can live with that," she agrees, bopping me on the nose. "And since you already roughed him up, I won't punish him for barging into my apartment like that."

I swat her hand away. "Seriously, though, he seems nice. And he's really ridiculously good-looking."

"All models are good-looking," she answers pertly.

"I beg to disagree. Some of them are only worth looking at from the neck down."

"Liza!"

Jeannie clutches at her chest. I roll my eyes.

"Don't look so shocked. I'm not as innocent as you think."

She gasps. "Does Mom know?"

It takes a second for her question to sink in. Heat floods my body as I backtrack.

"No, no! That's not what I meant! I just meant I read a lot of romance novels. Plus, you know, movies and TV and stuff."

She slumps against the couch. "Oh, good. You're too young for that, okay?"

"Now who sounds like Mom?"

"I'm just saying . . ."

I squint at her. "Don't tell me you're still—"

"No!" Jeannie yelps. "I mean, obviously, I've had boyfriends before, so . . . you know."

"I've had boyfriends too, but none as hot as Nathan," I can't help teasing.

I barely have time to duck as she aims a throw pillow at my head. I dodge it and tackle her to the ground, tickling her until she cries *uncle*. I poke her in the ribs one more time before relenting.

"Call your boyfriend and invite him to dinner."

"First of all, he's *just* my friend," she corrects. "Second of all, this is our weekend together. No boys allowed."

"Okay, but you gave him your spare key."

Jeannie sighs. "If I invite him to dinner, will you get off my back?"

"Maybe."

She narrows her eyes at me, and I heave a dramatic sigh.

"Okay, fine. I promise."

Jeannie shakes her head and gives Nathan a call. They talk briefly, and I don't miss the color in her cheeks as she hangs up. She wags a finger at me before I can say anything.

"He'll be here soon. Go get changed."

"Am I going to have to dress up?"

She peers at me. "If by dress up, you mean wear clothes that don't smell or have holes, then yes."

"If only that's how Mom defined *dressed up*," I complain.

"I'm guessing she's still after you to wear dresses."

"You guess correctly."

Back in my room, Jeannie searches through what I brought. Her eyes widen at the endless collection of T-shirts in my bag. She settles on a black *Deathly Hallows* shirt and tosses it into my arms.

"This'll work. Do a front tuck with your jeans and it's perfect."

"Isn't that what Tan's always doing to the shirts on *Queer Eye*?"

"It is." She grins. "I told you the Fab Five could teach you real life skills. Now show me your best tuck."

Jeannie waits patiently for me to put on the T-shirt, then tucks in the section just above the zipper of my jeans. A tug here and a yank there, and I meet her approval. While she gets ready in her room, I hear a knock on the door.

I open it and smile. "Hey, Nathan."

"Hi, Liza."

He eyeballs my hands. I hold them up for him to inspect.

"No weapon. I promise."

"Good to know." He pretends to wipe his brow. "One near beating is enough for me."

Jeannie walks out then, dressed in a blush-colored silk blouse with bow detailing. She's paired it with vegan leather black leggings and topped everything off with a black Chanel tweed jacket and ankle boots. He whistles.

"You look great, Jeannie."

She smiles shyly. "Thank you."

Nathan leans over to hug her, and it lasts a few seconds longer than is friendly. I resist the temptation to make kissy faces at Jeannie.

"So, where are we going for dinner?"

Nathan purses his lips. "Are you craving anything in particular?"

"Well, my friend Grace told me I had to try New York pizza."

"That's a *must*. In fact, we'll take you to Joe's."

My brows stitch together in concentration. "Wait. Is that the place Spider-Man works at?"

"I knew I liked you for a reason," he replies with a grin. "You're exactly right, but I'm taking you to the OG Joe's on Carmine."

"Aren't they pretty much the same?"

Jeannie laughs as Nathan balks at me. "I wouldn't say that too loud if I were you. New Yorkers are majorly divided on that one. But I swear the OG is better."

"Then what are we waiting for?"

# Chapter 11

Joe's Pizza definitely lives up to the hype, as does everything else Jeannie takes me to over the next few days. My Instagram account, previously full of memes and food pics, has doubled in size. We've done all the touristy stuff, including the Statue of Liberty, Ellis Island, the Empire State Building, and the World Trade Center. Yesterday was a whole day at the Met, followed by dinner and *Aladdin* on Broadway. By the time we got home, I went straight to bed and passed out.

Today, we've been taking it easy. I'm reading in bed when I hear a knock at my door before it swings open.

"Get dressed, Bunbun," Jeannie says.

She bounces into my room unexpectedly and throws herself onto the bed. She must have just walked in the door, though I didn't hear her come in. I put down my Julia Quinn novel and look her over. Jeannie's long black hair is pinned back into a twist, and she's dressed in another fitted white T-shirt and skinny jeans. On closer inspection, there's just enough makeup on her face to highlight her features.

Jeannie pokes me in the arm. "Come on, or we'll be late."

I check the time on my phone. How is it six o'clock already?

"Late to what? Where are we going?"

"It's a surprise."

I arch an eyebrow. "Uh . . . am I going to like this surprise?"

"Of course you are. In fact, I bet you'll say this is the best part of the whole trip."

That's a bold statement. Everything we've done so far has been pretty spectacular.

"Well?" She eyes me impatiently. "Are you gonna get moving or what?"

"This better be worth my getting dressed," I quip as I climb off the bed.

"Have I ever steered you wrong?"

A certain unfortunate hairdo in middle school comes to mind. Jeannie swore spiral perms were in, but I just looked like an overgrown poodle. She must guess what I'm thinking because she interrupts as soon as I open my mouth.

"About something other than fashion."

"Fine. I'll get changed," I relent, opening the closet door.

"Great!"

Jeannie flounces out the room. A second later, I stick my head into the hallway.

"One more thing."

She turns back to look at me. "What?"

"Don't call me Bunbun!"

• • • • •

Despite my best efforts, Jeannie adamantly refuses to give me any hints as to where we're going. It's a bit brisk when we step outside the building, so I put on my jacket. When we reach the corner, Jeannie hails a taxi. A few minutes later, we're headed downtown.

As we make our way past Rockefeller Center, traffic slows down enough that I'm able to grab a few pics of the gilded gold statue and beautiful fountains.

Jeannie taps me on the shoulder when we reach Bryant Park.

"Look! Right there. It's the New York Public Library."

Twin lions flank the steps leading up to the light stone edifice I've only seen in movies.

"It's beautiful!"

Jeannie smirks. "Wait until you see the inside. Remind me to take you before you leave."

We continue past the Empire State Building, though I don't recognize it immediately from ground level. Then, we come up on a distinctive triangular building next to a small park.

"That's the Flatiron Building," Jeannie informs me without being asked. "They call it that because it's shaped like one."

I tilt my head to the side. "I guess it is."

"How would you know? You've never used one."

Jeannie dodges the slap I aim at her arm before turning to direct our driver. He pulls to the curb a few feet away and lets us out. Jeannie leads me through the doors of Patisserie Chanson, a sleek French bakery. The decor reminds me of an airplane, with glinting aluminum squares jutting from the ceiling and white tile along both walls. My eyes flutter closed briefly as butter and sugar beckon to me from the clear glass cases on the right. I turn to her.

"This is the surprise?"

She grins. "Not quite."

Before I can ask any more questions, a blonde woman dressed in all black approaches us.

"Good evening. Do you have a reservation?"

"Yes," Jeannie answers. "Party of two for Jeannie Yang."

The hostess checks her computer, and then nods. "Follow me, please."

She leads us down a set of stairs into a dim, cozy room. Above us, exposed brick slopes across the ceiling and down to form the wall of a long bar. Oval booths line the opposite side, and colorful star-shaped tiles decorate the floor. The hostess brings us to two stools about halfway down the bar, where five other people are already seated.

"Enjoy."

I perch myself on the seat to Jeannie's right. When she's settled, I lean over and whisper in her ear.

"You know I'm not old enough to drink, right?"

She shushes me. "Just wait and see."

After a few more groups fill in the remaining open spots, a trio of chefs appears to join the bartenders. The tallest of the three, a stocky man with brown hair shaved along the side and blue eyes, begins to speak.

"Welcome, everyone, to the Chanson Dessert Bar. Tonight, we'll be preparing a six-course menu meant to delight your senses. If you've never been here before, get ready for a one-of-a-kind dessert experience."

He goes on to explain that each course will be prepared tableside from beginning to end. My eyes widen as they meet Jeannie's.

She winks. "Surprise!"

I don't stop grinning until the tasting begins. After the first course of olive oil gelato, the chefs move on to yuzu parfait with honeycomb. I'm enthralled by their use of liquid nitrogen, flame torches, and even Himalayan salt blocks. The chefs demonstrate techniques I've never seen before, and I take videos of them on my phone for later. The menu alternates between sweet and savory, but everything blends together like magic. During a lull in the courses, Jeannie cocks her head at me.

"So, are you excited about starting at Rice in the fall?"

I shrug. "I guess. I originally wanted to go out of state like you, but Mom nearly had a heart attack when I asked."

"Have you decided on a major?"

"Not yet." I play with the stem of my glass. "They want me to do accounting so I can help out at Yin and Yang."

"Is that what you want?"

I say nothing, but she reads the answer in my eyes and sighs.

"Why don't you tell them? They were totally cool with me still modeling in college."

"That's because you're the golden child. They'd support you even if you joined a cult."

She takes a sip of her wine before answering. "I doubt that, Liza. They're strict with me too."

"It's not the same," I tell her. "As far as Mom's concerned, I can't even make my bed right. You're good at everything."

"That's not true. I can't bake worth a damn."

"You're right. The last time I tried one of your cookies, I almost cracked a tooth." I press a hand to my cheek to emphasize my point.

Jeannie pokes me in the arm. "It wasn't that bad."

"My molars disagree."

She rolls her eyes and waves me off as the next dish appears in front of us.

• • • • •

When the tasting concludes for the night, we emerge onto the street outside the bakery, stuffed and happy. As we stroll along the sidewalk, Jeannie hooks her arm through mine.

"That was amazing," I say, glancing at her. "I wish I could bake like those pastry chefs."

"You could totally be as good as them," Jeannie insists.

"Maybe . . ." I answer, my voice trailing off.

She stops short. "I have an idea! Why don't you enter the contest? You'll win for sure, and maybe that'll help change Mom's mind."

I shake my head. "She'll never let me enter, Jeannie."

We keep walking. Despite what I said, her words echo through my mind. What if she's right? I can bake circles around those contestants, even the ones who've competed before. I have the trophies to prove it. What's the worst that could happen?

A few minutes later, I'm busy planning bakes in my head when I hear Jeannie yelp.

"Liza, watch out!"

She yanks me away just in time to avoid colliding with a couple.

"Hey! Watch where you're going!"

I open my mouth to apologize, but the words die in my throat. The girl I nearly bumped into looks like she could walk the runway with Jeannie. Tall, slender, and dressed in a gold bandage dress and five-inch stilettos, the only ugly thing about her is her expression.

"What is wrong with you?! You almost stepped on my shoes!"

"I'm sorry," I mumble, staring at the ground. "I didn't see you."

"Didn't see—"

"Let it go, Nina. She didn't do it on purpose."

I shift my attention to her companion, and I stiffen immediately.

"James."

He tips his chin. "Liza."

"You know her?" Nina asks.

"You know them?" my sister parrots.

"We met in Houston," James explains to Nina. "We have . . . mutual friends."

His dark eyes drop down and linger on the front of my T-shirt. I belatedly remember what's on it—a fox wearing glasses and FOXY NERD written across the bottom. He presses his lips together as if trying to hide a smile. Nina, on the other hand, looks down her nose at me. Tomorrow's newspaper headline flashes in front of me.

*Teenage Tourist Bludgeons Terrified Model with Own Stiletto*

I chuckle out loud before I can stop myself. Nina scowls. As she starts to say something else, James interjects.

"We were just leaving dinner."

I expect him to ask a question, but he just stands there and stares. A beat passes, and I square my shoulders.

"In that case, don't let me stop you. Good night."

I spin on my heel and walk off without checking to see if Jeannie's following. I'm halfway down the block when James calls out to me.

"Liza! Hold on a minute!"

I'm tempted to ignore him and keep going, but Mom's voice pops into my head.

*Don't make a scene, Liza. Remember, everything you do is a reflection of our family.*

My jaw clenches, but I turn back to face him as he jogs up to me. Jeannie moves to join us, but gradually enough it's obvious she's giving us some privacy.

I glare up at him. "What do you want, James?"

"Oh, uh, I wanted to apologize . . . for Nina," he answers after clearing his throat. "She can be . . . a bit demanding."

I have a different word in mind, but nod anyway.

"Sure. Whatever."

He rubs the back of his neck. "Um, so, I didn't realize you were in Manhattan."

"I'm here visiting my sister," I answer.

"Ah, right. You said that . . . before."

Jeannie finally stops beside me. She smiles warmly and offers her hand.

"I'm Jeannie. It's nice to meet you."

He takes it and gives it a gentle shake. "James, and likewise. Were you two having dinner?"

"Actually, I took Liza to the Chanson Dessert Bar."

"Oh, it's one of my favorite places," he says with a faint smile. "Did you enjoy it?"

I start to answer, but Nina is barreling toward us, and she looks positively murderous.

I make a face. "You might want to get back to your girlfriend. She looks pissed."

"My girlfriend?" James glances over his shoulder. "Oh, Nina's not—I ran into her at the restaurant. We know each other from school. She was alone, so I offered to walk her home."

I'm taken aback. James, who can't be bothered to be nice to a server, offered to walk someone home? He must really like her. Something about that makes my heart twinge, and I shove the thought aside. There are only a few seconds before Nina descends on us, and I don't want this to ruin my otherwise perfect night.

I look at him pointedly. "You should probably tell her then, because she seems to think otherwise."

Right on cue, Nina threads an arm through his elbow and tugs lightly at him.

"Come on, James. We should get going."

I glance over at Jeannie. She takes note of my clenched jaw before turning to the others.

"Us too."

A small crease appears between James's brows, but he ultimately nods.

"Good night, Liza. I hope you enjoy the rest of your trip."

"Good night."

He escorts Nina down the street, while Jeannie hails a cab. By the time our taxi merges onto the street, they're gone.

• • • • •

With two days left before I'm due to fly out, Jeannie and I make the most of the time we have left. After the trip to Patisserie Chanson, I'm inspired to try my hand at something new. She's all for it, and she takes me to a nearby Japanese supermarket once I settle on an idea—agar jelly cake. We pick up some *kanten*, canned lychee, and fresh fruit. Since I'm baking, Jeannie offers to make dinner in exchange, and we set up in different areas of the kitchen.

The mangoes, strawberries, and kiwi get diced first. Then I dissolve the kanten powder into cool water. Once the lychee juice is strained, I add it in before bringing it all to a boil. As soon as I pour the first layer of jelly, I spread the fruit evenly through the pan. The rest of the liquid jelly is poured over that. I put the cake aside to set and hop over to check on Jeannie's progress.

"What are you making?"

"If you must know, nosy girl," she states while setting the oven temperature, "I'm baking some sea bass and basting it with miso. I've already made some stir-fried spinach and a small pot of rice for you."

"Mmm. Smells delicious!"

She glances back at my pristine station. "Are you done baking already?"

"What can I say? When you're good, you're good."

She narrows her eyes at me, and I laugh. "Fine. It was a no-bake recipe."

"That's what I thought. What do you still have left to do?"

"I'm trying to figure out if I want to add a couple more layers to the cake." I chew on my lower lip. "It'd probably taste even better with some mango and coconut milk."

"Let's skip it. Less calories to worry about." Jeannie catches me mid-frown. "What?"

I grit my teeth. I've been trying to figure out how to broach the topic, and it's now or never.

"Jeannie . . . are you eating enough?"

Her head jerks up. "What?"

"You've lost a lot of weight. Plus, you barely had any bites of the dessert at Chanson. I've seen you diet before, but this is different."

For a second, it looks as though Jeannie won't answer me. Then she puts a hand on my arm.

"It's not what you think, Liza. It's my job to look a certain way. Designers expect you to fit their sample size or risk not being booked. Once you're hired, your weight has to stay the same until the show is done."

My eyebrows shoot up, and I cross my arms over my chest. She sighs.

"Ask Nathan. He'll tell you the same. It's just part of the industry."

I don't know what to say to that, so I take a different approach.

"Do you even like modeling?"

Jeannie bastes the fish with another layer of miso before turning to me.

"I've never thought much about it. Everything happened so fast, you know?" She cocks her head to the side. "I do love the clothes and the traveling. Plus, I'm good at it."

"You're good at other things too," I insist. "You're way more talented than me."

"No, I'm not. Not really." She pauses to stick the bass in the oven. "In fact, don't tell Mom and Dad, but I still haven't picked a major."

I gasp. "But you're about to be a junior!"

"I know! That's what I'm talking about. At least you're passionate about baking. I have no idea what I want to do. I guess that's why I keep modeling."

I lean my hip against the counter. "But do you actually want to make it your career?"

Her expression turns pensive. It's several minutes before she comes up with an answer.

"Honestly? I don't know. Part of me wants to walk away, but a bigger part wants to stay. I've worked really hard to get to this point. Plus, models only have a few years before they age out."

I reach over and take her hands in mine. "At least swear to me you won't get hurt."

"What are you talking about?" she asks, perplexed.

"I've seen the documentaries, Jeannie. I don't want you to do unhealthy things to stay thin. You don't deserve that."

Jeannie tugs me in for a quick hug. Her eyes are suspiciously shiny when she pulls back.

"When did you get so mature? You're like my personal Asian Oprah."

"Yeah, right. If anyone's good at listening to people's problems, it's you. Besides, you already have all those self-help books lying around," I joke, waving toward the bookcases.

"Don't sell yourself short," she retorts. "I know you don't always believe you're good enough, but trust me, you are. Just think about how great a baker you are."

"Yeah, and what am I going to do with that? Change the world, one cake at a time?"

"Why not? You can turn people's bad days into great ones with a single perfectly baked pastry." She gestures at herself. "I mean, look at me. I'm happy just thinking about taking a bite of that jelly cake."

"Oh! Speaking of which, I need to go check on it."

The top layer sloshes ever so slightly when I give it a nudge. It's not quite ready yet. Jeannie takes the moment to tend to the fish, so I plop down on the couch and pull up Instagram. My New York pics have gotten a lot of likes, especially the ones from the dessert bar. As I'm scrolling past one of Grace's memes, a picture of Brody and Melissa pops up. They're sitting by the pool, her arms wrapped around his waist while he kisses her on the cheek. My heart clenches.

"What's wrong?"

I didn't notice Jeannie standing over my shoulder. I toss the phone onto the cushion next to me.

"It's nothing."

"Liza. You know you're a terrible liar, right?" She sits down. "Talk to me."

"It's really not a big deal. It's a pic of my ex with his new girl-friend."

"I'm sorry to hear that." Jeannie reaches over to squeeze my hand. "How long ago did you guys break up?"

"Almost three weeks."

Her eyebrows shoot up. "And he's already dating someone else? That's kind of quick."

"Not if you consider he was cheating on me with her."

"Oh, Liza." She presses me against her. "I'm so sorry."

"Don't tell Mom, okay? She doesn't know I was dating him."

"Why not?"

I raise my head to look at her. "You know how she is. She'll just tell me it's because he's not Asian."

"Then why don't you date someone Asian?"

"Uh, I think I'll pass. The ones Mom picks are the worst," I inform her with a grimace.

"Maybe the next one will be good. Keep an open mind. There's a lot to be said for having the same background."

*Et tu, Jeannie?* I scrutinize her face.

"What about you? Have you dated anyone recently?"

She plucks at an invisible thread on her shirt. "Actually, I haven't dated much since I moved here. I've been busy."

"Busy pining after Nathan maybe?"

Jeannie reddens. "Liza!"

"You know, the way to a man's heart is through his stomach." I waggle my eyebrows at her. "I hear oysters and chocolate work really well."

"I'm going to pretend you didn't say that."

I make kissing noises at her. She looks ready to throttle me, but the oven dings, so Jeannie leaps up to check on her food. At the same time, the doorbell rings. I grin when I see who's on the other side.

"Nathan! Are your ears burning?"

Jeannie glares at me from the kitchen. "Stop joking around, Liza."

*I'm serious*, I mouth to her. Her eyes nearly pop out of her head. Nathan cocks his head to the side.

"Um, can I come in?"

"Yeah, of course."

He reveals a bouquet of calla lilies from behind his back. "These are for you."

"Thanks," I say, handing them right to Jeannie. They're really for her anyway. While she moves to give him a hug, I check the jelly cake once more. This time, it's set properly, and I slice it into six pieces before putting it into the fridge.

"I'm sorry. I didn't know you'd be coming for dinner," Jeannie bemoans. "I only cooked enough for two."

He frowns. "I texted you. You didn't get it?"

Jeannie picks her phone up off the coffee table and checks her notifications. She grins sheepishly.

"I did. I forgot I put my phone on vibrate."

He throws an arm across her shoulder. "Well, don't stress about it, babe. I'm actually meeting some people in a bit anyway. I just remember you mentioning Liza was leaving soon, and I wanted to stop by and say goodbye."

"Are you sure it's not because you heard I was making dessert?" I joke.

"I had no idea," he says with a hand over his heart. "But . . . if you happen to have extra, I wouldn't say no to taking some with me."

I roll my eyes, but go in search of a reusable container. I transfer two slices of jelly cake and hand it to him. Nathan holds it up and peers through the clear bottom.

"Is this one of your famed recipes?"

"Actually, this is the first time I've made it, so I hope it tastes good."

"Then let's find out."

He opens the box and takes a big bite of one piece. I hold my breath as he chews.

"Oh, oh yeah. This. This is *amazing*," he moans. "It's so light, and not too sweet. It's way better than some of the stuff my mom makes, but don't tell her I said so."

"She's got a gift," Jeannie tells him.

"Your mom bakes?" I ask.

He nods. "She used to bake all the time but not anymore. She's too busy with work."

Nathan gestures at me with the slice of cake in his hand. "Now that I know your secret, I insist you stay for a few more days so I can gorge myself on your baking."

"Sorry. Plane ticket's been bought. You'll just have to come to Houston if you want any more."

Nathan pops the rest in his mouth in two large bites before nodding.

"Done deal. I'll make it happen. Especially if I can find an easy class to take while I'm down there."

"Good. Then Jeannie can show you around," I say. "Since she'll be back all summer."

Nathan flashes a brilliant smile at us both. "Dessert *and* a personal tour guide? This is sounding better and better."

Jeannie's face flushes. I swallow a laugh. Now she knows how I feel whenever Mom tries to set me up.

"Well, I guess this is goodbye for now, Liza."

Nathan wraps his arms around me. I scrunch my nose at the smoke and sandalwood of his cologne before pulling away.

"Bye, Nathan."

With a parting smile, he leaves and shuts the door behind him.

"The fish!" Jeannie suddenly exclaims. "Oh no. It's cold."

She throws it back in the oven for a few more minutes. Then we sit down and have dinner in companionable silence. When

Jeannie scarfs down a whole slice of my jelly cake, I'm thrilled.

"Nathan's right, Liza. This is stunning. You should make it for Mom."

"You know what? I will," I tell her. "She did ask me about some ideas just the other day."

"See? I know you think Mom doesn't believe in you, but she does. That's why I think you should enter the contest. Show her what else you can do."

I don't reply, but a seed of hope sprouts within me. Maybe I can do this.

# Chapter 12

After having so much fun with Jeannie, it takes me a few days to get used to being home again. I'd forgotten how nice it was to have her around all the time, not to mention having seven wonderful days without Mom's criticisms. The fact that she bombards me with questions about Jeannie the minute I walk in the door only adds to my misery. I do my best to answer them but purposely leave out the parts about Nathan.

"Tell your sister she should stay longer next time she's here," Mom demands, watching me unpack. "Six weeks isn't long enough."

"Why don't you just tell her yourself?"

"I don't want her to think I'm nagging her," she answers immediately.

I bite back a retort as I start pulling things out of my suitcase.

"Fine. I'll text her."

"Don't forget."

Like I could even if I wanted to. Mom probably has it marked on her calendar.

The other thing I don't tell her about is how much the trip inspired me to bake again. The same day I get home, I dust off my old recipe book—leather bound just like Mom's, her gift to me—and get to work. Several nights a week, I stay late and practice in the bakery. My hands grow accustomed to working the dough, and my taste buds start to sharpen. When Mom conveniently forgets to hire more help, forcing me to work four days a week, I hold my tongue. If I want her to let me compete, I need to stay on her good side.

Every day of the week, the shop is packed from sunrise to sunset. The secret to our newfound success is the *taiyaki*. It's one of the only things on the list I made her that Mom agreed to try. The day after I post a pic of it on our Instagram and Facebook, people start coming in to order it.

Since it was my idea, Mom puts me to work making the fish-shaped waffles. I'm happy to oblige because I've always loved the smell of fresh waffles. When topped with ice cream in Asian-inspired flavors—taro, matcha, milk tea—it's even better.

Thankfully, summer isn't just about work. I get to hang out with my friends on my off days. Mom even agrees to extend my curfew the whole summer as a reward.

About a week after I get back, Grace brings Sarah by at closing time to try our new dessert. She examines it curiously and then ventures a bite. She squeals so loudly people nearby turn to stare at us.

"Where have you been all my life?" she asks the cone. "And how do you guys come up with all this insanely good stuff?"

"Well, *we* didn't," I clarify. "It's a big trend in Japan. We just brought it here."

As Sarah finishes off her taiyaki, Grace leans in with a conspiratorial whisper.

"Have you talked to your mom about doing the contest this year?"

"Not yet," I answer under my breath, one eye on Mom. "I was thinking tonight."

"Good luck, but I don't think you'll need it. That jelly cake was delicious."

I made a slightly different version of it a few days back, adding a layer of mango mixed with coconut milk like I originally imagined. Grace and Sarah both raved about it, so I sent them home with a slice each before hiding the rest in the fridge. It's been two days, and I still haven't drummed up the courage to show it to Mom.

Once Grace and Sarah leave, we lock up and head home while I consider a million different ways to ask about the contest. I'm so wrapped in my thoughts I barely notice Mom pulling the car into the garage. She's already stepped into the kitchen when I catch up with her.

"Mom! Wait. I wanted to show you something."

She sighs. "It's been a long day, Liza. Can it wait until morning?"

"It'll just take a minute. I promise."

Mom's about as enthusiastic for my reveal as I am when she's waxing poetic about the latest Asian boy. Nonetheless, she decides to humor me. I pull out a chair at the table for her to sit, and then retrieve the jelly cake from the fridge. Putting the prettier of the two slices onto a plate, I grab a fork and place it in front of her.

She stares at it with furrowed brows. "What's this?"

"It's fresh fruit in agar jelly. I made it for Jeannie while I was in New York."

Mom scrutinizes my creation for several minutes. Eventually, she presses the edge of the fork into the triangular tip. It slices through smoother than butter, jiggling happily as she picks it up. I tense as she tucks it into her mouth.

She chews thoughtfully before swallowing. "It's . . ."

*Please like it. Please like it. Please like it.*

". . . delicious. Quite good."

I pump my fist under the table. One hurdle down. One big one to go.

Mom tips her head to the side. "How did you come up with this?"

"Jeannie told me she's been eating really healthy for modeling," I hedge. "I wanted to do something nice for her before I left, so I tweaked a recipe I found on the internet."

"I'm impressed. This makes for a good summer snack. Light, not too sweet, fun texture."

She takes two more bites in rapid succession. Okay, this is it.

I take a deep breath. "I'm really happy you like it, Mom, because I was hoping to talk to you about something."

"About what?"

"I . . . I want to participate in this year's contest."

She purses her lips. "You are. You're going to help me set up and run everything just like usual."

*Why did I think this was going to be easy?* I try again.

"No, Mom. That's not what I meant." I sit up straight in my chair. "I want to compete."

"So you don't want to help me?"

I wince at her accusatory tone. "I didn't say that. I can still help you set up, but I really want to be in the contest."

We stare at each other for a long time. I brace for the rejection long before she delivers it.

"No. You can't be a contestant."

My heart sinks. "Why not? I'm good enough to win."

"Liza. You seem to have forgotten something very important. This is a contest I run and judge. If you compete and win, people will accuse me of playing favorites."

I don't want to admit it, but she has a point. Even though Mom is the last person who'd give me special treatment, no one else knows that.

I flatten my hands against the table. "But if I bake better than everyone else, then it won't matter."

"Of course it matters. It only takes one rumor of partiality to ruin everything," Mom reiterates. "This contest is too important to our family for me to take that chance."

"What about me? What about what's important to me?"

She scoots forward in her chair. "Liza, there will be other contests for you to enter. Besides, this is just for fun. Your focus should be on preparing for college."

"What if we got another judge? Then it would be impartial."

"Even if I were to entertain the idea, which I'm not, finding a qualified judge this late in the game is impossible."

"What about Mrs. Lee? She's a baker too."

I wince and squeeze my eyes shut as soon as the words slip past my tongue. Mom's eyes bulge, her nostrils flaring as she struggles to hold back. Dad happens to walk in then. He senses the tension immediately and glances from me to her and back.

"What's going on?"

"Your daughter asked to compete in the contest. I told her no," Mom answers icily. "And that's final."

I bow my head as she stands and storms off. Dad sinks into the chair she abandoned as tears gather in my eyes. I force them back.

"Liza . . ."

"I just wanted to prove to her I'm good enough," I say, eyes pinned on the floor.

"Good enough for what?" he asks softly. "Culinary school?"

I swallow and nod. He leans back against the chair.

"Liza, we didn't say no because we don't think you're good

enough to succeed. Whether you believe it or not, Mom's told me before that you're a better baker than she could ever hope to be."

That doesn't sound remotely like something she'd say, but I'm not about to correct him.

"Then why won't you let me try?"

He scratches his head. "Because we want more for you in life. Look at what Mom and I have to do just to keep Yin and Yang going. We work fourteen to sixteen hours, six days a week. We don't take vacations. We don't close for most holidays. It's backbreaking work. We do this so you don't have to."

I lapse into silence. Baking isn't a job. It's my passion. I'll never get tired of tempting complex flavors from simple ingredients. I dream about pleating beautiful designs into dough and coaxing fruits and vegetables into animals and flowers. Why can't they understand that?

Dad exhales. "I can see this really bothers you. Let me talk to Mom. Maybe we can come up with a compromise."

He cuts me off before I can offer a reply. "But I want you to try to see things from Mom's point of view. No matter what, she wants the best for you, and so do I."

With that, Dad walks out of the room, leaving me to mull things over.

• • • • •

The next day, I emerge from sulking two hours late for work. Mom and Dad have already left, so I drive myself to the bakery. I walk into utter chaos. With Houston sweltering in mid-June, customers are grumbling about the long line outside. Tina is manning the cash register but can't get the credit card reader to work. A stack of fresh pastries sits unattended behind her, and half the shelves are empty.

I slide behind the counter and reset the card reader. Tina switches to restocking the shelves while I clear the purchase line. Within fifteen minutes, we've got a fresh group of people inside in the cool air.

Tina throws her arms around me when things eventually calm down.

"Oh, I've missed you! It's been this ridiculous all day!"

I squeeze her back. "I'm going to go say hi to my mom for a minute, okay? I'll be back."

I find Mom in the kitchen, neck deep in ingredients and oven trays. Her eyes flicker over to me before returning to the vegetable buns she's filling, the hint of a smile on her lips.

"Those trays need to go into the oven for twenty minutes."

Obediently, I slide the prepped pastries onto the oven racks. I shut the door and set one of the egg timers she keeps on the table. Mom calls out the next task, and then the next, until nearly an hour has gone by. With the ovens full and four timers ticking down, Mom gestures toward the nearest stool with her chin. I perch myself on top.

"I talked to Dad. He said you were really hurt that I wouldn't let you compete."

I know better than to confirm or deny, so I stay quiet.

"I'm not changing my mind on that," she continues. "However, I've decided you can be the technical judge."

I freeze. "You're going to let me judge?"

"You know how it works, and you've seen me judge for years," she says matter-of-factly as she wipes down the prep table. "We can make anything you're not sure about and practice if you want. That way, you'll know what to look out for on bake day."

I have no words. A judging position? I mean, it's not what I wanted, but maybe I can work this to my advantage. It'll definitely look great on a future culinary school application.

"Can I come up with some of the recipes too?" I ask on a whim.

"No. You need to learn how to judge first. Besides, a good technical challenge depends on a reliable recipe. There's no room for experimentation."

Well, it was worth a try.

I look her square in the eye. "Okay. I'll be a judge."

"Good. You'll join the celebrity judge I'm bringing on this year."

That's another big surprise. Mom's not exactly known for delegating.

"Who's the celebrity?"

She rinses the towel in the sink before replying.

"Mrs. Lee."

I nearly fall off my chair. "Seriously?"

"Well, as much as I hate to admit it, you had a good idea. We haven't had as many applicants as previous years, and she's got a huge following," Mom explains, almost to herself. "It'll be good publicity for the contest. She also agreed to donate an additional ten thousand for this year's scholarship."

"Ten thousand dollars?!" My mouth falls open. "Does that mean you'll be extending the deadline for applications?"

"Just a couple more weeks. I want to give us enough time to garner interest. Mrs. Lee's arranged for us to be interviewed on one of the big news channels, and I've already paid for the ad in the *Chinese Times*."

She takes a moment to check the oven as her first timer goes off. Satisfied with the bake, she covers her hands with gloves and pulls the trays out one by one. Once the buns are on the cooling racks, Mom sits down on her stool.

"I'm thinking of adding another incentive."

"Like what?"

"Maybe . . . five private baking lessons for the winner."

She stares at me intently. I've been subjected to many of her trademark looks, but I don't recognize this one. It's quite unsettling.

I shrug. "Sounds great. I'm sure whoever wins will love it."

Her face breaks into a smile. "I'm glad you like it. I'll add it in."

The three remaining timers go off within seconds of one another, effectively ending our conversation. Once everything's cooled, Mom sends me out to bag the fresh pastries, but not before she shoots me another mysterious look.

I'm sure it's nothing.

● ● ● ● ●

The day Mom is due to appear on the local morning news show *Space City Live* to talk about the contest, she wakes up at four thirty in the morning to get ready. Mrs. Lee will show up impeccably dressed, and she doesn't want to look shabby sitting next to her. How do I know this? I'm currently perched on a chair in the master bath, watching Mom scrounge through her and Dad's walk-in closet while he's sleeping peacefully in the next room.

"What about this one?" she asks.

Mom emerges with a matching two-piece that resembles a dress from afar. Blue roses bloom across the otherwise white fabric.

She looks at me. "You like it?"

"It's my favorite of the ones you've tried on," I answer neutrally.

She examines herself in the full-length mirror. "Good. I'll wear this, then."

I stand, ready to answer the siren call of my bed. Instead, Mom's voice anchors me to the spot.

"I need your help with my makeup."

Makeup? She doesn't wear makeup. Not unless you count the tinted moisturizer she dabs on so she doesn't get skin cancer. I plop unceremoniously back on the chair. About thirty minutes later—ten of which were spent with her accusing me of trying to stab her eye with eyeliner—Mom is finally camera ready. She leaves for the studio while I quickly give up on the idea of going back to sleep. Dad finds me sitting in the kitchen nearly an hour later. His eyes widen to the size of dinner plates.

"Mom dragged me out of bed this morning to help her get ready," I explain.

"Ah."

"I'm going to watch the show. Want to join me?"

He nods. We move into the living room and turn on the TV. We're just in time. The hosts are coming back from a commercial break, and they introduce Mrs. Lee and Mom. Mrs. Lee, as predicted, is clad in a beautifully tailored two-piece navy suit. A baby blue silk blouse peeks out from beneath her buttoned jacket, a bow sash detail at the neck giving it a feminine touch. Her trusty black stilettos peek out from beneath the cuffs of her slim pants. Today, her hair is gathered in waves around her face, and red lipstick completes her power look.

Despite Mom's best efforts, she looks almost a decade older than her co-judge in her matronly dress and simple black flats. She squints at the bright lights of the studio as they walk onto the stage. When they sit, her spine is so stiff you could fly a flag off her. Tiffany, one of the show's two hosts, greets them with a smile.

"So, Mrs. Yang, tell us a little bit about the contest."

Mom perks up and launches into the speech she could recite in her sleep.

"This is the fifth year for the annual Yin and Yang Junior Baking Competition. Every year, we choose ten high school students to compete in a bake-off-style contest. Each round consists of an original bake and a technical challenge, and the winner will receive a trophy and a scholarship. As a special bonus this year, the winning baker will also get five private lessons to improve their skills."

"What a wonderful opportunity," Kirk, the other host, comments. "And I hear this is also the first year you've invited a celebrity judge."

Only those who know Mom well catch the tiny clench of her jaw before she answers.

"Yes. As an accomplished baker and businesswoman, Mrs. Lee was a natural choice. I'm very excited to be judging with her this year. In addition, my daughter Liza will be co-judging the technical challenges."

I gasp. She said my name on live TV! And she didn't embarrass me! Dad chuckles as I slap his arm excitedly. Mom exchanges a fake smile with Mrs. Lee as Tiffany turns to the latter.

"I hear you also have a surprise announcement, Mrs. Lee."

"Yes, I do," she answers before staring directly into the camera. "The Mama Lee Foundation will be donating extra money to bring the scholarship amount this year from five thousand dollars to fifteen thousand."

Tiffany and Kirk clap their hands like it's the best thing they've ever heard. Mrs. Lee preens as they switch to questioning her about the new bakery. To add insult to injury, the camera cuts Mom out of the frame as it zooms in on her co-judge's face. Once the commercial break hits, Dad turns off the TV. We sit, not speaking, for several minutes. Then he gives himself a shake and stands.

"I should get ready for work."

Mom comes home minutes after he leaves for the restaurant. She walks in with drooped shoulders and a frown. My stomach sinks. I know exactly what it feels like to be overshadowed by someone more successful. I start to speak but quickly change my mind. The door to the master bedroom shuts, and I stare at it for a while before retreating to my room.

# Chapter 13

After the *Space City Live* segment, applications come flooding in. It doesn't take long before our mailbox is stuffed fuller than a deep-dish pizza. As the pile on our dining table grows, Mom hoards her favorites like red envelopes on Chinese New Year. Tina spends an entire afternoon folding our new flyers so Mom can stuff them into customers' bags while I man the register. Even Dad and Danny get in on the action, inserting them in restaurant menus and to-go bags. The rest we take in boxes to our sponsor businesses.

"How do you choose who gets a spot and who doesn't?" I ask Mom one evening.

"Why do you want to know all of a sudden?"

"I just thought it would be good to know more about the contestants as a judge," I answer.

"If you really want to be a good judge, learn those recipes and practice your critiques."

One of the reasons the contest has grown in popularity is Mom's insistence on highlighting Asian-inspired recipes. With only ten bakers, the first seven rounds will eliminate one person each. The top three bakers go on to the finale. So far, I've tasted the recipes she's planned for bread, cake, cookie, and sweet bun. All that's left are tarts, puffs, rolls, and specialty.

"Okay, okay. I'll get it all done."

Mom pins me with her gaze. "Make sure you run any notes by me. It's important you judge at the same level as Mrs. Lee."

Since the interview, she's been more determined than ever to make sure everything's perfect. This isn't just about the bakers or the community anymore. This is personal, and she's not losing to someone whose idea of quality control is having the right font on her signage.

Her words, not mine.

• • • • •

Two days before the contest is set to begin, I'm back at Boba Life. Grace and I are supposed to meet Ben and James here, though I only agreed after she bribed me with a copy of Julia Quinn's latest book. I wasn't exactly thrilled with the idea after the awkward run-in in New York. While I'm waiting, I jot down some thoughts on Mom's tarts. When Grace slides into the booth, I jump.

"Sorry. I didn't mean to scare you."

"I was just thinking about something," I answer after giving her a hug.

"What are you working on?"

"Some notes for the contest," I say, closing the notebook. "My mom's letting me judge the technical challenges this year."

Grace gapes at me. "Wait. This is why you've ghosted me for days? She actually agreed to that?"

"Sorry about that. It's been super hectic lately." I lean back against my chair with a sigh. "And yes, but only because she won't let me compete. She said there's too much attention on the contest this year to take any chances."

With my cup empty, we head to the back of the line for another round of tea. As we wait, eyes stab into me like acupuncture needles.

"Everybody's staring at me," I whisper to Grace.

"It's probably nothing. Just ignore them."

I stare at the menu up on the wall until we reach the register. The redheaded cashier grins.

"Back again, eh?"

"You know we can't stay away, Lance," Grace states.

"You want your usual?"

We nod. He rings us up, and we step to the side to wait. The shop's owner, Kevin, rounds the corner.

"Liza! Grace!" He winks at me. "Hey, you're famous now! I should get your autograph and put it on the wall."

"What are you talking about?"

Kevin stares blankly at me for a moment, his dark eyebrows knit together.

"You haven't looked at the flyers, have you?"

I glance at Grace. "Um . . . no. Why?"

"It's probably better if you just look at it yourself. Hold on."

Kevin steps over to grab one off a pile sitting next to their cup-sealing machines. He hands it to me, and Grace reads over my shoulder. The flyer starts out normally enough—announcing the contest, rules, eligibility, and judges. Then I scan farther down to where the prizes are listed. There, in full color and taking up the bottom third of the page, is my graduation photo. Grace reads the accompanying text out loud, because I've lost all ability to speak.

"'The first-prize winner will also receive five private lessons with our technical judge Liza Yang, three-time champion of the Houston Junior Baking Competition. Salutatorian of prestigious Salvis Private Academy's Class of 2019, Liza speaks three languages and enjoys reading, nature, and, of course, baking.'"

The blood drains from my face, and I swallow the curse trying to claw its way out of my throat.

"Liza?" Kevin steps toward me. "Liza, are you okay?"

Without answering, I grab my things and make a beeline for the door.

"Liza! Liza!" Grace calls out. "Wait for me!"

I burst out onto the plaza with a gasp. My chest refuses to cooperate, as though an elephant is sitting directly on top of it.

Grace rushes to my side. "Liza, are you okay?"

"I can't breathe," I gasp.

"Oh my god. Should I call 911?"

Blaring sirens would only attract the one thing I don't want right now—more attention.

I shake my head frantically. "Don't . . . don't do that. I . . . I just need to sit down."

Grace scans the vicinity before tugging me over to one of the outdoor tables. She shoves me into a chair.

"Just . . . count to ten or something, Liza."

I look down at the crumpled paper still in my hand. My head starts to pound.

"I can't believe she did this to me! I knew she was determined, but this . . . this is a dating profile!"

"Maybe she didn't realize that's what it sounds like," Grace suggests.

"She knew exactly what she was doing." I put my head in my hands. "All those people inside . . . they're going to think I agreed to this."

"I highly doubt that, but if they do, so what? Who cares what they think?"

That's easy to say when it isn't her face plastered on every flyer in the city.

*Every flyer.*

I think back to the other morning, when Mom asked me to help with her makeup. The way she compromised and offered to let me judge. I thought maybe it meant things were changing, but now . . . this.

"Grace, she made hundreds of these," I wail. "We've even got them in every bag at Yin and Yang!"

"People don't pay attention to those things anyway. They probably threw it away," she assures.

"I need to go home," I say, standing up and searching for my car in the lot.

Grace grabs me gently by the arm. "What are you going to do?"

"I need to talk to my mom. She's gone too far this time."

I turn to leave, but as I step off the curb, the strap of my purse catches on something and yanks me backward. As I stumble, I grab on to the first solid thing I find.

"What the—"

I tumble against a warm body, and we hit the ground together. Footsteps come running up.

"Are you okay?"

I wince. I'd recognize that voice anywhere.

"Ben . . ."

Grace hovers just behind him, staring down at me with wide eyes. A pained groan reminds me of the person who broke my fall. I turn to utter an apology and come face-to-face with James.

*Oh no.*

I scramble to get up, and my knee accidentally hits him in the groin. He lets out a howl.

"Oh no. I'm so, so sorry!"

"Don't move," he hisses.

He grabs me by the shoulders and carefully shifts me off him before standing. Grace helps me up and dusts me off as James tugs his clothes back into place.

"You need to watch where you're going," he says gruffly.

"James, it was obviously an accident," Ben defends. "She didn't see you."

"I'm sorry," I repeat. "I didn't mean to . . ."

My eyes drop down instinctively, and I jerk them away. My cheeks burn hotter than the ovens at the bakery.

"Are you hurt?" I mumble.

James shakes his head, doing an admirable job of looking unharmed. His deep brown eyes meet mine.

"What about you?" he asks.

Is that . . . concern in his voice?

"Depends on what you're talking about," I reply without thinking.

"What do you—"

Before I can make something up, Ben leans over to pick up the paper I'd dropped in my haste. I groan to myself. Why does this day keep getting worse? His eyes skim over the page, pausing when he hits the lower half. Ben looks up at me, then back down, and then back at me again. He opens his mouth, but no sound comes out.

James takes the flyer out of his cousin's hand. "What's so interesting?"

I pray for the ground to open up and swallow me whole. As he reads, his lips part when he hits my dreaded bio. It's so bad all he can do is stare.

"Could I have that back, please?" I squeak.

James hands it to me. Silently, I fold it up and shove it in my pocket.

Then I dredge up my last bit of pride and square my shoulders.

"Please excuse me."

Grace starts to follow, but I brush her off. Ben grabs her hand and tugs her to his side. I feel their eyes on my back as I walk to my car in a daze.

• • • • •

I barely notice the strange car parked outside as I unlock the door and step inside my house.

"Liza!"

"Jeannie?"

Her arms come around me and smother me in her embrace. Jeannie's soft floral perfume tempers the bitterness of Mom's betrayal. It's a few minutes before I'm willing to let her go. As our parents walk into the living room, Mom freezes.

"Liza! Didn't you say you were spending the afternoon with Grace?"

The sound of her voice sets my teeth on edge.

I scowl openly at her. "I need to talk to you in private, Mom."

Jeannie glances between us. "Um, I'm going to go to my room."

"Actually, why don't you come into the kitchen with me," Dad tells her. "You must be starving after flying all day."

"Dad, I'm not really—"

"Come. Eat."

His tone invites no argument. Throwing a glance over her shoulder, Jeannie smiles encouragingly before leaving with Dad. I wait until they're out of earshot before marching across the room to Mom.

I wave the flyer in her face. "How could you do this to me?!"

It takes a second for things to dawn on her.

She juts her chin out. "You agreed to teach the lessons."

"No, I didn't! You asked me if I thought private lessons were a good idea. You never told me you wanted *me* to do it!"

"I thought it was obvious," she says, busying herself with the books on the coffee table. "I'm swamped at the bakery, and Mrs. Lee has her own business to run. As the technical judge, you're the only other person qualified to do it."

What kind of mom logic is that? The lessons don't even happen until after the contest is over. Besides, she's taught me everything I know about baking.

*Calm down, Liza. Remember, this is for culinary school.*

I suck in a deep breath through gritted teeth. "Okay, fine, but why did you have to write that bio?"

"What's wrong with it? I thought it was nice."

"You thought it was—" I pause, aghast. "There was no reason to mention how many languages I speak or my class rank! Why would anyone need to know that?"

She shrugs. "People need to know you're qualified."

I position myself directly in front of her so she has to look at me.

"Then what about my hobbies? What do reading and nature have to do with my ability to judge a baking contest?"

Mom says nothing, not that it matters. We both know why she really did it, though it's obvious to me now she'll never own up to it. That's it. This is my life, and I'm not going to let her do this.

"Take it back. Tell everyone you made a mistake, and I'm not teaching the lessons."

"I will do no such thing, Liza!" She crosses her arms over her chest. "We have less than two days until the contest begins, and I've confirmed almost all the contestants."

"Take it back or I quit!"

Mom rears back. I've never shouted at her like this before.

She glowers at me. "I will not, and you *will* be at the contest. That's final."

I twirl around and storm out of the room. The walls rattle as I slam my bedroom door closed. Shortly after, quiet murmurs seep in from the hallway, but I don't bother eavesdropping. Then someone knocks on my door.

"Liza? Can I come in?"

It's Jeannie. I ignore her, but just like everyone else in this house, she walks in anyway. She closes the door behind her and comes to sit next to me on the bed. I stiffen as she tucks my head into the crook of her shoulder.

"I'm sorry, Liza."

After a second, I relax. "Why would she do this to me?"

Jeannie sighs. "I don't know. I think she believes she's helping."

"Well, she's terrible at it," I say, burrowing against her.

Jeannie's chuckle rumbles through her chest. "That we can agree on."

I raise my head to look at her. "What am I going to do? I can't face these people."

"Then what would you rather do?"

"Run away?" I answer with a hopeful expression.

"I doubt that's going to work."

We sit side by side, staring out the window with our heads propped against the wall. Eventually, I roll my head to peer at Jeannie.

"I wish I could move out of state like you."

"Trust me. It's not as fun as it sounds. I miss having someone cooking and cleaning for me all the time." Jeannie smooths a hand over the blanket. "I have to do everything, plus go to school and model."

"So . . . wanna trade?"

She smirks. "Not on your life."

Laughter bursts from my lips like water from a broken faucet. When I catch my breath, Jeannie tugs me close.

"We'll figure this out. You and me."

"Pinky swear?"

She loops her finger through mine. "Pinky swear."

# Chapter 14

I spend the next two days before the contest in self-imposed exile. Thankfully, Grace volunteers to be my lifeline. She delivers tea from Boba Life, and even brings Sarah around one afternoon. It's the stories she regales me with that cheer me up the most, though. Apparently, people have been claiming to see me around Chinatown.

I guess that makes me the new Bigfoot.

Unfortunately, when the morning of the contest arrives, I have to make a real appearance. With all the extra attention this year, a few of the news channels are coming to cover opening day. After tossing and turning the night before, my eyes are duller than a bun without egg wash. So, I ask Jeannie to help me with my makeup. The last thing I need right now is to look like I crawled out of a grave. I sit patiently as she applies it all with a precise hand. At some point, she steps back with a faint smile.

"Take a look."

I turn to face the mirror and suck in a sharp breath. It's a miracle! Instead of a circus clown, I'm staring at a better version of myself. My eyes are bigger and brighter, my cheeks are rosy pink, and my lips are shaped like a bow. I meet Jeannie's nervous gaze in the mirror.

"What do you think?" she asks. "Do you like it?"

If my eyes could form actual hearts, they would. Instead, I throw my arms around her neck.

"I love it!"

I release her to examine her work more closely. How did she turn so many products into something that looks so natural?

"You're like my real-life fairy godmother, Jeannie."

She chuckles. "In that case, let me work my magic on your wardrobe."

She sifts through the hangers in my closet and tosses what she likes onto the bed. Then I put on an impromptu fashion show so she can decide what looks best.

"No, not that one. It's too long."

"I don't like this. It makes you look bigger than you are."

"Where the hell did you get *that*?!"

By the time she settles on an outfit, I'm ready to go back to sleep. I don't know how she does this for a living.

"Now go get changed." Jeannie piles everything into my arms. "You don't want Mom yelling at you for being late, do you?"

Alone in my bedroom, I crash from the momentary high of my makeover. My stomach churns as I pull the navy blue swing dress over my head, a gift from Jeannie for my sixteenth birthday. Next is the long chain necklace she's lending me for the occasion. The weight of the pendant lies heavy against my rib cage.

Jeannie also left me a pair of low heels to put on, but I trade them for my nicest white sneakers. I instantly feel calmer when I put them on. Everyone's waiting outside, so I head to the garage after a quick once-over.

Mom cocks an eyebrow in my direction as I walk out, the canvas bag with her notebook of recipes clutched against her chest like it's her greatest treasure. Jeannie whistles and winks at me. Once we're all in the car, Dad glances back at me through the rearview mirror.

"You look very nice, Liza."

"Thanks, Dad."

• • • • •

When we pull into the campus for Bayou City Culinary Institute, I squeeze my eyes shut for a second. Mom's grating voice rips through my last moment of peace.

"Get out of the car, Liza! We can't be late!"

"There's plenty of time, lǎo pó," Dad interjects with a hand on her shoulder. "No need to rush her."

I resist the urge to scream and trudge behind my parents as we cross the large but mostly unoccupied parking lot. Jeannie loops an arm through mine, bumping hips with me until I break into a smile. We're at the top of the front steps when someone calls her name. She turns, her lips parting.

"Nathan?"

He jogs the last few feet to greet us both with a toothy grin. "Surprise!"

Jeannie's eyes flit to where Mom and Dad are standing over her right shoulder.

"What . . . what are you doing here?"

"I saw your Insta post from last night about the contest, and I was in the neighborhood. Besides, I promised to come visit, didn't I?"

I bite the inside of my cheek to keep from laughing. There's no denying he wants out of the friend zone now. Why else would he fly all the way down to Houston just to see her?

She smiles tentatively. "You didn't have to do that."

"Well, I booked a job down here anyway, plus I'm taking a photography class at the University of Houston while I'm here." Nathan leans toward me and winks. "Maybe I'll practice taking pictures of you while you're baking."

He might be into Jeannie, but I still flush beneath his gaze.

"Who's this?"

Mom's voice teeters between intrigue and suspicion. The blood drains from Jeannie's face, but she has no reason to worry. Nathan is smoother than Yin and Yang's famous milk cream.

He flashes a brilliant smile. "You must be Jeannie's mom, Mrs. Yang. My name is Nathan. I've heard so much about you from her, but she forgot to mention how young you look."

"Oh! Well, thank you," Mom stammers. "How did you two meet?"

"At a fashion show. Jeannie and I were walking for different designers, but we ran into each other backstage."

She turns to Dad with stars in her eyes. "They met at work! Isn't that wonderful?"

He makes a noncommittal sound in reply before pinning Nathan with a firm look.

"And what brings you down here, Nathan?"

"I came down for work, but I remember Jeannie telling me about your contest. I thought I'd drop by and wish Liza good luck."

"You are too sweet! Thank you," Mom answers, reaching up to cup his cheek. "And so handsome too."

Jeannie gasps. "Mom!"

"What? What did I say? It's true. He's very handsome."

Jeannie looks to Dad for help, but he just shrugs. No one gets between Mom and a potential husband for her daughters.

"Thank you, Mrs. Yang. That's very kind of you," Nathan states without batting an eye.

"You two should go grab seats before we get started!" Mom

shoves Jeannie toward him. "Jeannie, why don't you show him where the bake room is?"

Nathan's head dips. "I'm afraid I can't stay. I have to get across town for my class."

It's hard to say who's more crestfallen—Mom or Jeannie. Mom pulls herself together first.

"Then we'll be sure to save you a seat in case you have some time to come back. *I* certainly hope you will."

Nathan glances at his phone, seeming to reconsider.

"Actually, maybe I can come in for a quick tour, if Jeannie's willing."

"Of course she's willing," Mom answers for her. "You two go and have a good time."

"Thank you again, Mrs. Yang. Mr. Yang. Liza."

He nods at each of us before offering Jeannie his arm. We enter the building together—Mom and Dad up front, me in the middle, and Nathan and Jeannie at the rear. Mom whispers into Dad's ear as we move down corridors covered with framed awards and posters advertising student organizations. It's hard to make out what she's saying with the click of her heels echoing down the halls. Nonetheless, I'm guessing it has something to do with plans for Jeannie's upcoming wedding.

We bypass the bakeshop where the contest will be held. I crane my neck to peek through the open doorway. Though the room is still empty, the stainless steel tables are already set up with the tools and ingredients for today's bake. Jeannie takes Nathan inside while the rest of us continue on to the faculty break room that'll serve as our backstage area. Metal lockers line one wall, and small appliances sit atop a row of kitchen cabinets. In the back corner, a refrigerator hums.

Mom drops her bag on the counter next to a pile of extra

contest materials. Jeannie joins us shortly after without Nathan. She's saved from interrogation when Mrs. Lee swoops into the room. Her armor of choice today is a sleek black power suit with a white ruffled blouse. Her shoes are red-bottomed, the heels ready to pierce the heart of anyone who dares to come for her. With Jeannie beside her dressed in a canary yellow short-sleeved jumpsuit, it's easy to mistake them for mother and daughter.

"Mrs. Yang!" Mrs. Lee exclaims. "I love your dress. It looks so . . . comfortable."

To her credit, Mom doesn't flinch at the backhanded insult. She greets her co-judge with a blithe smile.

"Mrs. Lee, do be careful around the contestants today. They're far less predictable than your fancy baking machines. I'd hate for any of them to ruin that beautiful suit."

Dad's lips twitch as he tries to hold in a laugh. Mrs. Lee's eyes narrow, but she's prevented from offering a scathing retort when BCCI's director pokes his head in the door. Chef Anthony, an African American man with imposing stature but heaps of warmth, is emceeing the contest again this year.

"Ladies! Are you ready to kick things off today?"

Mom, who's studying the treasured recipes in her red leather notebook, doesn't hear him. Mrs. Lee sidles over to him with a flirty smile.

"It's such an honor to meet the man behind Bayou City Culinary Institute! Many of my bakers are graduates from your program."

"Is that right? Then I'm grateful to you for giving them a chance," Chef Anthony answers.

"Have you stopped by my newest bakery yet? It's been open for a month now."

He rubs the back of his neck. "Unfortunately, between the contest and teaching classes, I haven't had time to make it out there."

"You *teach* too? What an accomplished man you are."

Mrs. Lee's compliments are cloying to my ears, but he puffs out his chest.

She lays a hand on his bicep. "Make sure you let me know before you come by. I'll give you a personal tour."

"Thank you, Mrs. Lee. That's so generous of you!"

Mom finally looks up and notices him for the first time.

"Chef Anthony, is everything ready to go?"

He straightens and tugs at his collar. "Oh, yes, Mrs. Yang. One hundred percent."

"Mmm. I'd like to take another look to be sure."

Over the years, Chef Anthony's grown used to Mom's neurotic tendencies. Despite this, his reply takes on a rough edge.

"You are welcome to do so if you feel it necessary, Mrs. Yang."

Mom stiffens. Realizing everyone is watching to see what she'll do, she puts a hand up.

"There's no need. I'm confident in your attention to detail."

A young woman wearing a polo with the school's name stitched into it suddenly appears in the doorway.

"Chef Anthony? May I speak with you, please? We're wondering where the camera crews can set up."

"Excuse me one moment," he tells us. "This is Gloria, one of the students helping out today."

Everyone murmurs a hello before the two of them step out to talk. There's still some time before the contest is to begin, so I excuse myself to use the restroom. In truth, I'm hoping to get a peek at this year's contestants. My sneakers squeak on the linoleum floor as I stroll through the familiar hallways, arriving outside the bakeshop where the contestants are waiting to get started. Snippets of conversation float out into the hallway as I slowly ease my head through the doorway to try to catch a glimpse of who's inside.

"I knew you'd be trying to sneak a peek."

I spin around to find Grace grinning at me.

I smack her on the arm. "You nearly scared me to death!"

"Only because you weren't paying attention. You should've heard me from a mile away."

For emphasis, she taps her tan suede ankle boots on the floor.

"Sarah's running late," she tells me before I think to ask, "but she's on her way."

I nod before leaning back through the door.

She laughs. "Did your mom not show you who she picked?"

"Are you kidding? I'm almost positive she locked up the final applications in the restaurant safe. I looked all over for them."

She purses her lips. "In that case, I think you're justified in taking a look. Let's go."

I turn on my heel, but I'm rooted in place when I spot two familiar faces walking toward us.

"Ben? James?" Grace says, eyes darting over to me before she smiles.

"Hey, Liza!" Ben gives me quick hug. "You look great today!"

James, in typical fashion, stands there without a word. Grace moves to stand next to Ben, their hands joining together like two pieces of a puzzle. They're disgustingly cute, and I love it.

"What are you guys doing here?" I ask.

Ben grins. "Grace, do you want to tell her?"

Wait. Grace has something to do with this? I level a glare that she deflects by nudging his shoulder with hers.

"You tell her."

"Okay." He turns to me. "Remember the other day when we ran into you outside Boba Life?"

"Uh, yeah. Vaguely," I lie.

How could I forget? It's only just the most mortifying day of my life so far.

"Well, after you left in such a rush, I asked Grace what was up with the flyer."

"I explained everything," she fills in. "How it's your mom's contest, that you wanted to compete but she wouldn't let you, and—oh!—how she wrote that bio hoping to find you a boyfriend in the process."

I shoot her a look—*seriously?!*—but she's lost in Ben's eyes.

"Anyway," Ben continues, sweeping a loose strand of hair off his brow, "since Eastern Sun Bank is one of your sponsors, I had my dad pull some strings and get me and James into the competition. You know, so you'll have two less guys to worry about."

I'm not quite sure what he means by the last part, but there are more pressing matters to worry about.

I glance between them. "Can you guys actually bake?"

"Don't worry about us. We'll make it work."

Ben's eyes slide over to his cousin, who obviously wants to be anyplace but here.

"I'm sorry you got pulled into this," I say to James.

"What are you talking about?" Ben scoffs. "He's the one who came up with the whole idea in the first place."

My eyes boomerang from him back to James. "Really? It was your idea?"

"Well, I . . . that is, there's . . ."

His cheeks splotch with color as he drags a hand through his hair. James mumbles something under his breath. I lean in to make it out, but he jumps back.

"I . . . I need to . . . check on something inside," he sputters. "Excuse me."

He twirls around and sprints into the bakeshop. I turn back to Ben and Grace with a puzzled expression.

"What just happened?"

They look at each other and burst out laughing. I want to ask what's so funny, but my phone goes off. I groan as I read the text message.

"Mom wants me back in the prep room."

"I'll go with you," Grace offers. "See you later, Ben?"

He brings her hand up and presses a kiss against the back of it before letting go.

"Can't wait."

As soon as he heads inside, she sags against me. "Ugh. Could he be any cuter?"

I roll my eyes and drag her down the hallway. We're greeted by a flurry of activity the second we step foot inside. In the best lit corner of the room, Mrs. Lee is being interviewed by a TV crew. Dad and Chef Anthony are going over the schedule one more time, while Jeannie is nowhere to be found. Mom rushes over as soon as she spots us.

"Ah, there you are! You said you were going to the bathroom!"

"Sorry, Mrs. Yang! I ran into Liza on her way back," Grace states, hugging her briefly. "It's my fault we lost track of time."

If the situation were reversed, Mom would be ripping me a new one. Instead, she immediately forgives Grace and points at her bag.

"Will you hold on to it for me until Jeannie comes back, Grace? Liza will be busy judging, and my husband is very forgetful."

"Of course! I'll get it right now."

She hoists it over her shoulder just as Chef Anthony gets off his cell.

"Okay, everyone! All the contestants have arrived! Let's get this show on the road!"

The reporters rush out ahead of us to get set up in the bake-shop. Chef Anthony then leads the way, with Grace and me following in the back. My heart pounds harder with every step we take, a fine sheen of sweat gathering at my brow. As we near the door, Jeannie pops out and gives us a wave. Grace hugs me briefly before heading inside with Jeannie.

The walls on either side of the door are lined with the camera operators, each working out the final recording angles in the room. Chef Anthony waits for them to finish before strolling in and starting his rehearsed speech.

"Contestants, welcome to the Fifth Annual Yin and Yang Junior Baking Competition! I am Chef Anthony, and I welcome you to Bayou City Culinary Institute. This year, we had a record five hundred applications in total! From that, we've narrowed it down to ten of the most talented junior bakers Houston has to offer. This will no doubt be our best competition yet, and we're very excited to see what you are all capable of."

He pauses for dramatic effect, and looks toward the door as he continues.

"Before we begin, let me introduce our esteemed panel. First up, we have the woman who single-handedly changed the landscape of baking in the city, co-owner of Yin and Yang Restaurant and Bakery in Chinatown, Mrs. Janet Yang."

Mom sweeps into the room like royalty, a welcoming smile painted on her lips. Chef Anthony waits until the applause has died down before continuing.

"Next, we are incredibly lucky to have a celebrity judge this year. Known for making it possible for hungry people to eat delicious pastries across the world, all while looking fabulous, please give it up for *the* Mama Lee herself, Mrs. Teresa Lee!"

As I watch her waltz in with an air of confidence I'll never achieve, my hands start to shake.

*Pull yourself together, Liza. Mom'll never forgive you otherwise.*

Just like that, my brain stops spinning. Nothing's more motivating than the fear of disappointing your tiger mom. Besides, if I mess this up, I can forget about ever convincing her to say yes to culinary school.

"Now, if you tuned in to *Space City Live* this past week, you know there is another exciting change to this year's contest. For the first time, the technical challenges will be co-judged by three-time champion of the Houston Junior Baking Competition—"

*Please don't say it. Please don't say it.*

"—Liza Yang."

I don't believe it. No embarrassing introduction? No rehashing of that humiliating profile? I'm so stunned I forget to move, but Mom's glare ultimately propels me forward. I enter the bakeshop at almost a sprint, so I force myself to slow down for the last few steps. As I move to stand beside her, Mom gestures at my mouth with her eyes. It takes a second to understand she wants me to smile. I stretch my lips tightly across my face as cameras focus in on me. It's only then that I sweep my eyes over this year's contestants.

"Holy s—"

I bite back the rest of the curse when Mom clamps her hand around my forearm.

"Don't you dare embarrass me," she hisses in my ear.

Me, embarrass her? Is she kidding? I glance back out at the bakeshop. Behind every station is an Asian boy. Most are staring openly at me, their eyes raking over my body and making me shudder. I steer my own eyes toward Ben instead, who grins and mouths a hello.

*You know, so you'll have two less guys to worry about.*

Gratitude fills me as his words finally click. Somehow, Ben knew this would happen and went out of his way to help me. Although . . . didn't he say it was James's idea all along? I lean slightly to the side and peer past him to where James is stationed. He's busy organizing the supplies on his workspace, but perhaps feeling my gaze on him, he turns. When our eyes meet, he glances away.

I turn my attention to the rest of the room. In addition to the camera crews, we have a live audience for the first time. Three staggered rows of chairs line the left wall, and nearly every seat is occupied. Besides my family and friends, the boys' families—or more correctly, their mothers—have come to cheer them on. They're no easier to deal with, inspecting me like some prize cow.

Great. This is going to be *so* much fun.

Chef Anthony clears his throat. "Now that the introductions are done, we'll move on to the rules."

My mind wanders as he gives the contestants a rundown. As much as I appreciate the guys for joining, Ben sounded less than confident when I asked about his baking skills. Neither seems like the sort who can tell the difference between a spoon and a spatula. That goes double for James, who looks far from enthused about getting his hands dirty. It's going to take a miracle to get them to the end of the competition. Chef Anthony's booming voice startles me out of my thoughts.

"Now for the moment we've all been waiting for! Let's meet our contestants!"

I close my eyes and pray for salvation.

# Chapter 15

I drag myself to the first station with Mom and Mrs. Lee. Contestant one stands about five foot five, which means his eyes land right at my chin. With shaggy black hair and shiny metal braces, he's definitely memorable. My smile falters as I notice the dirt under his nails.

"Contestant one, tell us a little about yourself," Mom encourages.

He scratches his head. "Uh . . . my name is Harold Chang. I'm seventeen, and I go to Memorial High School."

"Welcome to the competition, Harold! How long have you been baking?"

"Uh, I don't know," he mumbles. "Maybe a few months?"

I'm sorry, what? Did he say a few *months*? I glower at Mom, who steadfastly avoids meeting my eye as she presses him for more information.

"And what are you most excited about baking?"

Someone pushes a camera into his face, and he stares into it, lips opening and closing like a goldfish in a bowl. Mrs. Lee clears her throat, but he doesn't stir.

"Um . . . we'll get back to you, Harold!" she says. "Let's move on."

At station two, we meet Jay Huang. Dressed all in black, he's lanky, and his hair is shaved at the bottom and pulled into a pony-tail at the top. His nails are painted to match his outfit, making it impossible to tell if he's any cleaner than Harold.

"Are . . . are you sure you're Jay?"

He half shrugs. "Yeah."

"But your picture . . ." Mom swallows. "You look very . . . different in that one."

"What picture?"

"Um, you were wearing a white shirt and a black tie."

"Oh, yeah, that's, like, from way back . . . last year, maybe?" he admits with a roll of the eyes. "It's the one we send to my grandma every year for Christmas because she has a bad heart. But this is who I really am."

Mom is aghast, and she struggles to come up with a suitable reply.

*Serves you right for trying to set me up.*

Thankfully, Mrs. Lee steps in with a composed smile.

"Well, Jay. How do you think you'll do in the competition?"

He picks up a measuring spoon and frowns. "I'm sure I'll be the first to go. I'm only doing this because Mom made me."

"So . . . you haven't done much baking, then?"

"Only if you count the good stuff," he quips with a waggle of the brows. "You know, like brownies?"

Someone in the audience lets out a loud squeak. We turn to see a woman—I presume, Mrs. Huang—waving a finger at him. When the camera pans to her, she ducks her head and plays with her earring.

Jay rolls his eyes. "I'm kidding, obviously. My body is a temple."

Mom can't decide if she should laugh or frown. I do my best to avoid the former as Mrs. Lee ushers us to the third station. Contes-tant three is wearing a button-down shirt almost the exact shade of blue as my dress. He's tall, at least two inches more than me, with thin-framed glasses perched on the bridge of his nose. His brown eyes sparkle as he smiles, and I admit, he's cute in a geeky kind of way.

Not that I'm ever going to tell Mom.

"Good morning, judges."

He sticks his hand out for each of us to shake, though he hangs on to mine for a second longer than necessary.

Mom visibly relaxes. "Your name is Edward, is that correct?"

His eyes dart briefly to the camera over her shoulder before answering.

"Yes. My name is Edward Lim. I've just graduated high school, and I'll be studying pre-med in the fall at Rice University. I've mostly baked for fun in the past, but I plan on doing whatever it takes to win."

Edward utters the last part while staring hard at me. Lim . . . Lim . . . wait. Is he related to Reuben somehow? I take a closer look. Nah. He's too . . . normal.

"Wonderful!" Mrs. Lee replies. "It's so lovely to meet you. We look forward to seeing what you come up with."

Next up is a pair of twins, David and Albert Kuan. Honestly, I don't know who's who. They've shown up in identical clothes and parted their hair in the exact same spot. Mrs. Lee graces them with her signature smile.

"Hello, boys."

"Hello. We're really happy to be here, Mrs. Lee, Mrs. Yang, and Liza."

They talk as if they're one person, not missing a single syllable. I shudder at the major *The Shining* vibes. Mom must have picked them thinking she'd have twice the chance of success. I'd say she's twice as likely to fail.

The contestant who occupies station number six is considerably shorter than the three of us. Standing barely at five feet, he spends the entire introduction staring at my chest. Granted, he does the same with the other two judges, but it's still über creepy. I only catch his name—Timothy something—before deciding I'm going to eliminate him as fast as humanly possible. I'll take Dirty Harry at station one any day. Mom pulls a face.

"Timothy. Your application says you're eighteen."

"That's because I am."

Timothy raises his eyes in a silent challenge. If Mom could politely demand proof, she'd have his driver's license in hand by now. Instead, she flashes a half-hearted smile.

"Um, good luck to you today."

She quickly steps over to station seven before Mrs. Lee can follow up with a question. The boy looks ready to bolt the minute the spotlight is on him. His dark eyes are wide, and his flat nose and round cheeks are covered with a smattering of freckles that remind me of the sesame seeds we sprinkle on buns. It takes Mrs. Lee several minutes to coax an answer out of him.

"I'm . . ." His voice is so quiet, we all lean in to hear him. "Um, my name is Michael . . . Zhou. Sixteen years old. I just moved to Houston last month. I hope I'll make some friends here."

I feel bad for him. No amount of talent will save him if he folds under pressure. Mrs. Lee must sense this too, because she reaches over and pats him on the hand.

"Don't be nervous, Michael. Just relax, and take deep breaths. It'll be fine."

He shoots her a shy smile. "Thank you, Mrs. Lee. I'll try that."

We've barely come to a stop at the eighth station when the contestant behind it bursts into speech.

"My name is Sammy Ma. I'll be eighteen in September, and I'm looking forward to the bread round because I'll be using my grandmother's recipe." He turns and smiles into the camera, waving. "Hi, Grandma!"

Sammy's got the roundest cheeks I've ever seen. They overwhelm the rest of his features and look ripe for squeezing. He could totally be related to the son in that Pixar short *Bao*.

"Good, good. We'll be rooting for you to get there," Mom redirects. "Let's meet our next contestant."

It's finally Ben's turn. While he flashes a smile at Mom and me, it wavers when it reaches Mrs. Lee. Oblivious, Mom greets him.

"Hello! Why don't you tell us a little about yourself?"

Charming Ben reappears, though his eyes never stray from Mom's as he answers.

"My name is Ben Chan. I'm eighteen, and I recently moved from New York City."

Mrs. Lee interrupts, her voice so low I'm almost sure I imagined it.

"It's been a long time, Ben."

He nods politely. "Hello, Mrs. Lee. It's lovely to see you too."

"If I remember correctly, you have quite the knack for baking. I'll be keeping my eye on you."

It could be my imagination, but there's a slight sharpness to her tone. When Ben smiles, I can tell it's fake.

"Thank you."

I try getting his attention, but he drops his head. With no other choice, I make my way to the last station. James's apron is too short for his frame, something I hadn't noticed until now. Despite this, his rigid posture and firmly set mouth encourage no teasing.

"I should have known if Ben's here, you wouldn't be far behind."

I jerk my head toward Mrs. Lee. The animosity in her voice is unmistakable. Mom and I exchange a look. It's not like her to break out of her effervescent persona, especially in front of a camera. James's stormy glare is equally intense as he replies.

"Seems to me like you're the one doing the following."

"Ah, contestant number ten!" Mom interjects loudly. "What is your name?"

"James Wong."

Mrs. Lee starts to say something else, but he cuts her off with a sharp look. Thankfully, I'm too stunned to laugh. Chef Anthony breaks the tension with a clap.

"Well, how about we get started?"

Mrs. Lee glowers at James for one more second before marching over to join our host. Mom and I follow and stand on his other side.

"Okay, contestants, listen up! Round one's theme is cookies. Mrs. Yang, if you please?"

Mom steps forward, projecting her voice so the entire room can hear.

"For your technical challenge, you will be replicating my matcha tea cookie recipe. They should have a powdery texture, be not too sweet, and have just the right amount of matcha flavor. Remember, we've given you most of the recipe, but not all. You have one and a half hours, starting . . . now!"

Once all ten contestants start in on their bakes, she swivels her head toward me. I read the challenge in her eyes.

Okay, Mom.

Let the games begin.

• • • • •

A little over an hour later, we're nearing the end of the allotted time for baking. Mom and I stayed out in the hall to keep it a blind judging, while Mrs. Lee and Chef Anthony remained inside to ensure there's no cheating.

"What do you think of our contestants this year, Liza?" Mom asks.

I clench my fists in my lap and swallow my automatic reply.

"I think it's too early to tell how they'll do. We'll get a better sense of them after this technical round."

She frowns. "That's not what I meant."

"I know."

I resume staring at the opposite wall. The silence between us grows thick with tension. When Chef Anthony counts down the last seconds of the bake, I hop onto my feet.

"Three, two, one, step away from your stations!"

The clatter of bowls and utensils heralds the end of our first technical. We give the contestants a few minutes to arrange their bakes on the table. Mom replaced the gingham altar with a tablecloth printed with the bakery's logo. She'd shown it to me rather proudly when it came in the mail.

"It's good publicity."

I think hosting the contest and naming it after Yin and Yang is plenty, but she's always been extra like that.

In any case, I fidget with my sleeve until Chef Anthony pops his head out into the hallway. Mom and I take our places behind the table, while the contestants stand facing us in random order. I fight a wave of nausea when I spot the dirt still under Harold's fingernails. There are two more contestants with equally bad hygiene in the pack, not counting Goth Jay.

Without hesitation, Mom picks up the cookie on the right side of the table. She holds it up and examines it.

"I would have liked to see more of a flower shape," she comments, "but let's see how the cookie tastes."

If this is Dirty Harry's cookie, he's doing an admirable job of hiding it. I want to slap it out of Mom's hand, but cringe instead as she chews. When she side-eyes me, I grab a cookie with great reluctance and nip off a piece just big enough to judge.

She turns to me. "What do you think, Liza?"

It'll be okay. There's, like, maybe a seventy percent chance this baker's hands were clean, after all. But that does little to reassure me.

*You can always kill it with antibiotics later.*

I force myself to swallow the offending bite before speaking.

"The consistency could be better. I'm guessing you forgot to sift the dry ingredients. The flavor is okay, but too sweet. And the decoration . . . didn't make it onto the plate."

Mom smiles almost with a hint of pride. "I agree. Let's move on."

The next plate contains soggy blobs of dough, underbaked so badly I wonder if they even got the cookies into the oven. Neither of us is keen on trying one, but Mom sacrifices herself so I don't have to. Her face tells me everything I need to know. I look at the contestants.

"These are severely underbaked. Too little time in the oven. They also don't have the shape required. Major time management issues here."

One plate after another, we taste and I judge. Mom doesn't disagree with me once, and it makes me surprisingly uneasy. On the second to last batch, I finally lay my eyes on pristinely made cookies. Mom's eyebrows shoot up as she eats, which looks promising. When I bite down on my piece, it's like heaven exploding in my mouth.

"Whoever made this knew what they were doing. The thickness of the dough is just enough that it holds the shape of the cutter. It's baked all the way through, and the matcha flavor is just right. The orange-infused white chocolate stripes on top are clean and precise. This is a delicious cookie."

The cookies on the plate next to that bake are almost on par, but the decoration lacks the finesse of my personal favorite. We rank the cookies based on our taste test, and step back to announce the results. Mom does the honors.

"Number ten is this one," she says, gesturing at the dough blobs. "Who does this belong to?"

Jay raises his hand. His pants are covered in flour, and there are streaks of food coloring on his face and arms. Despite initial appearances, he must have put some effort into his bake.

"Ah. Well, it didn't go well for you this round, but there's always the highlight bake," Mom tells him.

Ninth place goes to Timothy. I breathe a sigh of relief when I realize his cookies weren't the underbaked ones. Mom runs through the rest in quick succession until we reach first and second place.

She points to the last plate we ate from. "Second place goes to the baker who made this batch."

Ben raises his hand with a giant grin, his nerves forgotten.

"Very nice. Only the slightest texture issue. When the cookie hits your tongue, it should almost dry it out."

It's obvious who the winner is before she announces it. I shake my head in disbelief.

"That means the winner of our first technical is James. Congratulations!"

He cracks a smile. There's a single twitch at the junction of his lips, his dimple making the briefest of appearances. I look away quickly, annoyed at myself for noticing.

"Okay! Let's take a one-hour break," Mom commands. "I would encourage you all to make use of the restroom, because once we start the next round, you won't get another chance."

All ten guys stream out of the room along with their families.

Nervous energy fills the corridor as the contestants steal glances at each other. Chef Anthony steps away to answer a phone call, while Mrs. Lee heads off to check on the progress at her new bakery. This leaves Jeannie, Grace, and Sarah sitting along the wall. Dad pops into the room a few minutes later. He grins and waves two white plastic bags in our direction.

"I brought lunch. Come to the break room."

The four of us race after him, but I pause in the doorway.

"Are you coming, Mom?"

She shakes her head. "I'm not hungry. You go."

I step out into the empty corridor. Correction: the near-empty corridor. Someone's footsteps are approaching me from the other end of the hall. I brighten when I realize who it is.

"Nathan?"

I wait for him to catch up to me. He grins.

"Hello again."

"I thought you were busy today."

"I was, but my shoot ended up finishing early because one of the cameras broke. I was going to pick Jeannie up for lunch, but she invited me to stop by instead."

"Oh, then you're in for a treat," I tell him. "My dad did the cooking today."

• • • • •

We finish eating twenty minutes before the contestants are due back. By then, Nathan and Dad have traded enough bad jokes to last a lifetime. Despite the puns, Grace and Sarah have decided he's worthy enough to be saved from future tenderizing. Jeannie walks him back to his car while the rest of us return to the bakeshop.

Mom may not have eaten anything, but she hasn't been sitting idly by. At least five of the ten stations have been completely cleaned off and readied for the highlight bake.

"I could use your help." She gestures at the empty carts nearby. "We don't have much time before they come back."

Dad and Jeannie each take a station, and I grab one too. We remove all the dirty containers and utensils and wipe down the counters. Then, we replace everything and measure out the ingredients listed on each contestant's original recipe. Grace and Sarah both jump in to help me, something Mom makes note of. We're down to our last two stations when Sarah excuses herself to run to the restroom. She passes Ben and James as they walk back in. Ben immediately rolls up his sleeves to clear off his station.

Mom clucks her tongue. "Ben, you don't have to do that. You're a contestant. This is our job."

"Please, Mrs. Yang. I insist."

He's looking at her so earnestly she acquiesces. I can tell Mom's scheming already, and I smile to myself. She'll figure it out at some point. As I predicted, when Ben tucks an errant lock of Grace's hair behind her ear minutes later, the glint fades from her eyes. Mom sighs as they talk quietly, their heads bowed together.

I'm so busy gloating I don't immediately notice James positioning himself on the other side of my station. As he unbuttons the cuffs of his sleeves, surprise heat billows through my body. I'm so sure the oven at the station is on that I double-check the knobs. Weirdly, everything's in place.

James clears his throat. "How can I help?"

I hesitate for a beat before gesturing at a clean towel on the cart. "I'll clear things off if you'll wipe it down."

He nods. I remove the used mixing bowls, utensils, and leftover ingredients so he can run the cloth over the stainless steel surface.

As he wipes in large swirling motions, I'm fascinated by the way his shirt stretches across his muscles. It's a second before I realize he's asked me a question.

"I . . . I'm sorry?"

He tilts his head slightly. "Can I help you do anything else?"

"Oh, uh . . . I just need to replace everything and make sure you have all your ingredients."

"I'll do the second part. I know the recipe by heart."

A few days ago, I would've heard conceit in his voice. Today, there's something . . . different in his words. I catch myself staring again and cough awkwardly.

"Okay, yeah. You check your stuff and I'll get the rest."

In my haste to retrieve a fresh set of utensils, I trip over a loose shoelace. My body tumbles forward at breakneck speed, but I'm scooped up and saved from a near face-plant. My heart beats double time as James gently sets me on my feet. With his arm still around my waist, he peers down at me.

"Are you okay?"

His breath, hot like steam from a freshly baked bao, brushes over my cheek. I nod once. I don't trust myself to speak. His grip loosens, and I pull out of his grasp. Afraid of what I'll see if I look up at him, I use the cart for support as I walk over to where the clean items are kept. Once everything is loaded up, I check off my mental list before wheeling it back to his station.

I focus on arranging everything in the exact position it was in before. His fingers brush mine when he reaches for the last item—a glass mixing bowl. I yank my hand back and fist it at my side. Something flits over his features before he carefully locks the bowl into place on the mixer.

"Thank you."

"You're welcome," I mumble.

Surprisingly, he smiles, and I follow the upward curve of his lips. James's warm brown eyes lock on to mine for a brief second, and heat washes over me a second time. Confused and desperate for some air, I break eye contact and quickly push the cart back to the corner. I duck out of the room, but not before catching Ben and Grace smirking at me nearby.

Once outside, I shut my eyes and lean against the cool wall. Not long after, I sense Grace sidle up beside me. The vanilla and honey scent of her perfume fills my nostrils as she leans toward me.

"So . . ."

"Don't even think about it."

She sputters. "How do you know what I'm going to say?"

"Because you're my best friend, and I know you."

There's a pause before she inhales. "Want me to ask Ben about it?"

"Not unless you want this to be your last day on Earth."

"Oh, come on! You guys would be so cute together!"

I finally open my eyes to look at her. "Please let it go, Grace. I already have one matchmaker on my ass."

"I just want you to be as happy as I am."

"Who said I'm not happy? I have the best friend in the whole world." I yank her into a hug. "That's good enough for me."

Grace tries to shove me away, but I hold on tight. Her voice is muffled against my shoulder.

"You're such a dweeb."

"But you love me."

She pulls back and grins. "But I love you."

Glancing at the door, I square my shoulders.

"All right. Let's get this over with."

# Chapter 16

As the break ends, the other contestants trickle in and join Ben and James back in the bakeshop. Edward walks in last, with Sarah by his side. She giggles at something he says, but when Mom narrows her eyes at him, he immediately abandons her and slips behind his station. Sarah stares at him in confusion before making her way back to her seat.

The reporters settle into their positions as Chef Anthony accompanies Mrs. Lee through the doors. With my part done for the day, I hug the wall to watch along with the audience. Jeannie pats the empty chair next to her in the back row.

"I saved it for you."

I smile gratefully. "Thanks."

Grace plops down on my right, and Sarah switches chairs so she's sitting directly in front of us. From my seat by the wall, I have a clear view of all ten portable bake stations. Jeannie lowers her voice so only the three of us can hear her.

"Am I imagining things, or is there something going on between Mrs. Lee and contestants nine and ten?"

I shake my head. "Definitely not imagining it."

"What did they say to each other?" Grace asks me.

"Nothing worth repeating." Then I frown. "Actually, that's not right. Mrs. Lee made some comment about James always being around Ben. That really pissed him off."

"Really? What did he say back?"

"Something about Mrs. Lee following them to Houston."

She frowns too. "That's weird. We'll have to ask them about it later."

"Contestants," Chef Anthony shouts, "this is your highlight round. Mrs. Lee and Mrs. Yang would like you to give us your interpretation of cookie art. All your individual parts must be edible, and eighty percent of your design must be made from cookies. They'd like to see at least two flavors, and your piece should be nicely decorated. You have three hours. Begin!"

The reporters hang around for the first fifteen minutes to record the baking, and then they leave one by one. Harold, who I'm now convinced will never wash his hands, makes a huge mess of his workspace within twenty minutes. His clumsy pours and careless mixing ensure large amounts of ingredients never make it into his dough. Even so, my heart stops when he sends a full batch of cookies to the floor while trying to pull a hot tray out with his bare hand.

In a flash, the pads of his fingers are covered in white blisters, and he releases a howl that brings everyone to a dead stop. Chef Anthony quickly sends him out into the hallway for medical care. Seconds later, a semi-hysterical woman fights her way down our aisle to go after them. She must be Dirty Harry's mom. Chef Anthony returns and whispers something to Mom and Mrs. Lee. Too bad I can't read lips, because for once, they seem to agree, wearing twin looks of concern.

Abruptly, someone utters a loud expletive to our left. Timothy is in the far corner, angrily dumping his tray of half-baked cookies into the trash. He's grabbed a ball of dough and is preparing to toss it in too when a woman who could be his older sister pops up out of her chair to shout at him.

"Stop it! Just start over!"

Her protest goes unheard. Timothy lobs his leftover dough into the trash. He then picks up the rest of his ingredients and stares directly at her.

She rises out of her chair. "Don't you dare throw that away, Timothy Allen Gao! You're here to win!"

"Ma'am, there's no coaching allowed," Chef Anthony warns. "If you do it again, you'll be asked to leave."

"Yeah, Mom," Timothy adds snidely. "I don't need you to tell me what to do. I quit!"

He proceeds to rip off his apron and toss it on the ground. A stunned silence blankets the room as he storms out. Mrs. Gao tries to play it off.

"He gets like this sometimes when he doesn't get enough sleep."

She runs out after him, barely making it to the door before screeching his name.

"Timothy! Get back here right now!"

Chef Anthony turns to the remaining contestants with a tight smile.

"Everyone, please continue."

For the next several minutes, even the sound of multiple mixers can't drown out the screaming match outside. Eventually, a door slams in the distance, and Mrs. Gao reappears in the doorway. Her cheeks are flushed and her hair disheveled, as if she'd tried dragging her son back inside. She waves Chef Anthony over, and I manage to make out some of the words she says.

"Timothy . . . not feeling . . . my apologies . . . another day . . . fresh start . . ."

He shakes his head slowly in reply. Mrs. Gao then insists on talking to the judges, repeating whatever she told him. Mrs. Lee tips her head deferentially toward Mom, who shrugs helplessly. Her options exhausted, Timothy's mom leaves in a huff. Neither of them comes back. I feel a tap on my shoulder.

"What do you think Mom's going to do now?" Jeannie whispers.

"Your guess is as good as mine."

Sarah twists around to look at us. "Has this ever happened before?"

"No. We've never had contestants drop out, much less on day one."

I chew on my lower lip. After making such a fuss about the contest being perfect, why would Mom pick such clearly inept bakers? Either she's totally convinced I'll bring home that tattooed Ed Sheeran lookalike or these guys lied about their baking skills. Then again, I wouldn't put it past some, if not all, of these moms to fill out their sons' applications.

The rest of the highlight bake winds down without any more drama. Ben, James, Edward, and Sammy all seem to be on track with their cookies. Jay is mixing an inordinate amount of black icing in his mixer, while Michael keeps talking to himself and glancing at his shaking hands. The twins are behind, with one—Albert?—still baking his cookies, and his brother struggling to get his icing to the right consistency and color.

"You have fifteen minutes!" Chef Anthony announces. "Fifteen minutes left!"

The room explodes into chaos. The mothers in the audience can't help cheering their sons on, shouting encouragement as the contestants frantically put the finishing touches on their cookie art. In comparison, James is parked on his stool, sipping coolly on a glass of water like the eye in a storm. There isn't even a spot of

flour or food coloring on his apron, and his station is clean and organized. I strain to catch sight of his cookie art, but he's blocking it
from view. Shortly after, Ben throws his hands up after laying down
his last line of icing, and the two cousins high-five in celebration.

"And . . . time's up!" Chef Anthony calls out. "Put down the icing and back away from your cookies!"

A few of the contestants mic drop their spatulas. Others are
staring at their creations as if expecting them to come to life. Chef
Anthony steps forward.

"It's time for our judges to see how well you did. Harold—"

He cuts off, belatedly recalling Dirty Harry's oven mishap.
"Right. Um . . . Jay, please bring your cookie art to the table."

I choke back a laugh as he steps aside to reveal a hairy black
spider with the letters R.I.P. scrawled in bright red lettering. His
piping leaves a lot to be desired, but that's the least of his troubles.
Neither Mrs. Lee nor Mom is willing to come within two feet of it.

"Um, Jay . . . what inspired you to make this piece?" Mom
squeaks out.

"I really like Aragog from Harry Potter. It's my homage to him."

Chef Anthony is forced to do the honors. He cuts two pieces and
hands the plates over to them for judging. Mom has to shut her eyes
to take a bite, while Mrs. Lee turns her back to the cookie altogether.
We wait in collective silence for their verdict.

"It's . . . very creative," Mrs. Lee finally says. "But a bit over-
whelming for me. The choice of design is not the most appealing."

Mom stares steadfastly at Jay. "Did . . . did you make the eyes
with chocolate chips?"

"Yep," he answers proudly. "It brings him to life, I think."

"That it does," Chef Anthony agrees amiably. "Thank you, Jay.
You may sit down now."

Jay turns to head back to his station, but Mom calls out to him. "Please take your . . . Arago with you."

"His name is Aragog."

"Sure, sure, whatever." She waves at it. "Please just take it away."

Jay does as he's asked but spends the rest of the judging period glowering at Mom. Perched on his stool with black-lined eyes and a tucked chin, he's one wand short of a Cruciatus Curse. Meanwhile, Chef Anthony nods at the next contestant.

"Edward, why don't you show us what you made?"

Edward saunters up to the front and places his entry onto the table. He's made a cameo out of his cookie and painted its subject completely out of icing. It's impressive, but it would be more so if he had colored the icing instead of defaulting to all white. Grace squints before slapping me on the arm.

"Oh my god. I think that's you!"

"No, it's not. There's no way . . ."

My denial dies instantly when Chef Anthony tips the giant cookie up slightly for everyone to see. The girl on the cookie is an obvious match to my flyer photo, down to the pained smile on my face. The edges of my vision begin to blur as Mom claps her hands together.

"Isn't this lovely! The likeness . . . it's so striking!"

The minute she proclaims this, everyone in the room turns to stare at me. With all the heat I'm taking, it's a wonder I don't spontaneously combust.

*Come on, Human Torch.*

I glance down at my hands. Damn it. Not even a tiny flicker.

Thankfully, Mrs. Lee clears her throat and draws the attention back to the front of the room.

"It is quite detailed, Edward. I'm impressed by the amount of work you were able to pull off. Of course, ultimately it'll come down to taste."

I wince as Edward snaps pieces off Cookie Me's head to feed the judges. When Mom chomps down on an eye enthusiastically, mine twitches in sympathy. I shake off the creep factor and focus on the quality of the bake. The cookie crumbles too easily in my opinion, and the icing layer is far too thick.

"What flavor cookie did you make this out of?" Mrs. Lee asks politely.

"The hair is sugar cookie, and the face is snickerdoodle."

"I think it was a mistake to choose two flavors so similar to each other," she tells him, putting the rest of her piece down onto the plate. "If you hadn't told me, I would have assumed it was all the same."

Mom's lips curl. "I was able to tell them apart without a problem," Mom comments. "You should have scraped off a little of the icing first."

A feline smile stretches across Mrs. Lee's face. "Oh, I agree one hundred percent. The icing is quite heavy-handed."

Mom's eyes flicker over to the kitchen knives as Mrs. Lee looks out over the room. Lucky for her, Chef Anthony swoops in with a distraction.

"Thank you, Edward. Very nice. Now, David, would you like to bring up your art?"

He makes a face. "Actually, my cookie is only half of the design."

"Who has the other half?"

Albert raises his hand. "Me!"

Mom pinches the bridge of her nose and sighs as murmurs sweep across the bakeshop.

"What a unique idea."

"That's not fair!" one of the moms shouts.

"Is that even allowed?" another one chimes in.

Chef Anthony raises a hand to quiet the crowd. "This is a highly unusual situation. Please give me a minute to consult with the judges."

They bow their heads together as the two boys wait. A gangly woman sitting in front of us strains to hear what they're saying. She looks to be in her midforties, and she's dressed in a custom jersey with the boys' names emblazoned on the back.

"She must be their mom," Jeannie says under her breath.

"You think?"

She rewards me with a poke in the ribs, and I clap my hand over my mouth to cover my giggle. The twins' mother hears it nonetheless and turns around with a scowl. I duck my head as Chef Anthony steps forward.

"The judges have made a decision. Since this is day one, they will allow David and Albert to present their pieces together." He levels a look at the twins. "However, should you move on, you will each be expected to prepare your own individual pieces."

David brightens considerably, while Albert's shoulders droop. The pair escorts their cookies to the table and places them side by side. Mom's eyebrows shoot up.

"Yin and yang. How . . . nice."

"No," Grace gasps. "They didn't."

As a matter of fact, they did. Each twin has one half of the symbol—David with yin, Albert with yang.

"I made mine out of lemon cookie and white frosting," Albert announces. "David's is chocolate cookie with black frosting."

"I see," Mrs. Lee comments. "Are the dots the opposite flavors?"

"Oh . . . uh . . ."

"See? I told you that's what we should've done!" David snaps. "But no, you wanted to make it easy!"

The two of them go from seventeen to seven in three seconds flat, bickering loudly right at the table. Their mom is either speechless or used to their fights because she watches the whole thing without moving a muscle. Mom finally breaks them up.

"David! Albert! This is not acceptable behavior from our contestants!"

They rear back simultaneously. Albert turns to his mom, but she averts her gaze. He crosses his arms over his chest and lets out a loud huff, while David sneers in his direction. Mrs. Lee attempts to get us back on track.

"I like the initiative you two took for your highlight. Using the name of the competition as inspiration. Very creative."

Albert beams, while David—possibly the more self-aware twin—is only mollified. She breaks off a small piece from each side, and Mom follows suit. Albert's cookie poses more of a challenge, and we watch the two of them chew for a while before swallowing. Mrs. Lee, after taking a swig of her water, glances at her co-judge.

"Mrs. Yang, what you do think?"

Mom pulls herself to her full height—five foot two—and squares her jaw. Though both boys can look down their noses at her, they cower beneath her intimidating gaze.

"It would have been better if you both added flavor to your icing rather than just coloring it. Albert, your cookie is overbaked and too dry. David, yours has the right bite to it, and the chocolate really comes through. Good job."

Neither brother clearly expected her forthrightness. Albert's ears turn scarlet, his cheeks billowing like a half-inflated balloon. David, on the other hand, finally smiles.

"I agree with Mrs. Yang on the icing," Mrs. Lee starts, "but I liked how much lemon I tasted in your cookie, Albert. If you make it to the next round, I hope you'll pay more attention to your bake time."

Chef Anthony shoos them back to their seat before Albert melts down. He then gestures for Michael to come forward, but the contestant shakes his head frantically. Chef Anthony walks over to his station.

"Do you need help carry—"

The rest of the words die in his throat as he stares down at Michael's creation.

"Aren't those your technical cookies?"

"I tried my best, but I spilled water on my paper," he bursts out, near tears. "Momma spent all night . . ."

A stout woman at the end of our aisle suddenly starts coughing violently. Michael abandons his station and rushes to her side.

"Momma! Are you okay, Momma?"

"I'm fine, sweetie," she says with reddened cheeks. "I'll be okay. Just go back and present your piece."

"But it doesn't look anything like your design!"

Gasps echo through the room. It's not against the rules to use family recipes, but the contestants must come up with their own designs. With Michael's cheeks stained with tears, Chef Anthony coaxes him up to the front table with his tray. Mom tugs at her sleeve as she considers what to say. Mrs. Lee steps forward and gives him a gentle pat on the shoulder.

"You were trying to think on your feet. I commend you for that."

"Um . . . that's right," Mom follows. "Very good attempt to recover after a mishap."

Despite their kindness, Michael folds like a cardboard box. He leaves his tray on the table and treads back to his seat. Chef

Anthony quietly moves his cookies back to his station for him.

"Sammy, why don't you—"

He's at the judging table before Chef Anthony finishes his sentence. Sammy—or Lil Bao, as I prefer to call him—grins with such unreserved joy it's infectious.

"My design is called 'If it fits, I sits.' It's a peanut butter cookie with white- and milk-chocolate icing. I dedicate it to my cat, Peanut."

I lean forward to get a better look. Sure enough, he's painted a picture of his cat sitting in a cardboard box. It's crude but also so adorable. When the judges have a taste of his cookie, they go back in for a second bite.

"This is actually quite good," Mom announces. "Peanut butter and chocolate go well together, and you've kept a good balance between the flavors."

Mrs. Lee nods. "It's got good mouth feel. I quite enjoyed eating it."

Their compliments are accompanied by light applause from the audience. Sammy walks back to his station with his chest puffed out. Now there are only two left to present—Ben and James. Ben is up first, and he carefully moves his piece over. Grace and I stand up for a better look, and she lets out a low whistle.

"Wow."

I agree. Ben's chosen to make a batch of cookies shaped like blocks to create a *Minecraft* scene. His piping is pretty neat, and his coloring is on point. Mom has no idea what she's looking at, so she reaches for something generic.

"You're the first one in the competition to try 3D cookies, Ben. It's a more advanced skill, and you nailed it."

"I wish we didn't have to take it apart," Mrs. Lee laments, "but this *is* a cookie challenge, so let's get to tasting."

It's funny watching them both try to Jenga their way into a piece without breaking apart the entire structure. Ben glued everything down with a sugar solution, but it doesn't take much to wreck it. I tense subconsciously as Mom bites into her piece.

Her eyes widen. "Now, that's interesting! I was expecting gingerbread, but this is more of a biscotti."

"Bold choice, Ben," Mrs. Lee adds, still chewing. "Crunchy, but not too dry. Did you decrease your baking time?"

He flushes. "Actually, I tweaked the recipe a little so it would be a softer bake."

Their comments tempt Chef Anthony to indulge in a piece of his own. He makes a happy sound after popping the biscotti block into his mouth.

"Now all I need is some coffee or milk!"

It turns out Ben came prepared. There are two cups of milk on his tray, and he hands one to our host. Chef Anthony gulps it down in three swallows.

"Thank you, Ben," says Mom. "Please return to your station. James, please bring your highlight up."

All eyes are on James as he transfers his cookies to the front of the room. Like his cousin, he's chosen a batch of cookies rather than baking one giant piece. Instead of a build, however, he's decorated them beautifully with sprigs of rehydrated cherry blossoms. Mom leans in to examine them more closely. She loves an understated presentation, so as long as the taste makes a big impact, he'll win her favor. Mrs. Lee is a totally different story. With their terse exchange earlier, I wonder how she'll judge him.

"Tell us about your cookies," Chef Anthony commands.

"They're inspired by my travels to Japan. The cookies are a variation on butter cookies and have cherry blossoms mixed into the dough."

Three cookies disappear off his tray as the judges and host each take possession of one. It's hard to decipher the play of emotions on their faces as they eat. It's totally quiet in the room, save for the soft sound of crunching.

"The balance of flavors is exceptional," Mom proclaims. "The slight saltiness—I'm guessing from pickling the blossoms—keeps the cookie from being too rich. Excellent."

The energy in the room shifts as jealousy radiates from the other contestants. It only grows when Mrs. Lee reluctantly agrees.

"I have to say, James . . . this is one of the best cookies I've ever had, and I've tasted a lot over the years."

You'd think their high praise would garner at least one smile, but James remains stubbornly stoic as he turns stiffly and heads to his seat. Chef Anthony brightens the room with a giant grin.

"The first day of the Fifth Annual Yin and Yang Junior Baking Competition has now concluded. Our judges will take a break to deliberate on who will move on and who will be eliminated. Good luck to each and every one of you!"

# Chapter 17

The tension of the bake evaporates the minute Mom, Mrs. Lee, and Chef Anthony exit the room to discuss things. Mothers spill onto the bakeshop floor to reach their sons, some of whom are sagging against their stations. Grace is making a beeline for Ben, while Jeannie turns to me with a sparkle of excitement in her eyes.

"Nathan just texted me. He wants to take me out to dinner!"

"Don't do anything I wouldn't do," I tease.

"That's not a lot to go on, Liza."

She runs off to call Nathan before I can smack her on the arm. Sarah scoots over and waggles her eyebrows at me before glancing at Ben and James, who are admiring each other's creations.

"So which one is the hottie who helped you with Brody?"

I point surreptitiously at James. "That one."

"Whoa," Sarah says, giving him a once-over. "I can't believe you're not into him. He's so hot, and not just for an Asian guy."

I grimace. "That sounds really bad, Sarah."

She shakes her head frantically. "I was only trying to say that he's really . . ."

"Hot. Yeah, I got that. But you make it sound like Asian guys are not as hot as other guys."

"I definitely wasn't trying to say that." Sarah cocks her head to the side. "I just meant that I'm not usually into Asian guys but—"

I groan. "Stop. You're making it worse."

Her face crumples, and she wrings her hands in her lap.

"I'm really terrible at this, aren't I?" she mumbles. "I never know how to explain myself. Mom calls it verbal diarrhea."

"First of all, that was a mental picture I didn't need," I answer. "Second of all, if you're not sure you should say something, just don't. Think about how you'd feel hearing someone say it to you."

"What do you mean?"

I twist in my chair to face her more fully. "Okay. For example, how would you feel if I told you that someone you like was only hot for a white guy?"

"Well, now that you put it that way . . ." Sarah freezes. "Wait. You *do* like James! You just admitted it!"

"What are you talking about? I was turning your words around to give you an example."

"No, not exactly. You added the part about 'someone you like,' which implies that you like James."

My head spins trying to keep up with the abrupt shift in our conversation.

I roll my eyes at her. "You're missing my point."

"I'm pretty sure I heard it loud and clear."

Sarah's giggling draws attention from those around us, including the guy in question. Luckily, I remember something that gives me the upper hand.

"You're one to talk. I saw you with Edward earlier."

Her eyes go wide. "Edward?"

"Yep. You were totally flirting with him."

"I wasn't," she denies, twirling a strand of red hair. "He was just—we were talking, that's all!"

With every stammer, her voice pitches higher until she reaches frequencies only dogs can hear. I lean in with a smirk.

"Does that mean you think Edward's hot, and not just for an Asian guy?"

Sarah's face ripens like a tomato from my teasing. I take pity on her and stick my hand out.

"I'm kidding. How about a truce? I'll even introduce you to the guys."

She pouts but shakes on it. I bump her shoulder repeatedly until she finally cracks a smile. I tug her to her feet and lead her over to the others. They're crowded around Ben's workstation. He and Grace are attached by the hand and whispering to each other, while James hovers close by like a hawk. I fall into place beside him but keep my distance.

"Hi, guys. This is our friend Sarah. Sarah, this is Ben and his cousin James."

She sticks out her hand. "It's nice to meet you! I've heard absolutely nothing about either of you."

Ben shakes her hand with a lighthearted chuckle. James nods politely.

"You guys did amazing today!" Sarah says with a smile firmly on her lips. "All your cookies look delicious."

"I want to try your cookie, Ben," Grace cajoles.

He gives her a heart-melting smile. "I'll pick the best one for you."

Ben also hands Sarah and me pieces without being asked. Just like Mrs. Lee said, it's a bit softer than typical biscotti, but in the best way. With the last bite softening on my tongue, I angle my eyes at him.

"Did you put a little cinnamon in there?"

His eyes widen. "How did you know?"

"Because she's just that good," Grace answers. "Liza's going to be a world-famous baker one day."

I wave her off. "She's exaggerating. The truth is, when you spend as much time as I do at a bakery, you pick things up that normal people won't."

"I don't know about that," Ben insists.

"Grace is right," James adds, stepping forward to join us in the circle. "No one else picked it up, including your mom and Mrs. Lee, and they're the professionals."

His words hit me hard. I hadn't really thought of it that way. A smile blooms on my face. My eyes meet his, but we both look away quickly.

"So how about yours?" Grace asks James. "Do you mind if we try some?"

"I guess," he answers with a shrug.

He puts four cookies on a plate and slides it across the stainless steel surface of the table. Grace and Ben take theirs immediately, while Sarah plucks hers up and examines it first. As I reach for the plate, James goes to move it toward me. His fingers brush against mine, leaving sparks along my skin like a struck match. My eyes shoot up, but he doesn't seem to have noticed.

*Focus, Liza. You're here for his cookies.*

*And his buns*, a mischievous little voice adds.

I'm pretty sure my face is redder than a char siu, so I stay focused on the cookie. On instinct, I bring it up and give it a sniff. The soft floral scent of cherry blossoms tickles my nostrils. Then I take a bite of the cookie and let it sit on my tongue instead of chewing. The butter melts in my mouth and releases the flavors, one layer at a time.

"So . . . what do you think?"

I lift my eyes to find James watching me intently. A tiny crease forms between his thick brows. I glance over at Ben and Grace, but they're too busy making eyes at each other. Sarah just makes a happy sound as she takes another bite.

"Um," I stammer. "It has a really delicate flavor. Infusing the cherry blossoms into the butter is a really nice touch."

"Wait, how do you know he put them into the butter?" Sarah asks.

I shrug. "It's just a guess. I thought I tasted the two flavors at the exact same time, instead of one following the other."

Ben eyes his cousin. "Did she get that right, James?"

"Yes . . . she did."

There's a slight hush to his voice, as if he's coming to the conclusion as he speaks. This time, James's deep brown eyes hold mine for a long second before he casts them down onto the table.

"I hope you like them. Since you've never seen cherry blossoms in person."

I don't know what to say first. I never expected him to remember one of the random things I blurted out trying to make conversation that night at Dumpling Dynasty. On the other hand, his cookies do evoke the picture of walking through sakura trees.

"I do. Like them, that is," I admit after swallowing the rest of the cookie. "They're very . . . thoughtful."

*Thoughtful? Of all the descriptions you could have chosen, you picked* thoughtful?

I half expect him to say something condescending or turn his nose up at me.

Instead, he smiles.

It's not a toothy one by any means, but enough to showcase the lone dimple on his left cheek. It's an open parenthesis wishing for a partner, and my fingers itch to trace a matching one on the other side. His features, once sharp, stretch and soften into something that sends my heart racing.

"Liza, right?"

I spin around and find Edward at my elbow. Apparently, he's decided this is the ideal time to butt in.

I force a smile to my face. "Yes?"

"I . . . uh . . . I just wanted to introduce myself to you properly." He sticks out his hand. "We didn't get a chance to talk earlier."

"Oh. It's nice to meet you," I reply as I shake his hand.

Edward's eyes keep darting over my shoulder. I resist the urge to turn and see what James is doing behind me.

"Your mom is very knowledgeable. Super nice too."

I blink at him. "Sure. Of course."

"Oh! I didn't mean you're not. I was just . . . that is . . ."

Edward implodes in real time as he forgets whatever speech he's prepared for the occasion. Grace jumps in with a brilliant smile.

"Hi. I'm Grace."

"I'm sorry . . . I should've asked your name," he mumbles.

"It's okay. You know it now."

Sarah's staring wordlessly at him, so I give her a gentle shove toward him.

"And you remember Sarah, don't you?"

"Yeah," he acknowledges, not quite meeting her eye. "We met in the hall earlier, right?"

"Congratulations on your bakes." She smiles shyly. "Your highlight, especially."

He perks up. "Really?"

"Definitely! I mean, the whole using the icing to draw Liza's face and everything . . ."

Sarah launches into a full-on review of his cookie. Her tendency to gesture wildly while talking overwhelms most people, but Edward doesn't seem to mind. In fact, he's laughing within minutes. Grace and I look at each other knowingly. Maybe I don't really have to worry about Edward.

Not long after, Chef Anthony enters the room, followed by Mom and Mrs. Lee.

"Everyone, please return to your stations and seats for our judges' decision."

Grace, Sarah, and I walk back to our chairs. Jeannie slips in just seconds later. Her lipstick is smudged, and half her hair has fallen out of its clip.

I elbow her to get her attention. "I'm guessing Nathan came by again, huh?"

She blinks. "What do you mean?"

"Check your makeup."

Jeannie pulls a mirror out of her purse. Her eyes widen with alarm, and she covers her face with her hands.

"This is so embarrassing!"

"Just be glad I saw you before Mom did."

She sneaks a peek toward the front of the room. "Are you going to tell her?"

"Of course not." I grin. "Not yet, anyway."

She narrows her eyes at me. "If you don't swear not to mention it to Mom, I'm going to tell her all about the boys you've been hiding from her."

"You wouldn't dare."

"Do you really want to find out?"

I put my hands up in surrender. "Okay, okay. I swear I won't tell."

Chef Anthony clears his throat loudly and waits patiently for us to settle down.

"Thank you. Now I'm going to turn things over to our judges."

Mom's up first. She pulls herself to her full height—still a good six inches shorter than her stiletto-wearing co-judge.

"Well, this was quite an unusual opening day for our baking competition. Unfortunately, due to the burns to his hand, Harold will not be continuing with us. Timothy's mother has also informed us he will not be back. Since this leaves us with two less contestants, we have decided not to eliminate anyone this week."

Mrs. Lee steps forward, clasping her hands in front of her as she scans the crowd.

"However, as the rules explicitly state all highlight bakes must be original creations by the contestant, I'm afraid we must disqualify Michael Zhou."

"That's not fair!" a shrill voice shouts from the audience. "My son worked so hard today!"

Mrs. Zhou climbs out of the row and stomps up to the front like a coach angry over a bad call. Chef Anthony attempts to intervene, but she just turns her rage on him.

"And don't get me started on you! Michael's practiced all week for this. If anyone's to blame, it's you and your shoddy workstations. If the table was level, he would have won this highlight!"

That's totally untrue, of course, but no one's about to contradict her. Michael, on the other hand, begs her to stop. He steps out from behind his workstation, hands up in front like a lion tamer.

"Momma, it's okay. Leave them alone. I wouldn't have won anyway. There are way better bakers in here."

"Don't say that about yourself! You're just as good as all these hacks in here!"

Things are spiraling rapidly out of control. We're just lucky the camera crews have left, or else we'd be splashed all over tonight's news. Hell, we'd probably end up trending on Twitter.

"Mrs. Zhou, there's no one to blame for this but your son," Mom states firmly. "As part of his application, he was required to acknowledge that he understood and would abide by the rules of the contest."

"Well, he didn't tell me!"

"That doesn't excuse his or your actions. We cannot bend the rules for your son, or any other contestant. I'm sorry, but he's disqualified."

"We don't need your stupid contest anyway!" Mrs. Zhou spits out. "Come on, Michael."

Michael slinks out behind her with muttered apologies. They leave behind an unsettling silence, only broken after Albert abruptly pipes up.

"I guess that's the way the cookie crumbles!"

The entire room erupts with laughter, the ridiculousness of the day having worn us all down. Mrs. Lee is laughing so hard there are tears falling down her cheeks. Mom is the one who recovers first.

"Why don't we end today on a good note? Before we were interrupted, I was about to announce our very first brilliant baker. James, your tea cookies were perfectly executed, and we enjoyed our trip to Japan through your cherry blossom–inspired highlight. Congratulations!"

Her declaration is greeted by applause. The other contestants are clapping as well, minus the twins, who are back to bickering. James smiles faintly without quite meeting anyone's eye.

"Enjoy the rest of your day, contestants," Chef Anthony adds.

"You've earned it. Our next bake day will be five days from now, and the theme of the day will be cake. We'll be looking forward to what you come up with!"

With the first bake day complete, people trickle out of the room. Notably, Sarah and Edward walk out together. Mrs. Lee announces she needs to leave as well, due to a meeting with her staff about opening a second location in Katy. Mom's lips thin as she nods once. It's hard to tell if she's pissed about Mrs. Lee's success, or that she's judging and running. Dad, Jeannie, and I stay behind to help with cleanup. Grace walks out with Ben and James, but she runs back inside a few minutes later.

"What are you doing here?"

"I'm helping," she says matter-of-factly. "Obviously."

I push her back toward the door. "You don't have to do that. Go hang out with Ben."

"I will. That is, we will."

"What do you mean 'we'?"

She shrugs a little too nonchalantly. "We're meeting the two of them later."

"Grace," I groan. "I don't even know if I can go out tonight. Mom gets super stressed during contest season and always wants us nearby."

Jeannie walks up then, holding a roll of paper towels and a spray bottle.

"What're you two talking about?"

"I'm trying to convince Liza to come out with me and the guys tonight," Grace tells her before transferring some dirty bowls onto the cleaning cart.

"Which guys?"

I stare hard at Grace, but she doesn't get the hint.

"Ben and James. They're contestants nine and ten. We met them right before graduation."

Jeannie turns to me with an oddly hurt expression. "You didn't tell me about them. Are you keeping secrets from me?"

"Of course not." I keep my eyes on the station I'm wiping down. "There was nothing to tell."

"Maybe not then," Grace insists. "But there's definitely something happening between her and James now."

"There is not!"

"There's not what?"

*Oh no.* Mom. Grace clamps her mouth closed, while I scramble for a reasonable lie. Ultimately, it's Jeannie who saves us both.

"We're talking about the contestants. Grace thinks we can already predict a winner, but Liza disagrees."

Mom glances at the three of us in succession before nodding.

"Well, Liza's right. No matter how well one of these boys does, there are plenty of chances to mess up later."

Grace fakes a convincing shrug. "I stand corrected. I guess we'll have to wait after all."

"We need to finish clearing everything out, girls," Mom goes on to say, pointing at the still dirty stations. "Chef Anthony needs to lock up."

"Yes, Mom."

"Yes, Mrs. Yang."

None of us relax until she's out of earshot. I slump against the table.

"That was close."

"Too close," Jeannie agrees.

We move quickly. Gloria and the other students clear the bowls, utensils, and equipment while we clean the stations. Even with all of us working, it's almost an hour before the room is put back together. We walk out as a group, but Grace, Jeannie, and I hang back so we can talk without being overheard.

"Jeannie, can you tell Liza she needs to come out with me tonight?"

I sigh. "Grace, I already told you. I can't come out. This is peak stress time for Mom. She'll throw a fit if I ask to go."

"Then let me handle it," Jeannie offers, threading an arm through my elbow. "She'll be fine as long as one of us is home. Plus, Dad will help me keep her calm."

"But you're on vacation! Besides, you were supposed to go to dinner tonight with Nathan, right?"

"We're actually meeting up tomorrow," she counters. "And don't change the subject. You deserve to relax. It's summer."

I nudge her shoulder. "Are you sure?"

"The world won't end just because Liza Yang actually has fun for once. Go. Enjoy being a newly minted adult."

I laugh. "You say that like it's a good thing."

"It is right now, but not forever. Make the most of your last summer before college. You'll never get this time back. Trust me, I know."

There's something forlorn about how she says this, but in a flash, she's back to her regular, cheerful self and shooing me toward the door.

"Fine, fine. I'll go." I wrap my arm around her waist. "Thanks, Jeannie."

"Always."

We reach the parking lot, and Grace tugs me toward her car. I pull out of her grasp.

"Hold on! I want to go home and change out of this dress. I'm sick of being in it."

"Actually, you should go with her," Jeannie comments. "It's

easier for me to convince Mom to let you stay out when you're already gone."

"Besides, you look great," Grace says. "James seemed to like it a lot too."

I'm glad it's already dark outside because my face flames at the memory of his smile.

"Let's just go and get this over with."

# Chapter 18

"It's a really nice night."

Ben glances up at the sky as he says so. I pause and take it all in. Houston was hit with a thunderstorm two days ago, and it washed away some of the sweltering June heat. Not that any of this helps with our current state. We've just filled our stomachs with bowls of piping hot noodles at Kingu Ramen, and we all stepped out onto the sidewalk with sweat beading across our foreheads.

"We should go for a walk around Hermann Park," Grace suggests.

Ben beams. "Oh, let's do it! I haven't been there yet."

Imagining the mosquitoes likely out in force, I prepare to back out.

"Will you come?"

The question comes from the last person I expect, and the answer just slips out.

"Sure," I hear myself say.

James smiles. I catch sight of his dimple, and I forget to breathe. Grace smirks devilishly, but I ignore her.

"Maybe we should take one car," she suggests, pointing in the direction of her tiny sedan.

"I can drive," Ben immediately volunteers. "I've got plenty of room in the car."

James, for once, doesn't object. The four of us follow the row of cars parked in front of the storefronts until we reach a black Mercedes SUV. Ben unlocks the car and helps Grace into the front passenger seat. That leaves me with James in the back.

I jump as he comes around and grabs the handle.

"Oh, I didn't mean—"

Too late. James already has the door open. I offer a sheepish smile and climb inside. Ben starts the engine and glances at us through the rearview.

"Seat belts, please."

I reach over my right shoulder, but when I tug the belt over my torso, it hitches halfway over. I let it retract and pull again, then again, but can't loosen it far enough to reach.

"May I?"

I press my back against the cushion as James stretches an arm across to grab hold of the belt. With one smooth motion, he secures it into the clasp at my hip. The movement brings his face so close I can make out the black outer rim of his eyes and smell the clean scent of him. It reminds me of warm laundry, mixed with fresh air. Not the overpowering body spray I'm used to with guys I've dated.

"Is that okay?"

*Oh yeah. More than okay.*

I swallow hard. "Uh-huh."

His gaze trails down to pause on my lips. My mouth is dryer than a bag of Saltines.

Ben clears his throat. "Ready back there?"

In a flash, James is back on his side like nothing happened.

"Uh, yeah, we're ready when you are," he says.

I turn to stare out the window as Ben backs out, my trembling hands clasped in my lap. He and Grace carry on a steady conversation on the way to the park, but it isn't enough to drown out the silence in the back. The air is stifling, and when we finally arrive, I can't get out fast enough. Unfortunately, I've forgotten I'm restrained, and I'm jerked back by the seat belt. My face burning with the heat of a thousand suns, I quickly release myself and stumble out into the night.

We make our way past the zoo and onto the path that encircles the man-made pond in the center. The moon is high and bright, and stars dot the usually hazy sky. Ben loops an arm over Grace's shoulder and pulls her against him. They walk ahead of us, talking with low voices as we stroll along the partially tree-lined path. At first, there's enough distance between James and me to drive a car through. As the minutes pass, he gradually closes the gap.

When we come around the first curve, my voice slices through the silence.

"So, where did you learn to bake like that?"

James turns to me, and a tender smile blossoms onto his face.

"My mom. She loves to bake," he explains. "It was one of the things my sister and I always did with her."

"I didn't know you have a sister," I reply as I match my steps to his. "What's her name?"

"Gigi. She's eighteen months younger than me."

"Is she here too?"

He shakes his head. "She's on a trip with her school abroad in Italy. She'll be back in a couple of weeks."

"I have an older sister. Her name is Jeannie."

"Yes, I know," he says, eyes twinkling. "We ran across each other when you were visiting."

"Ah, right. I . . . knew that."

*My, that lake looks awfully refreshing. Maybe I should swan dive into it.*

"So, how long have you been baking, Liza?"

I pull my eyes back to the path. "For as long as I can remember. Mom's always complaining I spent more time folding dumplings than laundry."

He laughs, a throaty sound that invites me to step closer.

I peer up at him. "Is your mom a professional baker too?"

He half shrugs. "She was, but my aunt—Ben's mom—needed help managing her commercial properties. That's actually why we're here. Mom and Aunt May are watching over a major renovation of one of her apartment complexes."

"Is that how you guys know Mrs. Lee? Through your mom?"

James hesitates. When he does speak, his voice is drawn tight like a bowstring.

"Not exactly. Our families ran in the same circles."

"Oh, does that mean you know her son? She mentioned—"

He cuts me off. "We should catch up to the others."

James strides forward, and I force myself to fall in line with him. As we continue along the path, my eyes keep straying over to him. Part of me wishes I hadn't mentioned Mrs. Lee. James was relaxing up until then. In fact, he was actually quite . . .

Likeable.

I trip on a crack in the path. Thankfully, I catch myself before James notices. My heart has just slowed to a normal rhythm when he suddenly turns to me.

"You and Grace seem really close."

I nod, the memories flooding back immediately. "We've known each other for years. I knew the day I met her that we were going to be best friends."

"Really? How?"

"Well, we met at the pool the summer before sixth grade. She was on one of the swim teams and was practicing in the deep end. I didn't actually know how to swim, so I was taking lessons," I reply softly as I glance at the water. "Some of the other kids were pointing and laughing because I was the oldest one there. Not only did Grace stand up for me, she offered to teach me herself."

"That was really nice of her."

"It was more than nice. I'm really lucky to have a friend like her."

James pauses for a brief moment under an oak tree. I come to a stop beside him.

"That's how I feel about Ben. Sometimes I forget we're only cousins. I always wanted a brother, but my parents weren't able to have another kid after Gigi."

"I hope you won't take this the wrong way," I say after a beat, "but it's funny when I see you guys together."

He leans against the trunk and eyes me curiously. "Why?"

"I guess it's because you're so different. Ben is so cheerful and friendly, and you're . . ."

I search for the right words. The ones I choose now don't match the ones I would have used just days ago.

"You're quiet, more reserved."

James smirks. "You know, I could say the same about you and Grace."

I open my mouth to deny it, but nothing comes out. He's right. Grace and I are pretty different. He smiles and pushes himself off the tree, and we start walking again.

"Ben complains I'm too serious," he admits. "But I can't help it. I feel responsible for him, even though we're only a few months apart. Ben tends to jump into things without thinking, and it's gotten him in trouble before."

Something clicks in my brain. "Is that why he moved down here?"

He says nothing for a long time. I'm beginning to think I overstepped when I hear his voice.

"Ben trusted someone he shouldn't have, and he got hurt."

That's something I know firsthand. Hell, James was there to witness it.

I cock my head. "And you? Why did you come?"

His attention shifts to Ben and Grace just a few paces in front of us. "I'm here to watch over him."

Their laughter floats through the air. Even from where I'm standing, I know Grace is happier than I've seen her in a long time.

I smile. "You don't need to worry about Grace. She'd never do anything to hurt him intentionally."

"Broken hearts are unavoidable," he says quietly. "Even when you do everything possible to protect yourself."

There's a melancholy to his voice I've never heard before.

My heart clenches. "Are you speaking from personal experience?"

"Actually, I've never really been in a relationship," he admits, rubbing the back of his neck.

I nearly trip on my own feet. "Why not?"

James shrugs. "I've been too busy. You already know that Ben wants to be a doctor. Believe it or not, he actually chose to do that. His parents didn't force him. My dad, on the other hand, wants me to follow in his footsteps." He stops, turning to me in the dark. "He's been after me to work on my résumé, which is why I've been working at the satellite site here. I think he's hoping I'll take it over one day."

I feel the answer in my bones, but I still ask. "Is that what you want?"

His head drops. "I'm not sure what I want just yet. Ben says I should go into medicine too, but—as you might have noticed—I'm not very good at talking to people."

I press my lips together to keep from smiling but give up when he flashes a disarming grin. I glance back at the lake with a shrug.

"I know how it feels. I really love baking, but my parents expect me to do something more practical."

"What would you do if you could?"

I've been asking myself that same question for weeks. What do I want to do? What if Mom and Dad never change their minds about culinary school? Worse yet, what if they're right and I end up working at Yin and Yang for the rest of my life? I swallow hard.

"I've always imagined going to culinary school and becoming a pastry chef. But now . . . I don't know. My parents are right about one thing, though. I don't want to spend the rest of my life working at some small local bakery." I sigh. "I think sometimes it's better to chase new dreams."

"Do you have one? A new dream?"

I don't know why I tell him. Perhaps it's the magic of the moon, or the boldness lent to me by the inky night.

"Something to call my own. Maybe a book. Not like a novel or anything. Like a baking book, with my own original recipes."

A long silence follows my admission. I start to regret saying anything. Then I hear James's soft voice just over my shoulder.

"There is one other reason why I haven't dated anyone."

As if compelled by our newfound connection, I turn to face him. With the moon at his back, I can't make out his expression, but I nonetheless feel the intensity of his gaze.

"I haven't met anyone worth risking my heart for."

The last word hangs heavy in the air, the sentence feeling oddly incomplete. James takes a step toward me, his face finally coming into view with the dip of his head. I lick my lips nervously, and his eyes trail down like a caress to settle on my mouth. Maybe he leans in, or maybe it's just my imagination, but slowly, the distance between us evaporates.

"Hey, you two! Keep up!"

I jerk back at the sound of Grace's voice. My cheeks burn hotter than Dad's Szechuan chicken as I spot her and Ben waving at us from the next bend. I muster a half-hearted smile and point in their direction.

"We'd better catch up."

We continue on to where Grace and Ben are waiting. We then walk, two by two, through the wooded area, with the scattered moonlight between branches our only source of light. It's about as peaceful as it can get, but I'm more on edge than ever before.

Slowly, Ben and Grace pull ahead again, but I barely notice. My mind plays my words to James over and over. At some point, the path takes a sharp turn, and in my distraction, I keep going straight.

"Liza, wait!"

James grabs me by the hand and pulls me back before my foot sinks into a large area of mud. I blush, grateful for the darkness.

"Oh, jeez. Thanks. I totally missed that."

He laughs. "Come on. It's this way."

He doesn't let go of my hand when we're back on the trail, but his grip is loose enough I could pull out of it. My grip tightens. I'm definitely better off sticking with him.

"Guys! Come look at this!"

We quicken our pace until the tree line opens to reveal a bridge spanning the stream that feeds into the pond. The moon glistens on the water's surface, waves rippling from the gentle breeze. The landscape looks totally different at night, the murky water turning into an indigo mirror. Grace is the first to notice our joined hands, and she pokes Ben in the ribs. His eyes go wide, and he stares at his cousin. I start to pull away, but James threads his fingers through mine and locks me in place.

"Are we going to keep admiring the view, or finish our walk?"

Ben laughs. "You don't have to tell me twice."

We resume our stroll around the rest of the pond, ending up back in the parking lot. I let go of James to get in the car. Before I can mourn the loss, he settles in and immediately wraps his fingers back around mine. I don't dare look at him, but there's no denying the tension between us. The air feels charged somehow, like some invisible force is pulling us together.

Ben has just parked beside Grace's car in the shopping plaza when something buzzes beside me. It's my phone. I accidentally left it in the car. Reluctantly, I slip my hand away to take a look. It's a text from Jeannie.

**Where are you? Mom is threatening to call the police!**

I check the time. Oh my god. It's almost midnight.

"Grace, I need to get home right now or my mom's going to kill me."

I tumble out of Ben's car in a panic. James hops out after me.

"Liza . . ."

Impulsively, I reach up on my tiptoes to hug him. His arms come around my back, and I catch a whiff of butter and cherry blossoms. Rather than bury my nose into his shirt—so, so tempting—I pull away with a strained smile.

"Good night, James."

Grace kisses Ben on the cheek. "I'll text you later."

She and I hop into her car and drive off into the night. The last thing I see is James waving goodbye.

• • • • •

I'm ambushed the minute I step through the front door. Mom unloads a night's worth of anxiety and stress by shouting at me for a solid half hour. If it wasn't my fault for worrying her, I'd walk away and lock myself in my room. Instead, I bear it without so much as a single flinch.

"Go to your room," she eventually demands with a choked voice. "Go!"

● ● ● ● ●

I startle awake with bleary eyes some six hours later and shuffle into the bathroom for a shower. As the water pours over me, I think back to the walk in the park. My hands still tingle from the memory of James's fingers in mine. It's so odd to think that just weeks ago, I would have slapped him for trying the same move.

Once I start to prune, I turn off the faucet and dry myself off. I wrap my hair in a towel and prop myself on my bed with my back against the wall. My phone, which has been on the charger, suddenly buzzes. It's a message. Then another. Then two more back-to-back. I tap to open a group chat with Grace and two unknown numbers.

**Is Liza up yet?** the first number asks.

**No, she's not a morning person,** Grace replies. **Maybe give her another hour or so.**

**I hope we didn't get her into too much trouble last night,** the other number texts.

> **I'm not gonna lie . . . her mom is super strict. But this is the first time she's broken curfew, so maybe it'll be okay.**

It doesn't take much to infer Ben and James are the other two in the chat. There's a lull in the conversation, so I decide to jump in.

> *Me:* Hey, guys. It's Liza.
> *Grace:* Liza! You're up early!
> *Me:* Couldn't sleep. Mom was super upset last night.
> *UN1:* I'm sorry we kept you out so late.
> *UN1:* This is Ben, BTW.

That makes the other number James. I quickly add them to my contacts.

> **Me:** It's okay. My mom's stressed about the contest, so it didn't help me any.
>
> **James:** Are you okay?

Just seeing his words appear on my screen makes me smile.

> **Me:** Yeah, I'll be okay. Just waiting to see what kind of punishment I get.
>
> **Grace:** I'm guessing you're gonna get grounded.
>
> **Me:** That's a fact. LOL
>
> **Grace:** Any idea for how long?
>
> **Me:** Pretty sure she thinks the end of time is too short rn.

Grace replies with a groaning gif. James sends a sad face emoji, while Ben chooses three sobbing ones. I chuckle. That's them to a T. My ears catch the sound of my parents stirring next door. It's time to face my fate. I leave one last text in the chat.

> **Gotta go. Mom's up. Will keep you updated.**

I toss the phone onto the bed and head back into the bathroom. Once my hair is dry, I run a brush through it and tie it into a pony-tail. I throw on my customary T-shirt, but pair it with some old jean shorts I only wear at home. Always an early riser, Jeannie is already at the table. She squeezes my hand as I sit down, and I smile gratefully. Mom's at the stove, preparing breakfast, and doesn't acknowledge either of us.

"Morning," Dad says after sitting down. "You're up early. Did you get enough sleep?"

I shrug. "I got enough."

We jump when Mom plunks down a pot of soupy rice. She goes

back to grab the pickled radishes, dried pork sung, and rice gluten. They plop onto the table with an equal amount of force, and I flinch. Instead of sitting down with us, she disappears into the bedroom.

Dad sighs. "Eat up. I'll go check on Mom."

He leaves the table. We hear the door open and close a minute later. I sag against the back of my chair.

"She's really pissed this time, isn't she?"

"You know it's not just about you, Bunbun," Jeannie assures me. "The contest went completely sideways yesterday, and you know how she gets when things don't go . . ."

"Perfectly. Yeah, I know."

I shouldn't say anything more, but the words tumble out of my mouth.

"This only happened because she went trolling for guys to set me up with. She normally screens the contestants to make sure they have enough skill and experience to compete."

"Even if that's true . . ." Jeannie starts.

"You and I both know it is."

"Even if that's true," she repeats, "she couldn't have predicted Harold's burn or Timothy's tantrum, not to mention Michael's disqualification. There's also co-judging with Mrs. Lee, which can't be easy."

"Now, that's something I don't get either. Why did she ask Mrs. Lee to judge anyway?"

Jeannie's fork freezes halfway to her mouth. "You don't know?"

"Know what?"

"She told me a lot of her sponsors weren't planning on donating this year," she informs me, food now forgotten. "They felt like the contest hadn't gotten them enough publicity. Getting Mrs. Lee on board was the only way to convince them to remain sponsors."

I frown. "Why didn't she tell me?"

"Apparently, you two weren't talking at the time."

"It must have been right after I asked to enter the contest." I groan and put my head in my hands. "I threw Mrs. Lee in her face too."

Dad returns shortly after with Mom in tow. She sits stiffly in the chair he offers her. I keep my eyes on my bowl and spread the condiments evenly over the surface of my rice so each bite tastes the same.

"You're grounded."

I don't look up but nod to show I heard her.

"Until the contest is over. You'll only be allowed to go to the bakery and out with the family."

"Can Grace or Sarah come over, at least?" I venture.

"No. I don't think they're good influences on you anymore. Especially Grace. Too Americanized."

I clench my fists. Mom's overreacting, as usual, but I know better than to argue with her. Jeannie does her best to talk Mom out of it, but as soon as she lets slip I was with two of the contestants, I'm done for.

"What were you thinking?! Do you not understand the importance of maintaining impartiality as a judge? If anyone had seen you with them, the contest would be over!"

"I'm sorry, Mom. I didn't think—"

"You're right! You didn't think!" Mom scoots her chair back abruptly, the legs screeching against the floor. "I shouldn't have made you a judge. It was my mistake trusting you."

Her words sting more than expected. I lash out.

"What about *you*? Why did you turn this into some ridiculous dating service?" I shout, waving my hands in front of me. "I don't need your help finding a boyfriend, and I definitely don't want it!"

"Really? Then why were you with those two boys last night?"

I start to say it was for Grace, but dragging her into the argument won't solve my problem. Jeannie interjects.

"Mom, I'm the one who told her to go have some fun. If you want to blame anyone, then blame me."

Mom points a finger at her. "I do blame you! You should have set a better example for your younger sister. Instead, this is what you teach her?!"

"*Hǎo le*, okay, no more," Dad says, finally stepping in. "I know you're angry, lǎo pó, but you're being too harsh. They're good girls, and they've never caused us any real trouble. Liza's already apologized, and you've punished her. That's enough."

While his words are gentle, his tone is firm. Dad rarely puts his foot down like this, and we all stop arguing to listen.

"You've been working nonstop to get this contest off the ground," he continues. "You need to take it easy and get some rest."

"You're right. I've been getting a lot of headaches," Mom agrees, a hand on her forehead. "Maybe I'll go lie down for a bit."

Mom excuses herself and walks off without touching any of her food. My heart twists in my chest.

Dad looks at Jeannie. "Didn't you mention you have plans with that boy Nathan today?"

"Oh . . . uh, yes."

"Then go. Just be back for dinner."

She peers at me before nodding. "Thanks, Dad."

He waits until she leaves before leaning against the table on his forearms and pinning me with his stare.

"You know Mom only has your best interest at heart, Liza. When you didn't come home on time, she thought something terrible had happened to you."

"I know." I bow my head. "I'm sorry."

He sighs. "If you really want Mom to back off on setting you up, there are other ways."

"What do you mean?"

"You've got to think more like her and less like you."

I squint at him. "That's an impossible task, Dad."

"Hear me out. How does Mom pick the guys she tries to set you up with?"

"Well, she has a checklist. Tall, smart, Asian, traditional, will make a lot of money, etc."

"Exactly. So use that to your advantage. Eliminate guys by finding their faults and exposing them." Dad taps his fingers on the table. "For example, Timothy. He acted like a two-year-old, and she hasn't stopped complaining about him since."

"So he's off the list."

Dad grins. "You bet he is."

"And Harold?"

"Maybe you didn't notice, but he's not exactly a clean boy."

I make a face. "Oh, trust me, I noticed."

"There you go, then. Two down, eight to go."

A light bulb goes off, and the weight on my shoulders grows lighter.

"Technically, it's four down. Michael's mom is probably too pissed to want anything to do with us. And contestant nine, Ben? He's dating Grace."

Dad cocks his head to the side. "What about the one who's always with him? The other boy you were out with last night."

"Oh . . . that's James, his cousin."

The second I utter his name, my cheeks grow hot. Dad raises his eyebrows.

"I'm guessing you don't have any objections to him?"

"Um . . . not yet," I say, looking down at my lap.

"Well, he does fit some of Mom's criteria," he says, ticking them off. "He's tall, handsome, and won the first brilliant baker of the contest. If you like him, you need to find out what else he's got going on."

I bite my tongue to keep from spilling the beans about our moonlit stroll.

"Okay, will do."

"There is one more thing." He glances at me and winks. "Contestant number three . . . Edward. I think he's your mom's favorite."

"I knew it! Why does she like him so much?"

"You mean other than the fact he's your age, going pre-med, and attending the same university as you in the fall?"

I snort. "Yes, besides that."

"I think he might be related to that Reuben boy. I overheard Mom talking to Mrs. Lim the other night." He leans forward. "Plus— and you didn't hear this from me—I think she's coaching him a bit."

"Why does this not surprise me?"

"I think she's definitely trying to help him win you over. Hence, the infamous cookie picture."

Great. For some unknown reason, Mom is determined to merge our families. Okay, I lied. I know very well why she's doing this. Mr. Lim is a US Representative for our state. I found out accidentally when I overheard Mom lamenting Reuben's canceled dinner with us to her friend over the phone.

"Will you help me convince Mom he's not a good match either?" I plead.

"All right, but this will be our little secret, okay? I'd like to live a few more decades."

I come around the table and throw my arms around his neck. He laughs and pats me on the back.

"Just promise me you'll try to be patient with Mom until everything is done, Liza."

I cross my fingers behind my back. "I promise."

"Okay. I need to head to the restaurant. Why don't you come and help me out today? Danny's on vacation with his family, so I'm shorthanded."

It would be nice to get out of the house. I shudder to think what else Mom might say to me if I stay behind.

"Okay," I say. "I'll go get changed."

# Chapter 19

After three days of Mom's cold shoulder, I'm ready to warm up with some baking. In fact, I spend most of the night before bake day working out the pandan chiffon recipe. I'd forgotten how challenging it can be to achieve that perfect airy texture. Despite the tension between us, I earn a nod of approval from Mom as she heads to bed. I'm still hours away from doing the same, determined to ensure I can judge this technical recipe in my sleep.

I pass out well after two a.m. Nonetheless, when my alarm goes off less than five hours later, I jump out of bed. With no cameras following us around, I get to wear my own clothes again. As I prepare to get dressed, I find myself flipping through my hangers.

"Looking for something to catch a certain baker's eye?"

I spin around to Jeannie's amused grin. At this point, the high color on my cheeks has become the norm. I grab a light blue sweater and my favorite pair of black skinny jeans. Jeannie raises an eyebrow.

"Are you sure Mom will be okay with that?"

"It's this or one of my geeky T-shirts from Tee Turtle," I answer with a grin. "You know how much she *loves* those."

"Point taken."

Once I'm dressed, she helps apply my makeup. Since Mom and

Dad left early to double-check everything at the school, I'm hitching a ride with Jeannie today. When we step out the front door, I'm surprised to find Nathan standing by the car. He lets out a low whistle.

"Look at you both!" He hooks an arm around Jeannie's waist to pull her in for a kiss. "Especially you."

"Stop it," my sister protests. "Come on, we don't want to be late."

Once we're all inside, Nathan ramps onto the freeway and weaves through the hectic rush hour traffic. He glances back at me through his rearview mirror.

"So, Liza, I heard it was quite an interesting first day."

"That's one way to put it," I answer with a chuckle. "I'm just glad no one set the bakeshop on fire."

"Are you rooting for anyone so far?"

"Nope. That wouldn't be very objective of me, as Mom would say."

He meets my eye in the mirror and smirks. "I promise I won't tell."

"Honestly, I'd say three or four of the guys have a really good shot at winning," I hedge.

"Maybe," Jeannie interjects, "but you wouldn't be upset if James won, would you?"

"I mean, he had a really strong bake, sure," I stammer, "but so did Ben."

Our car abruptly veers into another lane, and I clutch the door as Jeannie lets out a yelp. Nathan's knuckles are white as he regains control of the steering wheel.

"Is everyone all right?" he asks.

"Uh, yeah," I manage. "What happened?"

"Someone cut me off. Sorry about that." He meets my eye. "You were saying something about James and Ben?"

His words are stiff, and his eyes are pinned on the road in front of him. I don't blame him for being so shaken. Houston traffic is some of the worst in the country.

"Oh, just that they both did well during the first bake," I tell him.

"They're from New York City, like you." Jeannie grins and touches his arm. "In fact, we ran into James while Liza was visiting. That's actually why she got into trouble the other night. She was out with the two of them."

"Trouble that you encouraged," I retort, though I duck my head.

"I suppose that's true."

We pull into the parking lot. Nathan offers to walk Jeannie into the bakeshop, since he has a few minutes before he has to head to class. After saying goodbye, I make my way to the prep room. Mom, Mrs. Lee, and Chef Anthony are gathered around the dining table and finalizing the schedule when I walk in.

Mom's jaw drops open. "What are you wearing?"

I stare down at myself. "What's wrong with it?"

"I told you to wear something nice!"

"I think it looks lovely," Mrs. Lee says. "And very age appropriate."

That only incenses Mom more. Her threat to remove me as judge flits through my mind. Thankfully, she's too preoccupied with getting the day started to do more than send me a death glare. Gloria, the student we met on day one, bursts into the room.

"Chef Anthony! Something's—"

She skids to a stop at the sight of us all gathered together, her expression strained.

"Um, could I speak with you, please?"

"Of course," Chef Anthony answers immediately.

His eyes flicker toward Mom before he excuses himself. He shuts the door behind him, but hushed tones can be heard from the other side. Then Chef Anthony reappears.

"Mrs. Yang, I'm afraid we have a slight problem. The copies of the technical challenge have been . . . misplaced."

Mom squints at him, her voice razor-sharp.

"Misplaced? How? I thought you said everything was ready."

"It was," he insists. "I even checked it last night before I left. I'm not sure what happened. Maybe one of the custodians tossed the pile, thinking it was trash."

Mom retrieves her leather notebook of recipes and walks it over to him. Before handing it over, she issues a warning.

"Do not lose this."

"I'll make the copies personally," he swears. "It'll never leave my sight."

Mom grips it in her hands for one last second before relinquishing it into his possession. Her eyes remain on the door as the rest of the room goes back to chatting. I'm pretty sure she counts the minutes before he returns, and when he does, Mom snatches the notebook out of his hands and tucks it carefully into the bottom of her bag. On the plus side, things pretty much settle down by the time Chef Anthony moves toward the door a half hour later.

"Are we ready to start?"

I murmur my assent, and we head down to the bakeshop together. As before, Chef Anthony opens the day, introducing Mom, Mrs. Lee, and finally, me. As I stroll over to join them, my eyes laser in on James. He's dressed all in black, from the fitted button-down shirt stretched across his broad chest to the slim jeans and Adidas sneakers on his feet. It's a risky choice when baking, but I'm not complaining. James's gaze sweeps over me in a reciprocal fashion, and I see his mouth quirk up a bit, showing his dimple.

It's easy to linger on the guy who's managed to prove me wrong at every turn, but I peer past him to Ben. He's dressed simply as well, donning a graphic tee and dark wash jeans. He wiggles his fingers in a greeting, and I allow myself just a quick smile so Mom won't accuse me of impropriety.

"Who are we still waiting for?" Mrs. Lee asks out of the blue.

Chef Anthony notices the empty station at the same time. He frowns deeply.

"Anyone know where contestant two is today? Jay Huang?"

Mom snaps her head toward Dad, and he scurries out of the room. She leans across Mrs. Lee and mumbles something to Chef Anthony, who addresses the room.

"We're checking with Jay now to see where he is. Thank you for your patience."

Five minutes go by, then ten. Dad finally reappears in the doorway. The hope in Mom's eyes dies as he shakes his head forlornly.

"Should we wait a little longer?" Chef Anthony asks.

"No," she answers, her voice cracking. "Let's get started."

Clapping his hands together, he clears his throat to regain everyone's attention.

"Okay, thank you for waiting. Welcome to day two of the Fifth Annual Yin and Yang Junior Baking Competition. The theme for today is cakes. Mrs. Yang, the floor is yours."

Mom steps forward, but when she opens her mouth, nothing comes out. I look down and see her hands shaking slightly. She must be taking these mishaps even harder than I thought. Mrs. Lee stares at Chef Anthony with panicked eyes. Before I can convince myself not to, I walk to the front of the room and take a deep breath.

"For your technical challenge today, you have been given the recipe for pandan chiffon. The list of ingredients is short, but pay careful attention to your preparation. Miscalculate, and your cake will be flat and dense. You have one and a half hours. Good luck."

The six remaining contestants start in on the recipes. I cast my eyes downward as I walk past Mom and out into the corridor. Dad comes out with two chairs, setting them up against the wall.

"No point in standing for that long."

"Thanks, Dad."

He pats me on the head. "Go easy on Mom today. She didn't sleep almost at all last night."

At least that's one thing we have in common. Dad turns to walk inside but peeks back out with a grin.

"Four down, six to go."

I swallow my laughter as Mom emerges to sink down in the chair beside me. I steal a glance. Her eyes have lost their usual luster, and patches of dry skin exaggerate the lines on her face. I feel an unexpected surge of sympathy and nudge her gently on the shoulder.

"Are you okay, Mom?"

She doesn't answer for a few minutes. I'm about to ask again when she finally draws a breath.

"You did a good job giving those instructions. Very professional."

I grin. "I told you binging *The Great British Baking Show* would come in handy."

"It's not good for your eyes to stare at a screen for that long," she lectures, though the planes of her face soften. "You need to protect your vision."

"Okay, Mom."

It's a while longer before she twists in her chair to look at me.

"We need to talk about the other night."

I'd rather not, but I tense and wait for the impending lecture.

"Liza, I know you think since you're a legal adult, you can do whatever you feel like, but I'm still your mother. It's my job to protect and take care of you." She chokes back a cry. "When you didn't answer any of my texts or calls, all I could think about was if you were hurt, if you needed me, and I wasn't there for you . . ."

Guilt wrenches through me. I take her by the hands.

"I'm sorry, Mom. I just didn't realize my phone wasn't on me."

"It's hard being a mother, you know. Your children are your life." Mom takes a deep breath. "One day, you'll understand what it's like, Liza. Until then, try to be a little more considerate."

I bow my head. "Yes, Mom."

She squeezes my hands before tipping up my chin.

"Good. Now tell me more about Ben and James."

• • • • •

We're called back inside when the time is up. As soon as I step into the bakeshop, it's clear with a quick glance which bakers failed the challenge. Their chiffon cakes resemble either pancakes or bricks.

Mom side-eyes me. "Shall we give these a try?"

Since chiffon cakes can be tricky to master, Mom has decided to lead the judging this round. We begin with the plate to our far right. This one has held up decently well, though the top is too brown. Once we slice into it, there are only occasional air pockets.

I place it on my tongue and give it a second to soften before eating.

"It's a pretty good bake. A bit chewier than chiffon cake should be, but the flavor is there and it's got decent height." I look over at Mom. "What do you think?"

"I agree. The egg whites should have been whipped just a little more to give it the fluffy texture we're looking for. Good job."

The second one is flat and amorphous, rather than tall and bouncy. Mom has to saw the knife through just to get one slice, so we split it. The taste is off, more egg than pandan.

"Whoever baked this overworked the egg whites," Mom explains. "That's why the cake didn't rise."

My bite has a surprise—a sliver of the leaf. I hold it up for everyone to see.

"This is also where reading the instructions carefully would have helped. The leaves were supposed to be strained, not chopped into the batter."

Our third cake is on the flatter side but is improved by the lack of errant leaves. There's nothing remarkable about it otherwise. The fourth cake is quite lovely looking. When we bite into it, though, there's no hint of the grassy aroma.

Mom presses her lips together. "I think the baker forgot to draw out the juice with both water and coconut milk. The latter is too strong, and it overwhelms the delicate pandan flavor."

I duck my head to cover my surprise. That's something I wouldn't have known either, and I must have baked a dozen of those cakes last night.

Now over halfway through, we arrive at the fifth cake. Mom purses her lips with approval.

"This has a very appealing look to it. Let's see how it tastes."

When the chiffon first touches my tongue, something doesn't

seem quite right. The pandan and sugar are there, but there's an unknown flavor too. I close my eyes and take another bite.

Ah, there it is.

"This baker didn't properly measure the amount of baking soda used," I conclude.

Mom raises her eyebrows at me. "Liza is correct. She picked up on the hint of bitterness. This baker either added a little too much or it didn't get mixed in well."

When we pause in front of the very last plate, I'm positive it belongs to James. The chiffon cake looks every bit as good as the ones Mom and I have made. I give it a light tap with a fork, and it rebounds easily off the top. I grin and raise my head to make a comment about it, but all thought escapes me when I lock eyes with James. The look he's sending me could melt sugar faster than a culinary torch. My spoon clatters onto the table.

"Oh!"

I tear my eyes away to focus on slicing two pieces of cake. I pass Mom the first without meeting her eye. She'd catch on to how I'm feeling in a heartbeat otherwise. The cake bounces easily under her gentle poke. She cuts off a smaller piece and places it in her mouth.

"This cake. The height, the texture, the flavor. They're all there. Wonderful."

"Yes, it's quite delicious," I murmur.

With our tasting done, Chef Anthony steps forward.

"Fantastic. Our judges will now take a minute to rank the technical bakes."

It doesn't take long for Mom and me to come to an agreement, and she lets me deliver the final verdict. Once I reveal the order we ranked the cakes, it's Albert in last place, then David, Sammy,

Edward, and Ben. That leaves James as the last one standing, and when his win is announced, his grin raises more than a couple eyebrows.

Chef Anthony leads the audience in a round of applause before addressing the contestants.

"Great job, bakers. You are now released until this afternoon. Have a good lunch, and meet us back here in one hour."

Ben and Grace walk out hand in hand. James glances over to me before following behind them. I start to leave as well, but Edward steps in my path with an overly bright smile.

"Hi, Liza."

I bite back a curse. "Oh, hi again."

"You did a great job judging the technical today," Edward says. "I bet your chiffon cakes are perfect."

"Thanks, but yours could be good too, if you practice more," I answer politely.

"You look nice today. I mean, you always look nice . . ." He reaches up and tugs at his collar. "Sorry, that came out wrong."

I catch sight of Sarah standing by the row of chairs just over his left shoulder. She's watching us intently.

"Well, I'm going to grab something to eat," I say, jabbing my thumb toward the door. "You should too."

I turn to leave, but Mom quickly intervenes.

"Edward, didn't you have a question to ask Liza?"

He glances at me nervously. "Um, yes. I was hoping I could ask you . . . for some advice."

"Some advice?"

"Yes. About . . . something personal."

Oh no. She can't be doing this. Not now. Edward's eyes dart over to Mom again. I get an idea.

"Why don't we go talk over there in the corner? It's more private that way."

"Oh, I . . ."

I grab him by the wrist and drag him away from Mom. She has no choice but to leave us alone, though she inches her way slowly toward us while cleaning. I hiss at Edward under my breath.

"What did my mom promise you?"

"Ex . . . excuse me?"

"What did my mom promise you?" I repeat more firmly. "For trying to get me to date you?"

"I . . . erm," he stammers, casting his gaze to the ground with a sigh. "I don't actually know how to bake all that well, so she promised to help me out."

I press him. "What exactly do you mean by that?"

"You know, she agreed to . . . give me lessons. But I only did it because my mom and my aunt made me. I swear."

I ball my fists at my sides. Just when I thought I was getting somewhere with her, she goes and does this. He tugs at his ear.

"I figured I'd just flirt a little, convince you to go on a date, and then it'd be over. Simple as that."

"Simple as that?"

He withers under my glare. "I know how it sounds. That's why I didn't ask you out just now. Well, that and . . ."

"That and what?"

Edward works his way through every shade of red. When he replies, he keeps his eyes glued on a spot behind me.

"I . . . I met someone. Someone I actually like a lot. And I don't want her to think I like you instead."

My heart sinks. "Please tell me you're not into Grace. Or Jeannie."

"What?" he stammers. "No, no . . . I was talking about . . . well . . ."

He mumbles something under his breath.

I frown. "What?"

"Sarah," he grinds out. "I'm talking about your friend Sarah."

My eyes dart over to where she's still sitting against the wall, staring listlessly at her phone. A smile tugs at the corner of my mouth.

"Sarah definitely deserves a guy who isn't pretending to like another girl."

"I know. And I'm sorry." Edward bows his head. "I just wanted to get my mom off my back. She wants me to date a nice Asian girl."

I sigh. Now, that's something I can relate to.

"Look, I might have to listen to my mom, but you don't. Just tell her you asked me out and I said no."

"Are you sure? I'd hate to get you into trouble."

"I'm used to her getting mad at me. It won't be anything new."

He sags with relief. "Thanks. I really appreciate it."

Edward sprints out the door before Mom can intercept him. She throws a questioning look my way as I follow behind, but I ignore it. If I'm going to keep my promise to Dad, I need to get away from her for a bit.

I head down the main hall and shove the rear door open, ending up in a small courtyard shaded by trees. I hear what sounds like Grace's laughter and follow it to the left side of the U-shaped building. Around the corner, I screech to a halt. Grace is pressed against the brick wall, and her lips are locked on Ben's, whose arms tug her close.

"Whoops," I whisper.

I avert my gaze and spin around only to crash into James. Knocked off balance, he stumbles, and my legs get tangled up in his. We both hit the ground hard.

He groans. "Any chance you could find a less painful way to greet me?"

I shouldn't laugh, but I do. "I swear I'm not doing this on purpose."

We pick ourselves up off the grass. He plucks some loose blades off my head while I brush them off his shirt. I make a spinning motion with my finger.

"Turn around. Let me check your back."

He suppresses a smile as he does what I tell him. I dust the grass off his back, momentarily distracted by the softness of his shirt.

"Liza?"

As he turns to face me, I withdraw my hands and tuck them at my sides. His sharp intake of breath draws my eyes up to meet his, but nothing comes out of his mouth.

"Congratulations on your second win," I blurt out. "That was a great bake."

"You really think so? I wasn't actually sure I'd get it done on time."

"Why wouldn't you have?"

He rubs the back of his neck. "My first batter was really salty, and I couldn't figure out why. I was sure I measured everything correctly, so I double-checked my jars. It turned out my sugar had salt mixed in."

"What?" I frown. "Maybe one of the culinary students got distracted while preparing for today. I'm sorry about that."

"Either way, I'm just glad I had time to remake the batter and have the cake come out okay."

"That was *way* better than okay. It was perfect. Even my mom said so, and she never says that about anything."

James breaks into a dazzling smile. I stare, transfixed, at his crinkled eyes and that irresistible dimple.

"I think that's the nicest thing you've ever said to me."

I aim for a careless shrug. "Technically, I was complimenting your cake."

As he leans in, my heart slams against my rib cage like a bird trying to take flight.

"Does that mean I haven't changed your mind about me yet?"

"A-about you?"

"Well, I know I didn't make the best first impression, but I was hoping..."

James catches himself then, and I resist the urge to scream. Hoping for what? His face twitches as it tries to settle on an emotion, but it never quite finds one. Instead, he straightens and drags a hand through his hair.

"Anyway, I'm glad you liked my cake. It means a lot, coming from you."

It takes me a couple heartbeats to reply. Even then, I can only do it while staring at my shoes.

"Really? Why?"

"I... well, you're an amazing baker, for one."

"You've never had anything I've baked," I point out, smiling up at him.

"I don't need to," he answers immediately. "The fact that you noticed Ben's cake had too much baking soda is enough to prove you are. I never would have noticed."

"Yeah, well, you learn a lot about chiffon cakes after you've baked a dozen of them in a row," I joke half-heartedly.

Whatever he plans to say next is interrupted when Ben and Grace appear from around the corner.

"There you are," Ben calls out. "We've been looking all over for you two!"

I keep my voice light. "In each other's mouths?"

Ben blushes madly, while Grace just shrugs.

"The moment presented itself, so I took it."

I bite down on the inside of my cheek to keep from laughing. That's peak Grace. She's never been shy about going after what she wants. Besides, it probably would have taken Ben a year to kiss her. Grace's eyes boomerang from me to James and back.

"Wait. Did we interrupt something?"

My eyes snap back to James. He opens his mouth to say something, then closes it again.

"We were just talking about this morning's challenge," I finally say. "Anyway, we should leave soon if you guys want to eat. We've got almost forty minutes left."

"Do you know any place around here that's quick?" Ben asks.

"Actually, I do. How do you feel about pho?"

"Love it. James, on the other hand, can be . . ."

"I'm sure it'll be delicious," he interrupts. "If Liza says it's good, then it's good."

Ben and Grace lead the way back toward the building. I turn to follow, but James touches my elbow.

"Wait. You've got grass on the back of your sweater."

I still beneath his hands as he sweeps them across my shoulder blades and down my spine.

James clears his throat softly. "You've . . . you've got some on your head too."

He plucks the stubborn blades out of my hair before clearing his throat.

"All done."

I twirl around to thank him, but all that passes through my lips is air. He's standing so much closer than I expected. I follow his slender neck up over his angular jaw to finally meet his sparkling brown eyes.

"Should we . . ." I gesture back toward the school.

James shakes his head. "There's one more thing."

My breath hitches. "What's that?"

He takes another step forward. With a tilt of his head and a tip of my toes, our lips meet, and my eyes flutter closed. His arms encircle me and pull me against him. It takes my brain a second to catch up, and then my hands find their way up his chest. Somewhere in the back of my mind, I register how lightly he presses his mouth against mine, how he holds me like I might break. He tastes slightly of sugar and coconut, and I giggle without thinking. James pulls back.

"What's so funny?"

"You . . . taste good," I admit, cheeks flaming.

"In that case . . ."

He dips down to kiss me again. This time, his lips move the way he does—confident, measured, and without hesitation. Not to be outdone, I quickly figure out the recipe that makes him press even closer.

"Ben, look!"

Grace's gleeful exclamation pulls us apart, though not without a fair amount of reluctance. James grins down at me, his dimple on full display. I tuck my face into his shoulder as Ben playfully chides her.

"Look what you did."

"Oh no! I'm sorry. Go back to what you were doing," she insists. "Don't let me interrupt."

James is happy to oblige, but when he tries to steal another kiss, I turn the other way.

He pouts. "You're such a tease."

"I don't give those out for free, mister. You want another one, you need to earn it."

His eyes glint with mischief. "I do love a challenge."

*You and me both.*

# Chapter 20

Lunch flies by, and soon, we're all back in the bakeshop. It's time for the highlight cakes, and I can't wait to see what James has in store. I'm positive it'll be amazing. It's just too bad I couldn't coax it out of him while we were eating lunch. Once the remaining bakers are positioned behind their bake stations, time starts. Mom, Mrs. Lee, and Chef Anthony watch from their position at the front of the bakeshop, occasionally whispering to each other.

Wedged between Jeannie and Grace in our seats along the left wall, I do my best to pay attention to all the contestants in the room. It's just so hard when James is by far the most entertaining. He's deep in concentration, a frown painted on his lips and his sleeves rolled up past his elbow as he bends to check the oven temperature. Every so often, he walks over to the fridge and tucks something inside.

"Hey, why is Mom giving you the stink eye?" Jeannie asks.

"Huh? What?"

I swing my gaze over to Mom and find her scowling menacingly at me. I sink lower in my chair.

"Edward probably told her I refused to go on a date with him."

Grace spins around. "Wait, he asked you out?"

"No. Not really. It turns out she's been secretly trying to set us up the whole time, so I told him to tell her that so she'd get off both our backs."

"She doesn't look real happy," Jeannie observes, lips twitching.

"What else is new?"

"What if you tell her about James?" Grace suggests. "I'm sure she'll forgive you then."

She's got a point. James checks off pretty much everything on Mom's list. If she finds out he's interested, she might finally leave me alone. It's perfect.

That is, *if* I decide to tell her.

The truth is I'm not ready to say anything yet. I'm not sure if it's because everything's so new with James, or that she'd find a way to take credit for putting us together. No matter what, though, I know I want to keep this to myself a little longer.

I give myself a shake and turn back to the baking. Edward is busy cutting pieces out of his cake, and it's hard to tell what he's going for at the moment. Sammy has been working diligently on his three-tiered creation. He's chosen a naked cake, which is a bold move. It'll be impossible to hide any defects in his baking that way. From the looks of his tiers, though, he's done a good job.

David and Albert have at least decided on different flavors but are easily twenty minutes behind the rest of the group. Ben's been sitting on his stool while waiting for his cake to cool down, and now he starts in on his decoration. He doesn't notice how Mrs. Lee's eyes keep glancing between him and James. Not in the Mrs. Robinson way but definitely with a creepy vibe. James admitted to knowing her that night in Hermann Park, but there must be some bad blood between them if he won't say anything else about her.

"Bakers! You have fifteen minutes left. Fifteen minutes!"

Chef Anthony's warning sends the room into overdrive. David is doing his best to frost his cake, but it keeps melting. Albert, on the other hand, has slathered his on and is tossing sprinkles onto one side like Salt Bae. Edward is putting the finishing touches on his cake using flowers he brought in, while Sammy is doing something similar. Ben has opted to pipe his flowers, the ombré reminding me of the one Selasi made during season seven of *The Great British Baking Show*. I'm not able to get a good look at James's cake, because as usual, he's standing directly in my line of sight.

"Bakers! Time is up! Step away from your cakes!"

Icing bags are dumped, tools are dropped, and cake stands are cleaned as the contestants prepare their cakes for judging. Mrs. Lee and Mom step up to the table, and Chef Anthony gestures at Edward. He carries his creation over and places it down gingerly. I'll admit it's a pretty gorgeous cake. He's iced the top and sides using a smoother, leaving a spotless finish. Fresh spring flowers are arranged on top in a crescent shape, with the Chinese character for love written in red icing.

I have to hand it to Mom. She's an excellent teacher.

"Beautifully done," she proclaims predictably. "Tell us what flavors you chose."

"It's a fudge cake with fresh strawberry filling. I used strawberries in the frosting as well."

Mrs. Lee slices into it and gently works the piece out, but the tip of it stays behind with the rest of the cake.

"I think he sliced off the top to make the layers look even," I tell Grace under my breath.

"It's a nice shortcut, taking a little off the top to even out your layers," Mrs. Lee observes immediately after, "but I like the character of a slightly imperfect cake."

Mom scowls openly at her co-judge. I hide a smile behind my hand as Grace's elbow jabs into my side. After having a bite, both judges agree that it's a solid bake, though Mrs. Lee announces the cake itself is a bit dry. That only incites another glare from Mom.

David is up next. His cake is a hot mess, because he spent too little time cooling it. His frosting has fallen off in giant lumps, leaving only a separated layer on top. He's so distraught neither Mom nor Mrs. Lee knows quite what to say about it.

"You know, sometimes things don't pan out," Mom points out gently, "but appearances aren't everything."

*Yeah, right.*

I look around, but everyone's heads are still fixed on the front. I sag against my chair. For a second, I thought I said that out loud.

"Mrs. Yang is right. Let's cut into your cake and see what we've got," Mrs. Lee announces.

Once they get past the unappetizing exterior, the texture and taste of his red velvet cake are quite nice. David traipses back to his station with far less disappointment than he started with.

"Albert, if you please."

David's twin struggles under the weight of his thickly frosted cake. Chef Anthony rescues it from his arms and escorts him to the front of the room. His highlight has been baked as a whole sheet before being cut into messy blocks, each of which has been frosted within an inch of its life. If I didn't know better, I'd think he was trying to copy Ben's *Minecraft* piece from the first challenge.

Mrs. Lee smiles politely. "Albert . . . were you trying for petit fours?"

"What's that?"

She stares at him in disbelief for half a second. "Uh, never mind. What flavor is your cake?"

"White."

"You mean vanilla?" Mom asks.

He shrugs. "I guess. It's white."

I groan internally. Mom takes a deep breath and smiles.

"Right. Let's try it."

Each of our judges transfers a block onto their plate and slices through the center to take a look. As I suspected, there's almost as much frosting as actual cake, and my stomach turns at the sight of it. Mom is equally thrilled at the thought of having to put her piece in her mouth and ends up digging out just the middle to try.

"But the frosting's the best part!" Albert protests.

If he doesn't go home today, I'll be shocked. There's silence in the room as the two judges chew and swallow. Mrs. Lee gestures for something to drink, and Chef Anthony pours them both a glass of water. After a long sip, she takes a deep breath.

"I'm sorry, Albert, but your cake is dry. It's been overbaked, and the frosting is too thick. This was not your best bake."

He hasn't had a single decent bake yet, but I keep my opinion to myself. Mom bobs her head up and down alongside her.

"It was a good try, Albert, but Mrs. Lee is right."

I know it's bad if Mom is agreeing with her nemesis. Albert's face reddens, and his fists clench at his sides. Tension fills the bake-shop as we wait to see what he'll do.

"Albert."

Mrs. Kuan's quiet but firm warning pricks through his anger, and Albert deflates. He stomps to his table while grumbling under his breath the entire time. I shake my head. It's hard to believe he's only a year younger than me.

As with day one, Sammy's at the table and placing his high-light down before Chef Anthony calls his name. His naked cake is gorgeously decorated, the real flowers on the cake spiraling down the layers.

"Sammy! What a wonderful surprise," says Mrs. Lee. "Your cake looks like it could be in the display case at my bakery."

He presses both hands to his chest. "Thank you, Mrs. Lee! I feel so honored."

Mom's face might be unreadable to most, but I can tell she wishes she'd gotten to say that first. However, she bounces back with a bright smile.

"I'm excited to try this. What flavor did you pick?"

"Lemon poppy seed, with a cream cheese filling."

Oh, that sounds *amazing*. I'm going to have to figure out a way to sneak a bite later. This time, Mom takes the lead after they have a taste.

"This is so moist, Sammy! The cream cheese doesn't overwhelm the light flavor of the lemon at all."

"Like I said," Mrs. Lee adds. "I'd sell this in my display. No question."

Mom and Mrs. Lee stare each other down while Sammy floats back to his station with a giant grin, positively bursting with pride.

"Ben, please bring up your cake," Chef Anthony states.

Ben glances over at us as he moves to pick up his cake, but he stiffens as he spots someone over my left shoulder. I turn and am surprised to find Nathan tucked against the wall behind Jeannie, though I barely make out his face beneath the brim of his baseball cap. He looks like a celebrity who doesn't want to be recognized. I knew the two of them had lunch together, but she must have convinced him to check out the highlight bake.

I frown as Ben exchanges a look with James, whose expression hardens upon seeing Nathan. His eyes then flick over to me for a single heartbeat before facing the judges once more.

Chef Anthony clears his throat. "Ben, your cake, please."

Ben carries his cake across the floor, almost tripping at one point. My heart leaps into my throat, but he manages to right himself. He stands, ramrod straight, as he faces judging. Mom gestures at his cake.

"Your piping skills are incredible. Very nicely done."

He barely manages to smile.

"Tell us about your cake," Mrs. Lee states.

Ben doesn't quite meet her eye. "It's a Taiwanese sponge cake with fresh fruit filling. The frosting is actually colored whipped cream."

Mom's eyes light up. This is her specialty. She's quick to remove a slice, going so far as to swipe at the frosting with her finger to taste. Based on what I can see, it looks like a well-executed bake. Mom agrees, but Mrs. Lee aims a more critical eye at it.

"I think the fruit layers could have been more evenly distributed, but all in all, a delicious cake."

Ben practically rushes back to his station. If either judge notices, they don't make mention of it. Unaware of the strain around him, Chef Anthony grins at James.

"Time for your cake, brilliant baker."

Despite the way he just acted, I crane my neck to peek at his highlight. He's been hiding it from view the whole time. When he steps away, I gasp.

"It's a mousse cake," I say to no one in particular.

"It's a mango raspberry mousse cake," James confirms. "With a vanilla sponge base."

So that's why he was going back and forth to the fridge earlier. There's no denying it's an expertly executed cake, with a thin raspberry glaze atop alternating layers of mango and raspberry mousse. When Mrs. Lee presses the knife into the top, it glides down without resistance. All the sections hold their shape as the slice is removed.

My mouth waters. Mango is one of my favorite flavors. No one utters a word while eating. It's so good Mom closes her eyes for a minute to enjoy the aroma. Finally, she exhales.

"I don't know what to say other than this is exceptional."

This is high praise from Mom, who finds fault in anything and everything. He levels a look at Mrs. Lee as if expecting criticism.

"You're a perfectionist, James, and it shows in this cake. Excellent."

Her words take him off guard, but he recovers enough to offer a polite bow. Chef Anthony dismisses him back to his station and announces a short break for deliberation. Mrs. Lee and Mom head out of the bakeshop to discuss.

Grace and I are barely out of our seats when James approaches. The smile falls off my face as he brushes by me and heads right for Nathan.

"You've got a lot of nerve showing up here," James hisses. "Who put you up to this?"

"No one," Nathan replies calmly, though his jaw is tight. "I'm visiting my girlfriend."

Girlfriend? That seems a bit premature. I glance at Jeannie, but she's distracted by James as he spits out a reply.

"Like I really believe that."

She steps between them. "You should. I *am* his girlfriend."

He stares at her in disbelief before turning sharply toward me. "And you? How long have you known him?"

"We met during my trip to New York," I answer slowly. "Why? What's going on?"

He doesn't offer an answer. I sense the shift in him before his eyes shutter.

"I see."

James spins around and stalks over to Ben. He whispers something, and Ben shakes his head, but he repeats himself with urgency. The two cousins then leave the room together. Grace goes after them but returns almost immediately, her face riddled with shock.

I race to her side. "Grace? What happened?"

"He . . . he told me to stay away from him."

"Who did?"

She looks at me with glistening eyes. "James. He wouldn't let me talk to Ben."

"*What?*"

Now I'm pissed. I move toward the door, intent on chasing them down, but she grabs me by the arm.

"Don't go. I don't want to be alone right now."

A single tear trails down her cheek, and I know more will soon follow. I put an arm around her.

"Okay. Let's go for a walk or something then."

I lead her out into the hallway, careful to head in the opposite direction of where the guys went. Halfway to the end of the corridor, Grace breaks down. I pull her into my arms and hug her tightly as she cries. How dare James treat her this way? And Ben? What's his excuse for not standing up for her? My eyes are drawn back to the bakeshop. It's time to get some answers.

I murmur against her ear. "You okay?"

Her chin taps my shoulder. I duck down to examine her face. Her cheeks are streaked with half-dried tears.

"Let's go talk to Nathan," I suggest. "Maybe he can tell us what's going on."

I thread an arm through hers and drag her back to the bakeshop.

We make a beeline for Nathan. He's talking with Jeannie but stops when he spots us.

"You want to know what happened, don't you?"

I nod, and he gestures for us to sit down. I turn two chairs in the row in front of him around and guide Grace into one before taking the other. He scans the partially empty room before leaning in.

"Okay, the short version is I've known Ben and James for years. Our parents did business together, so we spent a lot of time around each other. We even attended the same academy in New York, but I was a grade ahead. James always acted like he's better than everyone else, but in high school, Ben and I started hanging out more. It didn't take long for James to become jealous of how close we were getting."

As much as I hate to admit it, I can see James feeling threatened by someone as easygoing as Nathan.

"Anyway, when Ben refused to stop being my friend, James did everything he could to make me look bad. He convinced Ben's parents I was the reason their son was partying so much, especially after he wrecked his car one night. They went so far as to contact my modeling agency and get me dropped. After that, Ben stopped talking to me too. It's been a year now, and I'm still having trouble booking jobs."

I fall back against my chair, and my chest starts to throb. Can this really be true? I glance at Grace, who's staring at Nathan with a pinched expression.

"I'm so sorry this happened to you, babe," Jeannie answers, pressing a kiss to his cheek. "It must have been awful."

"That wasn't even the worst part. I found out my dad was having an affair with Ben's mom too." Nathan drops his head. "I treated them like brothers, and they turned their backs on me. It's part of the reason why I came down for the summer, to get away from the drama. At least, that's what I thought I was doing."

My head is spinning. I remember him mentioning his dad's affairs, but with Ben's mom? This is only supposed to happen in Asian dramas. Nathan presses his face into Jeannie's shoulder, and she murmurs comforting words. Grace turns to me.

"Can I borrow you for a sec?"

"Yeah, sure."

She leads me out of the room and down the hall to the cafeteria. After checking to make sure we're alone, she gestures for me to sit down at the closest table.

"Do you believe him, Liza?"

"I . . . maybe?" I tug at my earring. "I don't know."

"I think he's lying. Or at least, not telling us everything," Grace says.

The conviction in her tone makes me raise my eyebrows.

"Why do you think that?"

She glances out the window. "It's something Ben told me a while back, that he almost got in trouble with the police because of a false accusation. That's why his parents suggested he move down here early."

"Did he give you a name?"

"No, but now that all this has happened, I'm sure it's Nathan."

I frown. "Maybe we should go ask him, then."

I start to head back, but she stops me. "Don't! He'll know that we know."

"How can he possibly know that we know?"

"I don't know, but I don't want Nathan to know we know what Ben knows."

My brain nearly short-circuits from the wheel of *knows*. Taking a moment to reorient myself, I consider her accusation. Can Nathan really be the reason why Ben fled New York? Conveniently, the one person who can clear this up isn't talking.

We head quickly back to the bakeshop to rejoin the others. As if summoned by our conversation, Ben and James enter the room together. Both steadfastly avoid meeting anyone's eye as they return to their stations. Mom, Mrs. Lee, and Chef Anthony return shortly after.

"The judges have deliberated. Mrs. Lee, if you please?"

She tucks her hands behind her back, but her eyes dim when they land on James's station. I don't have to see his face to know what's probably on it.

"Mrs. Yang and I were unanimous in our decision this bake. The contestant going home today is . . . Albert."

I tense. Rather than throwing a bowl or something equally breakable, Albert slouches on his stool and pouts.

"As for our brilliant baker this week, it goes to someone who already showed great promise on day one. Congratulations, James. You've done it again."

There's a smattering of applause in the room. He never takes his eyes off the front wall nor makes an attempt to smile. Mom is perplexed but smiles at the rest of the group.

"Well, contestants, it's been quite an exciting day. I hope you get some rest and relaxation before we meet again. Just don't forget to practice, because the next challenge theme is . . . bread."

Sammy pumps his fist. "Yes!"

The minute we're dismissed, Ben flees. James looks back at me once, eyes unreadable, before following his cousin out the door.

# Chapter 21

The next day, I'm startled awake just before ten by a series of back-to-back texts. As I unlock my phone with half-open eyes, it rings. I yawn before answering.

"Hello?"

There's crying on the other end of the line. I bolt up in bed.

"Grace? Is that you? What's wrong?"

Crying turns into full-on sobbing. I hear shuffling on the phone, and then another voice comes on.

"Liza? This is Mrs. Chiu. Do you mind coming over? I hate to bother you, but I can't get Grace to tell me what's wrong."

I'm out of bed and changed by the time she finishes talking. I had planned on inviting Grace to spend the night with me after what happened, but she rushed out of the bakeshop without even saying goodbye. When she didn't respond to any of my texts, I assumed she'd gone to sleep.

Mom and Dad are already at work, and Jeannie is out with Nathan again, so no one's there to question where I'm going. I hop in the car and head a few miles down the road. I pull into the driveway as Mrs. Chiu opens the door.

"That was fast."

It's said with concern, not accusation. I throw her a grin before toeing my shoes off and launching myself up the stairs to Grace's room. I knock twice and then barge right in. Grace's room is as familiar as my own. Ballet-pink walls are covered in canvas prints of glittery inspirational quotes and elaborate paper flowers. Her desk, positioned directly below a picture window, is cluttered with fashion magazines, and a bow-shaped chair is tucked against it. I turn toward her bed, where pink and cream throw pillows have been tossed to the floor.

"Grace? It's me," I say softly.

She's curled up in bed, surrounded by a mountain of used tissues. Her face is blotched and stained with tears, and dark circles rim her eyes. I climb into bed beside her.

"Grace . . ." I brush the strands of hair sticking to her cheeks to one side. "Tell me what happened."

She hands me her phone, too choked up to explain. "Read the text."

I open up her messages, instantly drawn to the one on top. It's from Ben, sent right after midnight. I brace myself.

**I don't think we should be together anymore, Grace. I'm sorry.**

"That's it?" I say, more to myself.

I scroll up and skim through dozens of saccharine declarations and random conversations between the two of them. The last one of those was sent yesterday before the baking began.

"I saw it when I woke up this morning. I . . . I don't understand," she says. "What did I do?"

I toss her phone aside and grab her gently by the shoulders.

"Nothing. You've done nothing wrong, Grace. Didn't you say James wouldn't even let you talk to Ben yesterday?"

Grace nods and wipes her nose with the tissue I hand her.

"I think this is his doing," I continue. "Ben would never break up with you otherwise."

"You . . . you think so?"

I nod. "I know so. Ben's liked you since the moment you guys met. There's no way he would change his mind just like that."

A knot forms in my stomach. I wanted so badly to believe that James was better than this, that Nathan was lying all along. But now? After what he's done to Grace?

She sniffles. "What am I going to do?"

"You're going to relax and get some sleep. I'll take care of this."

I roll off the bed, hell-bent on making James pay. She grabs my wrist as I'm about to head out the door.

"Liza, no. I don't want you to have to see James. Not for me. Maybe you can just text him or something."

I flinch at the stab to my chest. I've already tried that, and he completely ignored me.

"If James did this, he won't admit it unless I'm standing right in front of him. Besides, I'm just going to talk to him."

More like beat him into submission, but close enough.

"But you don't know how to find him," Grace reminds me.

This gives me pause, but then I remember something very important and grin.

"Mom has his address on file. It's on the application form. All the contestants have to fill one out."

After tossing all the dirty tissues into her trash can, I lean down to give her another bear hug.

"Get some sleep. I'll bring you some boba in a little bit, okay?"

"Thanks, Liza."

I shut the lights off and close the door. Downstairs, Mrs. Chiu is anxiously waiting in the living room. She perks up as I appear in the doorway.

"How is she?"

"She'll be okay. I have to take care of something at home, but I'll be back later if that's all right."

"Of course it is! Come back whenever you want."

I drive home as fast as I can without risking being pulled over. I might want revenge, but Mom will kill me if I get a ticket. Once I'm in the house, I go straight to the study. Piles of paper are strewn around the room, both on the floor and the desk, burying it beneath them. I can't believe Mom and Dad harp on me for not cleaning my room when it looks like a bomb went off in here.

I square my shoulders and begin on one end of the desk, flipping through the stacks of papers as carefully as I can. Most of them are receipts or bills for the restaurant or bakery, or letters from family back home in Taiwan. My graduation photos are also lying on the desk, missing the one Mom ultimately used.

My eyes land on a box holding at least a hundred more contest flyers. I have to physically hold myself back.

*Grace first. Arson later.*

I resume my search. Thirty minutes later, I finally find what I'm looking for in a small filing cabinet filled to the brim with this year's applications. They are alphabetized, but before I can search in the Ws, my phone goes off. It's a text from Sarah.

**Can we meet up somewhere? Need to talk.**

I think back to my conversation with Edward. Maybe a break wouldn't hurt. My first instinct is to suggest Boba Life, but the last thing I want is to run into James or Ben right now.

**How about Juiceland?**

**Sounds great. See you there in thirty.**

I put everything back mostly in place and stand up to stretch my aching muscles. With my purse and phone in tow, I drive over to Juiceland. A bowl of mango shaved ice sounds amazing right now. As I pull into the plaza, a grand opening across the parking lot catches my eye. It's another new tea place—Tea Bear. I glance at my watch. Sarah probably won't get here for another ten minutes. Might as well go check it out.

As I near the door, a familiar figure freezes me in my tracks.

It's James.

I duck behind a pillar. How the hell did we still end up in the same place? He's standing in line with Ben, and a pair of girls is chatting with them. Ben is polite but doesn't really seem interested. James, on the other hand, laughs at something the taller girl says. I hate the pain that rips through me and makes it hard to breathe. My plan to confront James suddenly feels insurmountable, an Everest-size hurdle more likely to conquer me than the other way around.

"Liza?" Sarah says from behind me. "Is everything okay?"

"Yes, yep," I answer, the words coming out in a rush. "Everything's fine. Totally fine. Let's go to Juiceland."

Not giving her a chance to answer, I loop my arm through hers and drag her away. As we step into the shop, we're greeted by clear acrylic tables spread across a room with bright yellow walls and painted navy concrete floors. We put in our orders—mango shaved ice for me, strawberry for her—and once they're ready, we bring our bowls over to a table in the back. I shove a bite of mango and ice drenched in condensed milk in my mouth before peering at Sarah.

"So, what did you want to talk about?"

She swallows. "Okay, I'm just going to come out and ask. Do you like Edward?"

"What? No!" I sputter. "Not in the least."

I hadn't noticed how tense she was, but it melts off her face with my answer. She fiddles with one of her auburn curls, and her green eyes dart up to meet mine.

"Well, he seems to like you a lot. He's always talking to you and baking things to impress you."

"That's not because he likes me. It's because our moms have been trying to set us up."

Her mouth hangs open. "What? Why?"

"It's a long story," I say after shoving another spoonful of mango into my mouth, "but you know how my mom feels about my ex-boyfriends."

"Wait, is this one of those arranged marriage deals?" she asks, waggling her eyebrows. "I saw a documentary on Netflix about it the other day."

I laugh. "It's not, and I don't want you giving my mom any ideas."

Sarah giggles. I eat more of my shaved ice, savoring the sweet flavors. When I look up at Sarah, she's lost in thought. On a hunch, I lean forward, my arms on the table.

"Wait. Why are you asking? Do *you* like him?"

"I . . ." She flushes scarlet. "Maybe? We've been talking a lot during the breaks, and he's really sweet. We've even hung out and listened to opera."

"Opera?"

Her eyes sparkle with excitement. "Yeah! In fact, he showed me some videos of Taiwanese opera, and it was . . ."

*Weird? Creepy? Annoying?*

"Really interesting! The elaborate costumes, the sets, and the singing! It's so unique."

I guess opera really does transcend culture, though I'm still not a fan. Since it's clear Sarah's gearing up for a full-blown analysis, I quickly pull us back to the topic at hand.

"Look, the point is Edward doesn't like me, and I don't like him." I wave my spoon at her. "Also, he listened to *opera* with you. And then showed you *more* opera. No guy does that unless he likes you."

Sarah starts to speak, but I cut her off.

"Even Asian guys."

She balks. "That's not what I was going to say!"

I smirk.

"Liza! I wasn't!"

I throw my hands up in surrender. "Okay, okay, I'm kidding. But not about this. I have it on good authority Edward only likes girls with curly hair. Actually, just one in particular."

The color floods back into her cheeks. As if on cue, her phone pings. Sarah gasps.

"It's him."

"Well?"

Her eyes move across the message, and she lets out a squeak. "He asked if I'd like to see a movie with him later."

A wide smile spreads across her face. I nudge her arm.

"See? I told you."

"I'm going to see if he wants to join us here for shaved ice first."

As Sarah's fingers fly over her keyboard, I catch Ben and James walking past the front door. The girls they were with earlier are nowhere in sight. My anger, momentarily forgotten, flares back hotter than the flames in Dad's kitchen. I'm on my feet and out the door in a flash.

"Liza! Liza, wait! Where are you going?"

I stop short on the sidewalk, and Sarah collides into me with a yelp.

"Sorry! I didn't . . ."

She trails off, her eyes landing on the subjects of my scrutiny. Ben's having trouble looking at me, while James delivers a dismissive glance my way. Shoppers brush past us as they make their way along the strip of stores we're standing in front of, but the two of them remain silent. I'm trying to decide which of my looks is the most lethal when the two girls come bounding over. The taller one takes hold of James's arm.

"Do you guys want to grab something to eat?"

If I didn't know better, I'd say I saw a flicker of regret on James's face. Sarah steps forward, but I warn her off with a subtle shake of my head.

"How is she?"

For a second, I'm sure I imagined Ben's whispered words over the noise in the plaza. Then he asks again, louder.

"How's Grace?"

I gape at him. Is he serious? He breaks up with her and now he wants to know how she is? I explode.

"I'd say ask her yourself, but that would require you to be less of a coward. A text? Really?"

James steps forward. "Liza, stop."

I shift the full weight of my rage onto him. He stills beneath my daggered gaze, while the girls murmur an excuse and run off. Sarah's still at my side, but she stays quiet.

"Don't tell me what to do. He broke Grace's heart, and since she's too busy crying at home to say anything, I'm going to."

I drag my eyes back to Ben. "Do you have *any* idea how hard it is for Grace to trust someone? She finally lets you in, and then you decide to dump her? Via text message? You didn't deserve her."

"Well, she didn't look all that sad when she was making out with Nathan," James abruptly interrupts.

*"Excuse me?"*

My outburst startles the elderly lady who walks by at that very moment. I shoot her an apologetic look.

"Before you defend her, I was there," James states. "I went back for my phone after we left yesterday. I saw Grace and Nathan making out by the bathrooms."

"I don't believe that for a second!" Sarah defends. "Grace isn't that kind of person."

James looks at her as if noticing her for the first time. Meanwhile, I think back to last night. It wasn't like Grace to run out like that, but I assumed it was because she was upset about Ben.

I shake my head. "Sarah's right. You must have seen someone else. Grace would *never* cheat on anyone."

"How can you be sure?"

*Because her first boyfriend cheated on her, asswipe.*

I ultimately say nothing, because it's not my secret to tell. James takes my silence for confirmation of his suspicions.

"Like I said. It's not Ben who doesn't deserve her. It's Grace who doesn't deserve him." His eyes narrow. "And as for you, I would have expected more than Nathan."

"Oh, so I'm somehow guilty by association? Really? Because from what I hear, you're the problem, not him. You tried to ruin his life."

"Is that what he told you? That *I* ruined *his* life?"

I flinch at the fury in his eyes. Ben grabs him by the arm.

"James, don't. He's obviously still lying about what happened. Maybe we should—"

James cuts him off. "No. You don't owe anyone an explanation. Especially anyone associated with Nathan. Let's go."

He drags Ben across the parking lot before he can protest. To my horror, large, fat tears trickle down my cheeks, and I swipe at them angrily. To make matters worse, Edward steps out of the car a few feet away and walks toward us.

"Hi, Sarah! Are you ready—" He sees me and freezes. "Liza? Are you okay?"

Sarah touches me on the elbow. "Maybe we should go back inside. We can talk about it in there."

I pull away from her and manage a smile.

"You guys go in without me. I . . . I have to go check on Grace."

I hurry back to my car, slamming the door shut in time for the dam to break.

* * * * *

It takes a few minutes to pull myself together. I end up driving to Boba Life to grab the tea I promised Grace. When I pull into her driveway, I check my reflection in the mirror. A girl with tired eyes and reddened cheeks stares back at me. I take several calming breaths before getting out of the car. I plaster a cheerful smile on my face as Mrs. Chiu answers the door.

"I'm back!"

She seems surprised by the change in my appearance but decides not to comment. I slip my shoes off and climb the stairs, knocking softly on Grace's bedroom door.

"Hey, it's me."

She opens the door from the inside, and I find her still in her pajamas. At least the curtains are open, and there's more a hill than a mountain of tissues around her.

"I come bearing gifts."

I ended up ordering four drinks total, so I place the bag on her desk before removing one and piercing the plastic top with a straw. The rest stay in the holder as I hand a lilac-colored drink to her.

"It's your favorite. Taro."

"You're the best," she says, managing a weak smile.

Grace settles back onto the bed and pats the spot next to her, gesturing for me to join. I grab my tea and climb next to her.

"How are you doing?" I ask.

She sighs and rests her head on my shoulder. "I really liked him, Liza."

"I know you did."

"I thought he was different."

The ache in her voice matches the one in my heart. I know exactly how she feels. I reach over the tissue box between us and squeeze her hand.

"I'm sorry, Grace. I'm so sorry."

A few more minutes pass before she tips her head in my direction. "Are you okay?"

I keep my eyes forward. "Yeah. Why?"

"It doesn't seem like it."

"What makes you say that?"

Her eyes bore into me. Sometimes I forget how well she knows me. I settle for a shrug.

"It's nothing."

"It's not nothing."

"Fine. I'll tell you, but you have to promise not to get upset."

She nods against my shoulder. Gradually, I recount what happened at the plaza. I pause when I get to the part about Nathan, unsure of how to broach the subject. At some point, I just go for it.

"James . . . accused you of kissing Nathan after we got out of the cake challenge."

Grace's eyes widen, and she looks away quickly.

"It's not what he thinks," she says eventually, fiddling with her comforter.

"So you two weren't kissing?"

"We were . . . but it didn't happen the way James thinks it did. Nathan is the one who kissed me. I went to the restroom and ran into him in the hallway. We started talking, and he said he was sorry about what happened with Ben. I was a little weirded out when he hugged me, but then he tried to kiss me and I had to shove him off."

Grace chokes up again, and I wrap an arm around her and pull her close.

"Why didn't you tell me?"

"I was afraid to. I thought . . . he's your sister's boyfriend. Besides, it was just the one time, and he apologized right away. He said he didn't mean to misjudge things."

I clench and unclench my fists. No one has a right to take what hasn't been freely given.

"Grace, if he made you uncomfortable, then you shouldn't have to hide it. In fact, I'm glad you told me. Jeannie doesn't deserve to be with a cheater."

"What if she doesn't believe me?"

"Of course she'll believe you! Why would she think you were lying? Jeannie's known you almost as long as I have." I soften my voice. "Look, we can talk to her together."

"What if she accuses me of trying to steal him? Remember what happened with Everly last year? All I did was work on a history project with Aaron, and she was convinced I wanted him for myself.

Please don't make me tell Jeannie. I . . . I just don't think I can handle that right now."

It kills me to say okay, but I don't want Grace to feel pressured.

"Yeah, sure."

"Thanks for being here, Liza."

"Are you kidding me? You're my best friend. I'm always going to be here for you." I throw an arm around her and touch our temples together. "Just make sure you give me a heads-up if you need help getting rid of a body."

She giggles, but the laughter fades as something comes over her.

"Does this mean you and James . . . ?"

I swallow the lump in my throat. "He showed his true colors today. I'm glad we're done."

"You don't mean that."

"It doesn't matter. Today's not about him." I gesture for her to drink her tea. "I'm here for you, and there are no boys allowed."

"What about girls?" she asks through a mouthful of boba.

I pretend to be offended. "What am I? Chopped liver?"

"You don't count. I don't stand a chance with you."

"Trust me. In that situation, you're the one way out of my league."

"Hmm," she answers, tapping her chin. "On second thought, I think you're right."

"Hey!"

It's good to see her laughing again. Since she's done with her tea, I grab both and take them to the kitchen to throw away. When I come back, Grace is staring pensively out the window.

"You know, it's kind of ironic."

I sink back onto the bed next to her. "What is?"

"People assume because I'm bi, I get to date all these people.

But all I really want is one person to love me, you know? I'm so tired of trying so hard and still getting my heart broken."

When the tears roll down her face this time, they're quiet and steady. I tug her against my shoulder.

"I wish I could make this go away, Grace."

"I'm really glad you're my friend."

"Best friend," I tease, pointing at a picture of us on her desk. "Don't be downgrading me like that. I worked hard to get here."

"Shut up."

"You shut up."

Grace pokes me hard in the ribs, and I shove her away.

"Keep doing that, and I won't tell you what happened with Sarah today."

That grabs her attention immediately. Tears forgotten, she sits up with greedy eyes. I grin.

"Well . . ."

# Chapter 22

Four days later, on round three of the competition, I shuffle into the break room with drooping eyes. It took everything I had this morning not to burrito myself in my covers. I was up late talking to Grace; she's decided to stay away for the rest of the contest. After arguing with my alarm for those precious extra minutes, I left the house in a black linen tee and jean shorts.

I expect Mom to disapprove, but she doesn't spare me a glance.

The contest must be really getting to her. I've never seen her look so dejected. We're only three challenges into this year's contest, but five contestants down. She's had to cut half the planned baking days out to compensate. As much as Mom grumbles about the preparation that goes into it every year, she takes great pride in how it comes out. It must have gotten to Chef Anthony too, because he barely musters a half-hearted smile.

"Everyone excited about today?"

Dad is the only one who answers in the affirmative. Mrs. Lee is glued to her phone, dressed in a sleek black pantsuit with freshwater pearls and another pair of sky-high stilettos. Jeannie texts me saying Nathan should be dropping her off soon. Seeing his name on the screen puts me on edge. I need to figure out how to get her away from him so we can talk.

Just like bake day two, Gloria abruptly flies into the room.

"Chef Anthony! Come quick!"

Chef Anthony runs out of the room behind her, and Mom immediately follows. I jog to catch up to them. We arrive at the bakeshop to see contestants and family members gathered outside the doorway. James and Ben are standing next to each other, leaning against the wall. James looks surly, his eyes narrowed as he glances around at the other contestants. Ben's lips are pressed in a thin line, his eyes pinned to his shoes. I ignore them both as I step into the room behind Mom. She comes to a full stop just inside the open door, and we both gasp aloud.

The entire bakeshop is in shambles. There's flour and sugar all over the floor. Towels and utensils are strewn across all the workstations, and even with a cursory glance, it's obvious ingredients are missing off every table.

"Who had access to this room?" Mom demands to know.

Chef Anthony rears back from the death glare she aims his way.

"Uh . . . before competition, just me and the volunteer students. But none of them would have done this."

"How do you know? Maybe one of them is racist." She points at her head. "The ones who wear the red hats."

"Mrs. Yang, that's a serious accusation," he intones, squaring his shoulders. "And I don't take well to you making it. My students are good kids, and they volunteer their free time to be here."

"Only because you're giving them course credit."

His lips press into a tight line. "Even so, getting into this school is extremely competitive. None of our students would risk their spot for something like this."

"Lǎo pó, let's not jump to conclusions." Dad lays a hand on Mom's shoulder. "We don't even know when this happened."

"Did anyone see anything?" Mrs. Lee pipes up.

None of us had noticed she joined us. A minute later, Jeannie walks in as well. Chef Anthony cocks his head toward Gloria.

"Were you the one who found it like this?"

She shakes her head. "No, Chef. One of the contestants alerted me."

"Which one? Show me."

We bottleneck at the doorway, trying to get out into the corridor. Mrs. Lee and Mom stop and let Chef Anthony pass first. My heart sinks when Gloria heads straight for Ben.

"He's the one."

James tenses as Chef Anthony levels a suspicious look at him.

"Can you tell me what happened?"

"It was like that when I got here. As soon as I saw it, I let one of your students know."

"Was anyone else here with you?"

James straightens to his full height, eyes challenging. "I was. We came in the same car."

After a pause, Chef Anthony turns his gaze to the rest of the group.

"Did anyone see anything?"

Heads shake around him. I stare at the cousins. Are they telling the truth, or did they do this as some sort of revenge? The thought makes bile rise into my throat.

"Are there security cameras we can check?" Mrs. Lee suggests.

"We only have them at the entrances and exits. There's never been a break-in until now."

The contest was scheduled to begin fifteen minutes ago. Now unsettled murmurs rise from the group gathered in the hall. With Mom dazed and staring off into space, Dad takes charge.

"I think it's best if we get things cleaned up so we can start without further delay. Chef, can you escort the contestants and their families to a different area for the time being?"

"Of course." Chef Anthony points down the hall. "Everyone, if you'll please follow Gloria to the auditorium."

His student leads the crowd away. Mom, Dad, and I head inside to help clean as much of the mess as possible. Mrs. Lee volunteers to stop by the nearby grocery store for more ingredients, and Jeannie offers to go with her.

We manage to get everything swept up decently fast, replacing all the broken and dirty utensils with fresh ones. Once Jeannie and Mrs. Lee return, we distribute the ingredients based on each station's need. Stepping back to admire our handiwork, Dad smiles.

"Anything else we might be missing?"

"Oh! The recipes for the technical challenge," Chef Anthony notes. "The copies we made were damaged by the mess."

"My book's in the break room," Mom tells him.

"Okay, I'll just tell Gloria to bring everyone back in."

"I can do that," Jeannie volunteers. "That way you guys can get everything ready faster."

"I'll stay here, just in case," Mrs. Lee adds.

We head in opposite directions: Jeannie to fetch the others, and the rest of us heading to the prep room. As we near, I see something move around the corner at the other end of the hall, but when I look again, there's nothing. I shake it off and head inside behind Mom, who grabs her canvas bag off the back counter. Her face pales as she sticks a hand into it and pulls items out. Impatient, she turns the entire bag upside down. The contents tumble out unceremoniously—pens, pads of paper, her wallet, her cell phone, and some random knickknacks, but no recipe book. She glances around in a panic.

"Where's my book? It's supposed to be here. I swear I put it in here this morning. I even double- *and* triple-checked it."

"Maybe you took it out and forgot." Dad gestures toward the row of metal lockers and boxes of baking supplies that line the perimeter of the room. "Can everyone check the area around you? Look on the floors and behind furniture. Make sure you didn't also pick it up by accident."

"It's a leather notebook with a red cover," Mom adds, voice shaking. "It has Chinese writing on the inside."

We search high and low, but other than some dust bunnies and crumbs, there's nothing to be found. Mom is on the verge of a melt-down, and we all know it.

"Maybe it fell out in the car," Dad tells her. "I'll check."

"No, I'll do it," I interrupt. "You stay."

He reaches into his pocket and tosses me the keys. I jog down the hallway and past the bakeshop. Jeannie is standing against the wall, but I don't have time to explain.

"I'll be right back!"

The July heat slams into me like a brick wall as I step outside. I ignore the discomfort and make my way over to the car. Despite searching every crevice, I find nothing. This is bad. This is apocalyptically bad. How am I going to break this to Mom? I decide to text Dad first. At least he'll know how to calm her down.

I drag myself back to the prep room. As expected, Mom is in hysterics. Jeannie and Mrs. Lee have joined the others, and they're all watching helplessly.

"Lǎo pó, are you sure you put it in your bag?" Dad is asking. "Maybe you left it at home."

"I didn't leave it," she says in a stage whisper. "Someone must have taken it. Maybe that's why the room was trashed too. What if they're trying to ruin the contest? Ruin my reputation?"

"I'm sure that's not the case."

"Why is this happening to me?" She continues wailing like she didn't hear him. "I've worked so hard to make this a success!"

"Don't worry, we'll fix this," Dad tries again.

"Your husband's right. I'm sure we can figure this out," Chef Anthony adds. "Do you maybe have a backup recipe? Or we can google one."

"No! It has to be the original recipe." Mom sinks into a nearby chair. "Not to mention we don't have time to get another set of ingredients."

He turns to Mrs. Lee. "Do you have a recipe we can use?"

"I'm afraid not. They're all trade secrets, so we keep the only copies in a safe back at my New York headquarters."

I rack my brain for a solution. There has to be something we can do. My head snaps up.

"What if we reverse the bake order today?"

Every pair of eyes in the room zeroes in on me. Dad is the first to speak.

"What did you say?"

"What if we have the contestants do the highlight before the technical?" I say with the slightest tremor in my voice. "That would give us time to either find the book or come up with a new recipe."

"That's brilliant!" Chef Anthony crows. "What do you think, Mrs. Yang?"

Mom stares at me like I've got something on my face but says nothing.

"I think that's a great idea," Mrs. Lee fills in. "Let's do it."

"Then we should head to the bakeshop and get started," our host answers.

We trek there as a group, but pause outside as Chef Anthony whispers instructions to his culinary students. As they scurry in and start trading out the ingredients at the stations, he walks into the bakeshop with his brightest smile.

"Welcome, everyone, to day three of the Fifth Annual Yin and Yang Junior Baking Competition. I know we got off to a rough start this morning, so the judges thought it might be fun to shake things up a little bit. Bakers, you will be starting with your highlights today."

Confusion spreads through the room, igniting mumbles and whispers from the audience already seated along the wall. Chef Anthony continues without pause.

"Why don't we bring in our esteemed judges? First up is the generous and talented Mrs. Yang of Yin and Yang Restaurant and Bakery!"

When Mom is summoned, she treads in looking stiff and uncomfortable. Mrs. Lee is introduced next, and she puts everyone at ease with a clever joke. I'm the last to be brought into the room, and nerves hit me just before I step inside.

"Our last judge has experience both in front of and behind a baking station. Please help me welcome back Miss Liza Yang!"

Some light applause accompanies my entrance. I take my spot next to the other two judges, consciously avoiding the right side of the room. Mrs. Lee takes a minute to look every contestant in the face before speaking.

"Today's theme is bread, so knead that dough, heat up that oven, and roll up your sleeves. You have three hours, beginning now!"

There's a moment where no one moves, as if Medusa herself has rendered them all stone. Sammy is the first to break the spell, dumping some flour out of his jar and sifting it into his mixing bowl. Over the next few minutes, the rest of the contestants join in, but the mood in the room is somber. Dad waves me over to him.

"I'm going to go home and look for the recipe book. Keep an eye on Mom, okay?"

He sneaks out while Mom's looking the other way. I ease into his seat and cross my fingers. Hopefully, he'll bring good news back. About thirty minutes into the bake, I feel my phone go off in my pocket. Two words pop up on the screen.

**No book.**

I swallow a litany of curses as I raise my head to find Mom staring expectantly at me. Her shoulders slump as I shake my head imperceptibly. My heart aches for her. Just like *The Great British Baking Show*, bread day is the trickiest to pull off. Without a clearly written recipe and properly measured ingredients, the bakers won't have a chance to get it right. If today doesn't go as planned, the contest could end here and now. As much as I hate the fact that Mom used the contest to find me a boyfriend, I don't want her to be publicly humiliated.

That's when the idea comes to me. It's tantalizing but also downright terrifying.

It might also get me grounded for the rest of my natural life.

Perfect.

I make my way to Mom's side and lean down to whisper in her ear.

"Can you come outside with me for a minute? I want to talk to you."

"Why?" she asks in a tired voice.

"Please. Just trust me."

Mom excuses herself and follows me into the hallway. My heart pounds loudly in my ears, and the hem of my shirt is bunched in my fists. I rush into speech, afraid I'll lose the courage otherwise.

"Mom, I want you to let me come up with the technical recipe."

"Liza, I don't think—"

"Please, Mom. I can do this," I tell her. "I won't let you down. I know how important the contest is to you."

My words echo through the empty corridor. Mom says nothing, staring at me with an unreadable expression. As the seconds fall away, so does my confidence. So much for not letting anyone steal my shot. I stare down at the ground.

"Okay."

My eyes bounce back up to her face. "What?"

"I said okay. I'll let you try."

Am I dreaming? I reach down and pinch myself. Ow! Shock gives way to a smile so big my cheeks hurt from the effort. This is really happening. I mean, maybe Mom's only agreeing because she's desperate and figures things can't get worse, but I don't care. I throw my arms around her and give her the biggest hug. She pats me awkwardly on the back until I let her go.

"This isn't a game, Liza. I hope you're really taking this seriously."

"I am! I am!"

"And I get final say on the recipe. If it's not good enough, then we won't use it." She checks her watch. "I need to get back inside for the judging."

"I'll start working on the recipe right now."

She heads inside, and I run back to the break room. I know exactly what I'm going to do, and I text Dad to stop by the grocery store on the way back to pick up what we need. Then I go in search of Gloria and her fellow students. I find them sitting in the cafeteria, playing a board game. Gloria lets me into Chef Anthony's office so I can type out and print eight copies of my recipe. I thank her for her help and head back to the prep room. Dad's waiting inside, and he looks at me with a puzzled expression.

"Did you get everything?"

He nods. "Yes, but why does Mom need all these things?"

"She doesn't. It's for my technical recipe."

He stares at me with surprise. "You're doing the technical? Does Mom know about this?"

"Yeah. I talked to her about it earlier."

With the recipe copies in hand, we walk to the bakeshop together. I hear Mom and Mrs. Lee critiquing James's bread, and what I hear startles me.

"I have to admit, James," Mrs. Lee says. "This is an off day for you. You overworked the dough, then underbaked it."

"The flavor is good," Mom adds, "but not as nuanced as your usual bakes."

I don't hear his reply. It's likely he doesn't give one. With the final highlight judged, Chef Anthony announces the lunch break. People file out of the room, murmuring about the surprising turnout for this morning's bake. Sarah and Edward walk out together, their hands brushing against each other. She and I share a quick smile as they continue down the hall.

Ben and James trail out last, and the latter's eyes flit over me as he passes. I keep mine on the papers in my hand until they're gone. Dad and I then enter the room with everything in tow. Mom and Jeannie are there, along with Mrs. Lee.

I hand the papers over to Mom for inspection with shaky hands. Dad pats my shoulder as her eyes flit quickly across the paper. When she looks up and nods, the tension inside me cracks like a fried wonton, and I finally exhale.

Mrs. Lee raises an eyebrow. "What's this?"

"Our technical recipe," Mom explains. "Liza's going to take the lead on this one."

"I know we're short on time, but are you sure this is a good idea?"

A faint smile appears on Mom's face, and I stand a little taller.

"Yes. I have full confidence in her."

"Okay, then," Mrs. Lee utters with surprising ease. "What can I do to help?"

"If you could put a copy of this recipe on each workstation," I explain, "we'll work on measuring everything out."

She accepts the pile of papers, eyes skimming over what I've written down.

"You came up with this recipe on your own?"

"Technically, it's one we use at the bakery, but I made some changes."

Mrs. Lee peers at Mom. "Your daughter is very talented."

"Yes, I know."

I bask in the rare compliment for a second before getting back down to business. Placing one copy of the recipe on the nearest workstation, I set up an assembly line of ingredients and measuring tools.

"Mom, please measure out the bread flour. Dad, you've got the sugar, salt, and yeast. Jeannie, if you could help out with the water and milk, that would be great. I'll take care of the rest."

When each batch is complete, we transfer it to an open workstation. Once we're done, we remove the extra ingredients and repackage them. The contestants stroll back in right as we're putting everything aside. Mom tips her head toward our host.

"We're ready when you are, Chef Anthony."

"Great! Let's do this."

His booming voice interrupts the various side conversations and brings silence back into the room.

"Contestants, it's time now for your technical challenge for bread day. Mrs. Yang—"

"Actually, since this is one of Liza's recipes, she'll give the instructions."

"Oh! My apologies." He tips his head toward me. "In that case, the floor is yours."

With all eyes now on me, I step into the spotlight.

# Chapter 23

"Contestants, today you will be baking Hokkaido milk bread, otherwise known as *shokupan*. This popular Japanese bread is made using the tangzhong roux method, which gives it a light and fluffy texture. The recipe you're working with also incorporates orange zest and ginger, so remember to balance those flavors. You have one and a half hours. Good luck."

I wait until the bakers have begun working on their recipes before sagging against the display table. The adrenaline that kept my voice steady seeps out of my system, leaving behind shaky hands and weak knees. I manage to escape to the hallway and collapse into a chair. A wave of sweat suddenly takes hold, but the cool wall grants me reprieve as I lean against it.

Mom steps out a moment later, and she puts a hand on my forehead with concern.

"You don't look so good. Are you coming down with something?"

I gently move her hand away. "I'm fine, Mom. Just tired."

"Were you up talking to Grace again? What could be so important at that time of night?"

"Noth—" I stop myself. "Her heart's been broken, and she needed someone to talk to."

"And what do you know about a broken heart?"

Her tone is sharp, but not condescending. Rather, it's threaded with worry, and for a second, I'm tempted to tell her the truth about everything. Ultimately, I keep things vague.

"A heart can be broken in lots of ways. I don't have to feel exactly the same to sympathize."

"You can do that without staying up all night," Mom chides, "but I know you're trying to be a good friend."

It's a small acknowledgment, but it's enough.

"Thanks, Mom."

She tsks. "Can you tell her to get upset during the day, though? You need to sleep."

"Mom!"

She says it with such a straight face I almost take her seriously. I roll my eyes but chuckle along with her. It's a nice change from yelling at each other.

"You picked a very good technical," Mom comments a little while later, her eyes flicking to the open doorway. "Milk bread is easy to get wrong."

"Well, I figured this was the best way to find out who's going to *rise* to the occasion."

I can see the wheels turning in her head, and then her eyebrows shoot up.

"You're quite funny, you know?"

I chuckle. "Are you surprised?"

"Actually, no. Jeannie's always been the quieter one. Too serious, I think. You're full of life."

I've never heard anyone describe me this way before, much less my own mother. It's jarring to hear her say it without a hint of criticism.

"That's why I worry about you. You want so much, so fast. You need to slow down."

And . . . she's back. I was starting to think she'd hit her head or something.

Mom regards me with a slight frown. "Your dad says I've been too hard on you. That I hurt you when I compare you to Jeannie. Is this true?"

Not trusting myself to speak, I stare down the corridor and nod. She exhales deeply.

"I only ever wanted the best for you—for both of you. You might not believe it, but I worry about Jeannie too."

I turn back to her. "You do?"

"Of course."

"Then why are you always after me?" I ask, picking at a loose thread on my shorts.

"Because I'm preparing you for the road ahead. Jeannie sticks to what she knows, but you like to dream big. That means life is going to be harder for you. You have to learn to take the falls and get right back up."

"It doesn't mean you have to do the shoving."

I slap a hand over my mouth. I didn't mean to say that out loud. Mom stares hard at me then, but she nods.

"Okay. I'll try. But only if you promise to listen to me more."

Did we just have a heart-to-heart like I see on TV? The one where the mom hugs her daughter to the swell of touching music? I twist toward Mom with an expectant smile, my ears perked for the sound of a faint melody.

She recoils in her seat. "Why are you looking at me like that?"

Right. So much for that idea. I make a show of adjusting my shirt.

"Nothing."

She shifts her attention to a spot on the wall across from us. The sunlight streaming in from the windows highlight lines and wrinkles I've never noticed before. Bags have taken up permanent residence beneath her eyes, a sign of the stress she's endured.

Most people would have closed up shop or delegated their work while hosting this contest. Mom has kept the bakery running like normal except the nights before competition rounds. On those days, she's in the kitchen preparing for the next day.

"I'm sorry the contest didn't go as planned this year," I say.

She pats me on the arm. "It's my own fault. I didn't screen the contestants as carefully as I usually do."

"Because you were trying to set me up with one of them?"

Once again, the words slip past before I can stop them. I haven't confronted her again since the night I came home late. Her hand stills, but she twists in her chair to face me.

"You never see the good in yourself, Liza. You only try to be like everyone else, to be more American, to date outside your race. I wanted you to be proud of your own culture. To know there's nothing wrong with dating someone of your own background."

I feel a sudden lump in my throat. She thinks I'm ashamed of myself. But that's not true. I mean, hell, I was kissing an Asian boy just the other day.

The memory sends my thoughts in a completely new direction, one I was not prepared to visit just yet, and my chest tightens. I shove it back into the dark corner I relegated it to before.

"I know who I am, Mom, and I'm proud of it. All of it."

She frowns. "Then why won't you give the boys I bring around a chance?"

"Because you only pick them based on your criteria! I'm the one who has to date them, and you've never asked me once what I like or want."

"What you want isn't always what you need, Liza. You're not old enough to understand that."

"Maybe, but I am old enough to know what makes me happy, and that's getting to choose who I date," I insist, pulling my hand away. "I need to learn for myself what's right and wrong for me. Isn't that what you want for me too?"

For once, Mom's staring at me like she's really seeing me. She draws a breath, but Chef Anthony sticks his head out.

"Fifteen-minute warning, ladies."

We stand up to stretch our legs, and I lean a shoulder against the wall.

"Is there at least one boy in there you would date?" Mom asks softly.

*There was. But he turned out to be worse than all the others.*

"I don't know," I mumble, scratching my ear. "I haven't exactly gotten to know any of them that well."

"Not even James or Ben? That's who you were out with that night, right?"

I know she won't let it go if I don't say something, so I lie.

"We spent most of it eating and talking about random things."

*And taking a moonlit walk. And holding hands.*

"Shut up," I mutter to myself.

"What did you say?"

"Uh, just that it's time to go in."

I lead us back into the room, and five completely different breads greet us on the table. Some are weirdly shaped, and others are dry or soggy. To be honest, none of them look appetizing. Nonetheless, we slice two pieces from each for judging, and

Mom sticks to her promise to let me do all the talking.

"This one wasn't proofed for long enough. That's why there's not a good rise."

"Whoever baked this one left it in too long. It's burnt."

"There's no orange or ginger in this one. Not sure what happened."

"Oh! Too much ginger. It overwhelms the other flavors."

"We can't eat this one. The dough is raw in the middle."

When Mom and I turn away to deliberate, it takes us far longer than before. There are no clear winners this round. Not even James pulled off a decent bake from the look of things. It's like he's purposely trying to get eliminated. A terrible thought enters my mind.

What if he's the one who sabotaged the bake this morning?

Mom's voice pulls me back to reality. "Do you agree with this ranking?"

"Yeah. It looks good."

We face the contestants and announce the plates from worst to best. David's bread is at the bottom, and bakes from Ben, James, and Edward are above him in that order. Surprisingly, Albert doesn't gloat when he hears David is at the bottom. In fact, he gives his twin brother an encouraging smile.

When Sammy is announced as the winner of the technical, he lets out a whoop as his family claps loudly in the audience. Part of me is glad I don't have to congratulate James on another win, but a tinier part of me is disappointed he'd accept such lazy baking. I would never present something I wasn't a hundred percent happy with.

"Well, this has been quite the turnaround," Chef Anthony comments. "I don't envy you judges. Please go deliberate on this week's bake."

Normally, Mom and Mrs. Lee would make the final decision, but since the milk bread recipe was my idea, I'm invited to join. Once we're seated around the table in the break room, the negotiation begins. Mrs. Lee is quick to critique James's bread right off the bat.

"His highlight lacked finesse. And his technical? How do you forget to set the timer on your oven? I expected a lot more from him, especially having won two bake days in a row."

"But that's just it. His baking has been solid until now," Mom counters as she scoots forward in her chair. "And so has Ben's. Today was a bad day for everyone."

"Not everyone. Sammy did really well on this challenge," I offer. "Plus, I snuck a taste of his grandmother's orange cranberry loaf, and it was delicious."

"I agree," Mrs. Lee states. "It was a phenomenal bake, and his technical came in first too."

Mom taps her pen on the table. "That leaves Edward and David. To me, Edward tried too hard to one-up the rest. Both of his breads tasted the same."

I'm surprised she's being so hard on her golden boy. I hope it's not because he wasn't successful getting me to agree to a date. Mrs. Lee purses her lips.

"Yes, but Edward came in second on the technical. His flavor did need some work, but the bread itself was well baked. On the other hand, David's highlight wasn't too bad. It was simple, but well executed."

"Yet he came in dead last on the technical," Mom points out.

I glance from one woman to the other. Have all their judging sessions been this . . . civil? There's still a chill in the air, but at first, they could barely stand to look at each other.

"What do you think, Liza?"

I freeze in the middle of scratching the back of my head. Mom wants my input? She arches an eyebrow.

"Well?"

"Uh, we should consider the bigger picture, maybe," I say, clenching my hands to keep them still. "Like, look at their past bakes. To determine who should go home."

Mrs. Lee leans back with a smile. "You're quite good at this judging thing."

"I watch a lot of *Great British Baking Show*. I learned it from them," I confess.

Mom smirks. "Yes. For once, her obsession with Netflix has paid off."

After several more minutes of discussion, we make our decision and return to the bakeshop. It's Mom's turn to announce this week, so she positions herself slightly in front of the rest of us.

"Bread is extremely tricky to get right, and it showed today. Every one of you had difficulties, and only some of you overcame them. I'm sad to say the one who will not be continuing on to the next bake is . . . David."

He doesn't look remotely surprised, and he acknowledges the decision with a subtle lowering of his eyes. His mom and brother are in the audience, and Albert hugs him impulsively as he walks by. I guess blood is thicker than batter.

"As for our brilliant baker today, we have someone who stepped up to the challenge and made his grandmother proud. Congratulations, Sammy!"

I clap in earnest, happy to see him win this round. On our walk back from deliberating, Mom explained he'd been close to being a runner-up the last two weeks. If anyone knows how it feels to be second-best, it's me. I press a hand to my heart when he runs into the audience to hug his grandmother. I hadn't noticed she was here until now, but her wrinkled smile lights up the whole room. When his family asks me to take a photo for them, I oblige. By the time I hand them back the phone, James and Ben are gone.

With the day over, we all pitch in to clean things up. I kind of wish Nathan wouldn't, because with every kiss he gives Jeannie, I get more and more annoyed. I know I promised Grace I wouldn't get involved, but Jeannie deserves to know the truth.

When we finish, Mom, Dad, and I head home in one car, while Nathan offers to drop Jeannie off. Mom stops by my room as we're all getting ready for bed. She leans against the doorframe in her favorite pajamas, a striped linen set one of her friends brought her from Taiwan.

"Thank you for helping out. It could have been a disaster."

"You're welcome."

"I was thinking. How would you like to create the technicals for the rest of the competition?"

What did she just say? I stare, motionless, like a scared guinea pig. Mom doesn't notice and keeps talking.

"I never did find the recipe book, and I—"

"Yes, yes! Um, I mean, I'd be happy to help," I answer.

"Good, good. Then I need you to start working on filled-bun recipes in the morning, so get some sleep. That means no talking to Grace until dawn, got it?"

"Okay, Mom."

It's a white lie, but I think of it more as a half-truth. If Grace is fine when I check in with her, I'll go to bed. Otherwise, I can't abandon her.

Mom tucks a lock of my hair behind one ear, cupping my cheek with her hand.

"I'm proud of what you did today."

"No buts?"

She smiles wryly. "No buts."

Once she closes the door, I jump up and down on the bed to celebrate. I wince when my head accidentally bumps into the ceiling fan. Mom's voice pierces through our shared wall.

"What was that?"

"Nothing!"

I sit back down and grin. So this is what it feels like to win.

I like it.

•  •  •  •  •

"So, what did you want to talk to me about?"

Jeannie props her chin on her hand. It took me two days to drum up the courage to talk to her, and now we're here for a late lunch at Morning Thai on the pretense of a sisters' day out. I picked it because it's small and typically quiet outside of peak lunch hours. Now, sitting beneath the dim lighting and banana-leaf-shaped fans, my stomach twists into knots. Our waitress stops by to grab our orders, which buys me a few more minutes. I ask for the basil chicken with brown rice. While Jeannie glances over the large menu, I fiddle with the straw of my Thai iced tea.

Once we're alone again, Jeannie wiggles her fingers at me.

"Am I going to have to tickle it out of you?"

I try to smile, but it ends up like a grimace. "Before I tell you, you have to promise me you'll listen to the whole thing before making a decision."

"Okay," Jeannie says slowly. "Now you've got me worried. What's going on? Is it James?"

The mere mention of his name is a knife to my chest. I force myself to answer.

"No . . . I mean, yes. Kind of?"

She drapes her napkin across her lap. "That's not helpful, Liza."

*Just do it. Just tell her.*

"Grace told me Nathan tried to kiss her the other night."

I wince instinctively, expecting her to pelt me with the utensils at her side. Instead, there's nothing but silence. I chance a peek at Jeannie and find her frowning at her glass of water. Maybe she didn't hear me.

"Jeannie, I said—"

"It's not true. She's lying."

"What?" I stare at her, slack-jawed. "Why would you say that?"

"Because Nathan told me this would happen. He warned me James was the type to hold a grudge, and that he wouldn't stop trying to ruin his life."

Nathan's version of James doesn't sound at all like the one I know, even with everything that's happened since last bake day. Of course, I keep that to myself as I cock my head to the side.

"So? What does that have to do with Grace?"

"Come on. You're smarter than that." Jeannie crosses her arms over her chest. "It doesn't take a genius to see Ben goes along with everything James does. Now that he's dating Grace, they probably convinced her to say Nathan kissed her so I'd break up with him."

I gasp. "Jeannie, that doesn't even make sense! It's Grace we're talking about. You've known her almost as long as I have. She would never lie about this sort of thing."

That gives Jeannie pause. She's the only one besides me who's aware of what happened with Eric. Doubt flickers in her eyes, but she ultimately shakes her head.

"Nathan has been nothing but the perfect gentleman since we started dating. He wouldn't do that to me. He cares about me."

Her voice cracks, and she casts her eyes down to the table. I lean forward so I can look her in the eyes.

"Jeannie, he had me fooled too, but just because a guy's nice to you doesn't mean he's not cheating on you. I know that firsthand."

Unexpectedly, she recoils. "And just because your boyfriends cheated on you doesn't mean mine will."

That stings. Since I had to hide my exes from Mom, Jeannie's been my closest confidante. I've told her things even Grace doesn't know.

"That's not fair, Jeannie, and you know it."

Our argument has caught the attention of several nearby tables, and they stop what they're doing. At this point, I don't care if they hear everything. Jeannie narrows her eyes at me.

"What's not fair is my baby sister trying to ruin the one good thing in my life."

I swallow the acid in my mouth as our food arrives. It's not like I have any appetite left.

"What the hell are you talking about?" I hiss across the table. "You've got *everything*. The best grades, a gorgeous apartment, a modeling career, and you're Mom's favorite."

"Oh yeah? For your information, the guy who owns the apartment is moving back in the fall. I'm going to be homeless unless I can find another place to stay. And that modeling career you're so envious about? I haven't booked a job in months because I'm too 'generic' looking."

She pauses, chest heaving. I can do nothing but stare. Why didn't she tell me any of this before? Jeannie nails me with accusing eyes.

"Maybe James is the real reason you're saying all this about Nathan."

I gape at her. "Excuse me?!"

"Maybe *you're* the one who doesn't want to believe your perfect guy is in the wrong."

I'm stunned. Tears spring into my eyes, but I make myself say the words anyway.

"For your information, James and I aren't even talking. The minute he found out *my sister* was dating Nathan, he dropped me. The only reason I came today was to protect *you*, but I guess you'd rather get your heart broken too!"

I stand up and storm out before belatedly remembering we came in one car. Rather than having to ask Jeannie for a ride home, I walk a little ways down the shopping center and call an Uber. I duck behind the corner of a building when Jeannie rushes out the door. She gets in the car, and a few minutes later, my phone starts going off.

It's her.

I decline the call, and the three that follow. She eventually gives up and pulls out of the plaza. Good. Let her explain to Mom why she's coming home without me.

I get a text saying my driver is close, so I step back onto the walkway to wait. The door to the cafe on my left opens, and someone takes a few steps before stopping.

"Liza?"

*Ugh! Why now?*

"Ben."

I swivel toward him with a guarded expression. At least he's alone this time. His face is taut, but hope shines in his eyes as they dart around me.

"Um . . . are you here by yourself?"

"Yes, I am."

Hearing my tone, the smile falls off his face, but he manages to resurrect it.

"Are you going somewhere?"

I glance toward the main road. "Home."

"Right now?"

I squint at him. "Why do you care?"

"Well, um . . . can we talk?"

"Are we going to talk about why you broke up with Grace?" I challenge. "Because if not, I'm leaving."

A black sedan pulls up, and the driver rolls down his window.

"Are you Liza?"

"Yep. That's me."

I step off the curb as the driver gets out and opens the door for me.

"Liza, wait! Please."

I try to make myself get in the car, but the desolation in Ben's voice roots me to the spot. Damn it. He steps around me and hands the driver a fifty-dollar bill.

"Here. Take this for your trouble. She won't be needing the ride anymore."

The driver peers at me through his sunglasses. "Miss?"

I squeeze my eyes shut before smiling apologetically at him.

"Thanks for coming, but I'm going to stay with him."

"Are you sure?"

"Definitely. I'm fine."

Once the car turns out of the plaza, I eye Ben warily. He rolls his shoulders.

"Is there somewhere we can go to talk in private? You can pick where we go."

It's a weekday, so Boba Life should still have a couple of booths available. I point in its direction.

"Take it or leave it."

# Chapter 24

We walk all the way to the other side of the plaza. In the early afternoon sun, the trek is unbearably hot. By the time we step inside the teashop, I'm ready for a cold drink. I get in line, but Ben shakes his head.

"It's my treat. Go grab a table and I'll get your drink."

I head to the back room and drop into a seat. Ben pops in about ten minutes later and hands me a drink before sitting down. He pierces the top of his cup with his straw but doesn't take a sip. I suck some boba into my mouth to chew away my irritation.

Ben tugs at the collar of his T-shirt. "Thank you for giving me a chance to explain things."

"I'm only promising to listen. That's all."

"That's totally fair. I get it, and I appreciate your time."

"So? What do you want to say?"

"Okay, I'll just start from the beginning." He drags his hand through his hair. "I've known Nathan for almost ten years. He attended Superbia with us. We all became friends, but it didn't take long for things to change. Nathan thought James was always showing off how good he was at everything, and James didn't like how often Nathan broke school rules. It got so bad I started hanging out with them separately so they wouldn't fight. Still, when my mom needed an actor for the TV spot promoting her condo complex, I convinced her to hire Nathan."

So far, his story is lining up with Nathan's. Ben picks up the plastic wrap he removed from the straw, rolling it between his fingers absently as he continues.

"Last year, Nathan started inviting me to all these exclusive parties, and I was so impressed by how popular he was. There were even celebrities who knew his name. Sometimes he'd lie and say we were both twenty-one so he could drink. I never did, though. I swear."

His eyes flit briefly over to me, conflict and fear stitched across his features. I keep my expression carefully neutral.

"My grades started slipping and my parents noticed, but I told them I just forgot to turn in some assignments. James was the only one who knew the truth, and I swore him to secrecy. I managed to pull everything up before the end of the semester, and things went back to normal. At least, until last Christmas."

"What happened then?" I ask.

"Well, for one, Mr. Lee—Nathan's dad—showed up drunk at my parents' annual holiday party."

I stiffen in my chair. "Wait. Did you say Mr. Lee?"

"Yeah. Nathan is Mrs. Lee's son. You didn't know that?"

My stomach flips, and I shake my head. Mrs. Lee mentioned her son the first time we met, but Mr. Lee is the only person I've seen a picture of. All of Mama Lee's ad campaigns are like Hallmark holiday movies—the two of them, arms linked and smiling, holding their signature pastries. My mind flashes back to Nathan hiding behind his baseball cap during the highlight bake, and I realize it's the only time he's been in the same room with his mom. Was it just Ben and James he was hiding from? Or Mrs. Lee too?

"Liza?"

Ben's voice tugs me out of my thoughts. "Oh, I'm sorry. Keep going."

"Well, I should explain something first. Nathan's parents got divorced a few years back. They agreed to keep it out of the papers and keep up appearances for the business, but my parents stopped inviting Mr. Lee over out of respect to Mrs. Lee." He takes a breath. "So when he showed up to the party uninvited, they got into an argument. Mom walked Mr. Lee out, but then he made a move on her and Nathan saw it."

Like father, like son, apparently.

"Nathan started cursing and calling Mom names, and Mrs. Lee took Nathan home. After that, Mom called his agency and canceled the contract she gave him for the TV ads. That's when everything fell apart."

My heart lurches in my chest as Ben rushes through the next part, his eyes pinned on his still-untouched cup of tea.

"A couple of weeks later, Nathan asked if he could borrow my car for a party in the Hamptons. I said no, but then he started crying. He said he was really depressed about what happened and really needed the distraction. In hindsight, I shouldn't have said yes, but he swore he'd be careful. I didn't find out what had happened until the next day."

I clutch my stomach as it churns in anticipation of what's to come.

"The police came to my house and told my parents that my car had been found at the scene of an accident. Apparently, Nathan had a lot to drink at the party and ran into a telephone pole on his way back before passing out. Thankfully, no one else was hurt, but when the police got there, he failed the Breathalyzer. That's when Nathan told them I was driving and had left so I wouldn't get into trouble."

I gasp. It's hard to believe the same guy who charmed me and Jeannie could be so underhanded.

"What an ass," I say.

Ben smiles wryly. "My parents and I ended up going down to the station for an interview. Our family lawyer had my blood alcohol level taken to prove I hadn't had anything to drink, and my parents vouched for me being home when my car was caught on the toll cameras heading out of town. Ultimately, I was cleared of everything, but as you can imagine, my parents were furious. If I had been charged, it could have ruined my family's reputation."

"What happened to Nathan?"

"Nathan was charged with a DUI. He had his license revoked for six months and had to go to rehab for a month. He was lucky his lawyer convinced the police not to file additional charges for lying to them about me. After that, my parents forbade me from talking to him ever again. I felt bad about it, but I was already in so much trouble with them."

I take a sip of my tea while I process this. "Was that it, then?"

He sighs and leans back in his chair. "I wish it were, but a few weeks later, my parents received an email from Nathan blaming us for getting him dropped from his agency. We had nothing to do with it, but he was convinced either me or James had leaked information to them. He threatened to talk to a reporter about it unless they gave him money to keep quiet."

Impulsively, I reach across and grab him by the hand.

He grips my fingers in his. "My parents didn't want to give in to his demands. Mom tried talking to Mrs. Lee first, but she wouldn't even answer the phone. I guess Nathan must have found a way to convince her we were at fault."

"What did you guys do then?"

Ben's mouth tightens into a line as he recalls what happened.

"My parents ended up consulting our lawyer. He drafted a letter to Mrs. Lee threatening legal action if Nathan didn't back off. Within a day or two, she called to apologize and promised she would take care of it. I found out later that they had a huge fight, and Nathan had to move in with a mutual friend for a while. After that, we didn't hear anything from him again, but later James told me he had a run-in with Nathan outside his house. He wouldn't tell me what happened between them, but afterward, our parents decided it would be best if we stayed away for a while. That's why we ended up coming down here early."

This whole thing has more twists and turns than a Korean drama, and I'm getting a headache trying to keep track of what I've heard. One thing is clear, though: Nathan is a liar. Abruptly, Ben glances at something that comes across his Apple watch.

"Do you need to go?" I ask.

"Oh, no, no," he says, shaking his head. "It's nothing."

We sit in silence for a while. Ben finally takes sips of his tea, and I consider what to do next. I suppose after hearing him pour his heart out, the least I can do is try to mend it.

"Grace didn't cheat on you with Nathan. He was the one who tried to kiss her, and she pushed him off. James didn't see the whole thing."

"What?" Anger sparks in his normally soft eyes. "Is she okay? Did he hurt her?"

"No. He didn't. But you did, when you broke up with her without explaining why."

I let that sink in for a minute. Ben slouches in his chair.

"I never wanted to hurt her. I just thought . . . James was worried

Nathan was using her to manipulate me. James and Nathan have never gotten along, even before all the drama."

"Well, I have some choice words for him."

"Don't blame him, Liza," he begs, sitting up and leaning toward me. "James was trying to protect me. He's always treated me more like a brother than a cousin."

"Either way, he could've just asked me for the truth."

"James doesn't trust easily. A lot of people have tried to take advantage of him because of his family's wealth. It's not an excuse, but I wanted you to know." Ben sighs. "He's actually the reason I came looking for you today."

"What do you mean?"

"Ever since your fight with him, he's been downright intolerable. He hasn't slept or eaten much in days. It's why he bombed those bread challenges."

Ben pins me with an earnest stare.

"Please give him another chance, Liza. You're special. He's never looked at anyone the way he looks at you."

I open my mouth, but he cuts me off. "Just promise you'll hear him out."

After a beat, I sigh. "Fine."

"Great!" Ben glances at his watch as another text pops up. "I'll be right back."

"I . . . wait a minute. What?"

Ben shoots out of the booth in a flash. When he returns, he's not alone.

• • • • •

"Are you two planning on glaring at each other forever?"

I roll my eyes over to Ben, who looks ready to throttle us both.

We've been sitting in the booth for a good fifteen minutes without exchanging a single word. James is slumped against his chair, his arms folded across his chest and his jaw set in a firm line. I've been staring at a torn piece of wallpaper as if it's the most interesting thing I've ever seen in my life.

When neither of us replies to his question, Ben throws up his hands.

"You guys are the most stubborn people I've ever met. You're made for each other, if you'd only open your mouths and talk."

He gets to his feet, jostling the empty cup in front of him.

"I'm going to use the bathroom. You guys better be talking by the time I get back."

Two minutes after he leaves, I rise from my chair. I'm done waiting for an apology that will never come. I'm halfway across the room when chair legs scratch against the floor. The sound is accompanied by the sensation of fingers wrapping gently around my wrist.

"Don't," James utters in a low voice. "Stay. Please."

I'm torn between yanking my arm away and sitting back down. James takes advantage of my indecision and steps closer, his hand sliding down to grasp mine. He takes a deep breath and looks me straight in the eye.

"Liza, I'm sorry."

He strokes a thumb across the back of my hand. The resultant warmth that streaks up my arm and down my spine reminds me why it's been so hard to stop thinking about him. Still, I know better than to let down my guard.

"Why should I believe you?"

James glances at the seat I vacated, but I don't move. He swallows hard, his Adam's apple bobbing up and down.

"I was an ass. I should have believed you instead of jumping to conclusions, but I was trying to protect Ben. He's been through so much already. When I saw how hard he was falling for Grace, I . . . I didn't want him to get hurt again."

This time, I do pull away, my chin jutted out as I glare at him.

"So you decided to break my—I mean, Grace's—heart instead?"

"I honestly didn't think she would take it that hard," he explains, taking a step forward. "I mean, they had a lot of fun together, but I never saw anything that made me think Grace was serious about Ben."

"Really? Not the fact that she texted and called him all the time? Or how she was always holding his hand? Oh, what about the nonstop hugging and kissing? That doesn't count for anything either?"

He has the decency to look ashamed as he drags a hand through his hair.

"I . . . I guess I didn't think about that."

"No, you didn't," I assert. "But I did, because I know my best friend. Just because Grace likes to flirt and have fun doesn't mean she isn't serious about Ben. If anything, she was worried that he wouldn't like her as much as she liked him."

"But what about Nathan?" he asks stubbornly. "I saw them kissing."

"What you saw was Nathan taking Grace by surprise and kissing *her*. You missed the part where she told him off."

James stills at that. My piece said, I turn and head for the door. Ben shouts for me to wait, but I pretend I don't hear him. Outside, I remember again that I don't have a ride. I'm sure as hell not calling Jeannie, so I decide to head to Yin and Yang.

It's a twenty-minute walk, but with the heat, it feels like forever. I've probably made it a third of the way when a car slows next to me.

The window on the passenger side rolls down to reveal James inside.

"Liza, please get in the car. We'll take you wherever you want."

I scowl at him from the sidewalk. "I don't need a ride from you."

"Liza, don't be ridiculous. It's almost a hundred degrees out-side."

"Go away."

After a second, the window goes back up, and Ben moves the car forward. He doesn't go far, though, pulling into a parking lot about twenty feet ahead of me. James gets out of the car and intercepts me.

"Please get in the car, Liza."

"I told you. I'm not going anywhere with you."

"Fine. Then Ben can drive you, and I'll call an Uber."

James is wearing a button-down navy shirt and dark wash jeans. He won't make it ten feet before being drenched in sweat. At least I'm dressed for the weather in my light blue T-shirt and white shorts.

"I'll be fine."

He presses his lips together, the movement reducing his dimple to a slash on his cheek.

"Stay here."

I don't want to listen to him, but he keeps one eye on me while walking back to the car. He ducks his head through the window and mumbles something. Ben protests, but James shakes his head. Seconds later, the car rolls away and James returns to my side with a determined look.

I gape at him. "What are you doing?"

"Walking with you."

"I don't need—"

He produces a bottle of cold water from behind his back. "Here. In case you get thirsty."

I don't know whether to punch him or kiss him.

*Liar. You know exactly what you want to do.*

I continue stomping down the sidewalk. I ignore him and keep my eyes on Yin and Yang in the distance, the sound of passing cars filling my ears. He quickly matches my pace, his longer legs striding effortlessly while my legs ache from the effort. All of a sudden, my calf clenches mid-step, and I fall to my knees with a hiss. James is on the ground in a flash.

"What's wrong? What happened?"

The pain is excruciating, the cramp's vise-like grip making it hard to breathe. Without a word, James helps me over to a table outside one of the cafes lining Bellaire Boulevard. Tears well in my eyes as he lowers me into the chair. All I can do is clench my fists and pray for it to end.

He peers at me. "I can try to help if you want. I used to get them when I ran track."

Desperate, I nod. James kneads my calf with gentle, circular motions, starting behind my knee and working his way down. Little by little, the tightness begins to ease until all that's left is a dull, aching weakness.

"It'll be best if you stay off it for a little while," he instructs. "Have something with potassium too, like a banana."

I'm so grateful to be rid of the pain that I forget I'm supposed to be angry with him.

"I thought Ben was the pre-med major."

He flashes a toothy smile. "Who do you think taught him everything he knows?"

His hands are still on my leg. Despite the sticky heat of the day, my brain registers the firm pressure of his fingers against my skin. James's warm brown eyes beckon me closer, and I have to look away before I drown in them.

Ben's car pulls into the parking spot in front of us. James tips his head toward it.

"Will you please get in the car now?"

I narrow my eyes at him. "Fine."

"*Thank you*. I feel like I'm in hell."

I bite back my retort. He must read it in my eyes because he chuckles softly.

"I guess I deserve that."

He helps me over to the car, and Ben opens the door for me. Both guys wait until I'm settled before climbing in themselves. The air inside is on full blast, and I sigh happily. Ben glances at me through the rearview.

"So, where to, milady?"

I consider asking for a ride home, but I'm struck by a better idea.

"I was going to meet Grace. We're supposed to hang out at the Water Wall. Want to come with?"

"Um . . . sure," Ben answers with a shaky smile.

I give him the address. As he enters it into his phone, I pull mine out and text Grace.

> **I've got a surprise for you. Meet me at the Water Wall in thirty minutes?**
>
> **Ok.**

Let's hope she doesn't kill me.

• • • • •

We make it there before Grace, so I have them park in one of the mall garages close by. Ben and James follow me across the street to Waterwall Park, a semicircular wall sixty-four feet in the air. Water cascades down in large sheets along the inside, rolling down a series of steps near the bottom and gathering into a channel below. A triangular tipped gate with three Roman arches stands guard in front of it, and a grassy park lined by oak trees connects the Water Wall and Williams Tower.

Families and couples are having picnics and playing nearby as we enter the main viewing area. The sound of rushing water surrounds me on all sides, white noise hiding the daily traffic driving past. I smile as drops of water sprinkle onto my head and face and revel in the reprieve from the heat. Ben gestures excitedly at different parts of it while shouting something unintelligible to James. My phone buzzes, and I pull it out.

**I'm here. Where are you?**

I send her a reply and then tuck it back into my pocket.

"Okay. She's coming," I say to Ben. "Don't screw this up."

"I won't," he says, though a nervous smile plays on his lips.

I grab James by the elbow and tug him away.

"What are you—" he starts.

I shoot him a look, and he relents. I don't stop until we're tucked around the corner of the wall. We're just far enough away to not be seen but close enough to watch how things play out.

I spot Grace rounding the corner before Ben does. When she sees him waiting near the center of the falls, she stops in her tracks, eyes wide. Grace turns to leave, but he catches up to her and throws his hands out in front of him. He says something, to which she shouts something in return. Ben continues to talk, alternating between shaking his head and pleading with her. I take an unconscious step forward when Grace bursts into tears, but James touches me on the arm.

"Let Ben handle it."

He's right. I'm the one who arranged this meeting, but he needs to do the rest. With every word, Ben inches closer, eventually enveloping her in his arms. She stiffens for a second and then relaxes into his embrace. He presses a kiss into her hair before leaning down and touching his mouth to hers.

"Looks like they worked it out."

I twist halfway and find James over my left shoulder, a smile tugging at his lips. His gaze slides over to me, and he leans in so I can hear him over the water.

"I am truly sorry, Liza. For hurting Grace. For making assumptions about your family." He pauses. "For hurting you."

It's hard to focus with his face so near mine, and his breath tickling my ear. His arm snakes across my waist and turns me so I'm facing him fully. His hand remains at my hip as our eyes lock.

"I hope you can forgive me."

My fingers itch with the need to touch him, to smooth the furrow between his brows and trace the outline of his dimple.

"I forgive you."

He steals the last word from my lips, his mouth capturing mine. My hands wrap around his neck as I press close, overcome with the need to prove this isn't a figment of my sleep-deprived imagination.

This kiss is different. More frantic. More intense. Like we're reclaiming each other. His hand trails up the back of my shirt. I intertwine my fingers in his hair. We only break apart for ragged gasps of air, our foreheads pressed together to stay connected. James smiles, the special kind I realize I've only seen when he's looking at me.

"I missed you."

"I missed you too."

His lips meet mine again. "I'm sorry."

"You said that already, but feel free to keep repeating it."

James tosses his head back and laughs. I giggle as a sudden breeze sends mist our way, burying my face into the crook of his shoulder.

His voice rumbles against my cheek. "Do you think your mom would mind if I asked to date you?"

"Are you kidding?" I tilt my head back to gawk at him. "You check off all her boxes. She'd be thrilled."

"What about your boxes?"

I pretend to think it over, and then shrug. "Meh."

James proceeds to tickle me until I break free, running over to Ben and Grace and using them as shields. I try to fake right, but he catches on and captures me in his arms, effectively ending my escape.

"Gotcha!"

I reach up and brush the hair off his brow, and he goes in for another kiss. It's a while before my feet land back on the ground.

"I see you guys have made up too," Grace says with a chuckle.

Ben smirks. "And not a moment too soon. He was driving me up a wall."

"I was getting tired of Liza's moping myself."

"Hey!" James and I protest at the same time.

"See? Totally made for each other," Ben teases.

The four of us walk around the park, sticking to the shade of the oak trees. My phone rings suddenly. It's Mom. Oh no.

"I'm sorry, Mom," I say before she can start in on me. "I should have called earlier. I'm out with Grace at the Water Wall, and I'm fine."

I don't mention Ben or James. I'd like to keep the latter to myself a little longer. Rather than yelling at me like she usually would, Mom sounds oddly calm over the phone.

"I'm glad you're okay. I was worried. Jeannie said you two had an argument."

I lean against a tree trunk. "Yeah, we did. It's a long story."

"Are you going to come home soon?"

"I'll leave in a minute."

"Dinner will be waiting," she tells me before hanging up.

Grace eyes me. "You gonna survive?"

"Sounds like it, but I should probably go home anyway."

"Ben and I can drop you off," James offers. "It's not out of the way."

As much as I'd love a few more minutes with him, I'm not ready to tempt fate just yet.

"Actually, I'm going to ride with Grace, if that's okay."

Somehow, James guesses what's on my mind. "I thought you said your mom would approve of us dating."

"I think she would, but with everything that's happened with the contest . . ."

I freeze. Wait a second. The contest. I glance from Ben to James and back. Grace touches me on the arm.

"You think Nathan might be the one who stole the recipe book and trashed the bakeshop, don't you?"

I nod. The two cousins exchange a look.

"Now that I think about it, it could also explain why I had salt in my sugar jar on cake day," James says.

"I definitely wouldn't put it past him," Ben adds, staring across the grassy lawn. "Especially if he thought it would help him get back at us . . . or at least, back at James."

"Why would ruining Mom's contest do anything to James?" I ask.

Ben raises his eyebrows at me. "*Because.*"

I follow the path of his eyes over to James, who's giving the buttons of his shirt rapt attention. As I watch, he turns more crimson by the minute.

Oh. *Oh*.

I thread my fingers through his, and he gives me a lopsided smile. I turn back to Ben.

"If he's really the culprit, how are we going to prove it? I've already tried talking sense into Jeannie. She won't listen."

James brings my hand up to press a kiss to my knuckles.

"Don't worry. I have a plan."

# Chapter 25

After returning home from the Water Wall, I spend most of the night waiting for a lecture that never comes. We even make it through an entire family dinner without Mom offering a single criticism. I'm totally weirded out by this kinder, more trusting version of her, even though I've wanted this my whole life. Jeannie and I still aren't talking, so I can't really ask her about it.

When I glance across the table at Dad, he only shrugs. Half of me expects to wake up in the middle of the night to her standing over my bed with a butcher knife. Needless to say, I don't get much sleep. It's just as well, because I'm super anxious about telling Mom and Dad about Nathan.

The next day, I pull them into the kitchen before Jeannie gets up and confess my suspicions about his sabotaging the contest. Dad's so stunned he can only shake his head.

Mom rubs her face and frowns. "Are you sure Nathan is to blame for this? He seems so . . ."

"Perfect?"

Her eye twitches before she replies. "I was going to say *nice*."

"I'm sure that's how he gets away with doing these things."

With a little pleading, Mom agrees to help me convince Jeannie to hear Ben out. Within a couple of hours, Ben and Jeannie are sitting in the study with the door closed. Grace is perched on the couch, staring blankly at the fireplace while wrapped in her own thoughts. She wanted to be there in case Jeannie had any questions. James, who insisted on coming with Ben too, moves to stand by me. He's wearing a white button-down shirt with the sleeves rolled up, paired with slim-cut jeans. I glance at him.

"Do you always dress like this?"

He winks. "Only if I'm trying to impress someone."

"So . . . this is your 'meet-the-mom' outfit?"

His grin melts my insides. "Do you think it'll work?"

"It's working on someone," Grace quips.

I scowl at her, but it's rendered ineffective by the flush of my cheeks.

James laughs. "I'll have to keep that in mind for the future."

I go to shove him, but he captures my hand in his and tugs me closer. My head tilts automatically, but we're interrupted.

"Liza."

I twirl around at the sound of Mom's voice. She gestures for me to join her in the kitchen, but I'm rooted to the spot.

James touches my arm. "Are you going to be okay?"

"She's not going to murder me with guests present, if that's what you're asking," I half joke.

"Seriously, Liza. Do you want me to go with you?"

I smile and cover his hand with mine. "Thanks, I'll be okay."

Mom is sitting at the kitchen table when I walk in, and I lower myself into the seat she's pulled for me. For a few tense minutes, I'm a bug under Mom's watchful eye. Finally, she tips her head and speaks.

"Are you doing this so I'll leave you alone?"

It takes my brain a second to deduce what she's really asking, but then I shake my head.

"No. I really like James."

There's another long pause before she nods.

"Good. Then his mom and I approve."

*Wait . . . what?*

"You talked to his mom?"

"Of course I did," she says, arranging the mail Dad left on the table. "When you came home so late that night, I called his parents to check if you were with him. His mom answered the phone."

"You—" I gasp. "Did you call Ben's parents too?"

"Why would I do that? It's obvious he likes Grace." She laughs at my hanging jaw. "I do pay attention, Liza. Especially when it comes to the people my daughters spend time with."

My mind circles back to what she said first. "What do you mean James's mom approves?"

"While we were on the phone, Mrs. Wong kept asking questions about our family, so I asked her why. Apparently, James had explained how the contest worked, and when he mentioned your name, he lit up. Mrs. Wong said she'd never seen him look so happy before."

My face burns hotter than Szechuan peppers hearing this. If Mom notices, she chooses not to comment. She sets the mail on the kitchen counter behind her.

"Anyway, she asked to hear more about you, so I told her all about the things you've accomplished. She was very impressed to hear about your baking skills, by the way. It seems Mrs. Wong's quite the baker herself. Of course, I asked about James too, and I have to say, he sounds like a very nice young man."

I'm speechless. For once, Mom's matchmaking worked to my

advantage. She must be thinking along the same lines because she lets out a triumphant laugh.

"See, Liza? I knew he would be the right one. You should have more faith in your mom."

Apparently, Mom's just going to pretend like she didn't have a whole help-Edward-win-Liza's-heart scheme, but I'll let it slide. After all, she did talk me up to Mrs. Wong.

"Thanks for having my back, Mom."

"You're welcome."

Mom goes to check on Jeannie and Ben, while I head back into the living room to update James on our conversation. When I get to the part about what happened between our moms, his cheeks redden.

"They really did that? Shit," he says a little loudly.

He claps his hand over his mouth. It's so unexpected, I just about die laughing.

James grins sheepishly and rubs the back of his neck. "Ah, sorry. I shouldn't have said that."

"Are you kidding?" I poke him in the ribs. "I've been waiting for this since the day we met!"

His eyes twinkle as he threads his arm around my waist.

"Is that all you've been waiting for?"

I giggle as James dips his head down to meet mine, but the door to the study opens, and we pull apart. My heart sinks when I spot Jeannie. She reminds me of a wilted flower, crumpled and broken. I wanted her to know the truth about Nathan, but seeing her hurt like this makes me question if I did the right thing.

"What he did to you was terrible," Jeannie tells Ben with fervent eyes. "I swear. I had no idea."

"I know you didn't. I'm just glad you were willing to hear me out."

They share a tentative smile. Then Ben moves over to sit by Grace, while Jeannie looks over at me. I don't know which of us moves first, but a second later, we're hugging and talking over each other in the middle of the room.

"I should've believed you," she says. "I should've known who to trust."

"It's okay," I answer back. "He's a really good liar."

"All those things I said to you . . ."

I shake my head against her cheek. "Already forgotten."

"Will you forgive me?"

"There's nothing to forgive."

Jeannie squeezes me hard and then steps over to Mom. She bows her head in shame.

"I'm sorry. I'm the one who brought him into this and ruined the contest. He wouldn't have even come down here if it wasn't for me."

Mom strokes her cheek. "It's not your fault. He was the one who decided to do this. Not you."

"It certainly seems like he's been trying to make James and me look like the guilty ones," Ben adds. "After all, he made sure I was the one who found the trashed bakeshop."

This only adds to Jeannie's distress. She pulls her phone out of her pocket.

"I am going to break up with him right now."

"Actually," James interjects, "I'd prefer if you waited a while."

"What? Why?"

Everyone turns to stare at him. He leans casually against the doorway.

"If we're going to catch Nathan in the act, he can't know we suspect him. He needs to think you still believe him."

"James is right," Grace states. "The only way we're going to stop him is to have concrete proof he's behind all this."

"So what do you suggest?"

"Give him a perfect opportunity to do something more, and get it on video," James explains.

"Do you think Mrs. Lee is part of this?" Mom interrupts quietly. "Did I make a mistake bringing her on board?"

I'm across the room in the blink of an eye. Jeannie takes one of Mom's hands in hers.

"Mrs. Lee never knew he tried blackmailing me," Ben assures. "And honestly, she would never risk her or her company's reputation like this."

I smile gratefully at him. Grace slips her hand into his, and he relaxes against her. Jeannie and I exchange a look before she turns to James with a determined set to her jaw.

"What can we do to help?"

• • • • •

Our plan is put in motion before everyone gathers for the next round of competition. After letting Chef Anthony in on the situation, he agrees to help us spring the trap. Jeannie texts Nathan, pretending to be too busy to meet up because the contest is almost finished. The night before bake day, she texts and asks him to stop by the bakeshop so they can spend some time together. Luckily, he agrees.

• • • • •

In the morning, everyone gathers around the table in the prep room. A short time later, we hear Jeannie's voice in the hall.

"I just need to grab my purse," she says. "You mind coming with me?"

"Sure, babe."

Jeannie enters first, her face etched with tension. Nathan steps in a second behind her, and his eyes go wide when he sees we're all inside.

"Nathan?" Mrs. Lee scowls. "What are you doing here?"

"Er . . . Mom! I . . . I . . ." he stammers. "Remember how you wanted me to take some summer courses to catch up on my credits? Well, I found some down here that I could take since I was in town for a shoot."

I can tell Mrs. Lee is gearing up to yell at him for not telling her sooner, but Mom distracts her by explaining Ben has been disqualified for stealing the recipe book and trashing the bakeshop.

Mrs. Lee's hand covers her mouth. "Are you sure it was him? I've known him and his family for a long time. He's not the type to cause this sort of trouble."

I peer at Nathan, and my blood boils at the smirk on his face.

Mom leans against the table. "I'm afraid so. He's the only person who had the opportunity and time. One of Chef Anthony's students came forward and told us she saw him in the building thirty minutes earlier than he said he was. Plus, while the rest of us were trying to piece together what happened, Ben excused himself to go to the bathroom. That's when my recipe book went missing."

"Did you ask him why he did it?" Mrs. Lee asks.

"All he would say is that he wanted to get back at Nathan for what happened before."

"What do you mean?" She turns to her son. "What happened? I thought you two were back on good terms."

Nathan manages an innocent shrug. While I'm glad Mrs. Lee doesn't know anything, seeing how easily he manipulated everyone makes me even angrier.

"I tried to get Ben to say more," Chef Anthony adds with a shake of his head. "But he clammed up after I told him I might have to press charges for the damage he caused."

Mrs. Lee's eyes harden. "And James?"

"He wasn't involved. Ben acted alone," Mom affirms.

Mrs. Lee is less than convinced, but she relents. "What does that mean for us today?"

"I'd like to get ahead of the negative publicity." Mom presses a hand to her temple. "It's only a matter of time before word gets out about what happened."

Chef Anthony jumps in and offers the suggestion we practiced with him early this morning.

"In that case, since we only have three remaining contestants, how would you feel about making the technical the semifinal round? That way, we can have the highlight as the final and crown a winner before anyone catches wind of the situation."

Mom pretends to consider it before reluctantly agreeing with a heavy sigh.

"I don't see any other choice, unless you can think of something, Mrs. Lee."

"I'm just here to judge," Mrs. Lee defers. "Whatever you think is best."

There's not a hint of malice in her reply. I glance between Mom and her. It's nice to see the competition has turned them from enemies to friendly competitors over the past weeks.

"We should give them time to prepare. Not to mention for us to make the necessary changes," Mom states as she walks over to Chef Anthony. "Maybe we should delay the bake until this afternoon."

"Sounds fair. I guess there's nothing left but to update the contestants," he replies.

We file out of the room in somber silence, and I stick to the back of the group as we head toward the bakeshop. Jeannie and Nathan are walking directly in front of me. I'm proud of how well she's holding up, considering I'm one domino away from full-on collapse.

Jeannie whispers something in Nathan's ear with a giggle, never giving away the fact that she knows exactly what kind of person he is.

"Oh, really?"

Predictably, he glances over his shoulder and waves me toward them.

"Come on, Liza! Keep up!"

I pick up my pace and force myself not to cringe when he throws an arm over my shoulder.

"Jeannie tells me you've got something special planned for the last technical."

"Yeah. I was saving it for the final, but since we're cutting things short, it'll make it easy to weed out the weakest contestant."

"Who do you think will win?" Jeannie prompts.

I count five steps before answering. "Things could always change, but I think James will take it."

Nathan's eyes jerk back to me. "James? How do you figure?"

"Well, I know he didn't win the bread challenge, but of the three bakers left, he's been the most consistent."

"That's true, and we both know how much Mom loves consistency," Jeannie adds in a stage-whisper.

I don't need to read Nathan's mind to see the wheels turning in his head right now.

"What about Sammy?" he asks. "He won the bread challenge. Or Edward?"

I scoff. "I think Sammy got lucky last time. As for Edward, he's a solid third place. It would take a lot to knock James off the podium."

Nathan's eyes dart over to Mom, and a frown deepens on his face. We arrive at the bakeshop, and Jeannie tugs him inside. Chef Anthony announces us in order; I enter last. My eyes immediately lock on James. I wink at him, knowing Nathan's watching us from the sidelines. Though it's for show, my heart flutters at his smile.

"Contestants, families, and friends," Mom begins. "In the five years since I created this contest, we've never faced as many challenges as we have this time around. Unfortunately, I must announce more bad news. After a thorough investigation, we've determined contestant number nine, Ben Chan, was responsible for sabotaging last week's challenge. As such, he has been disqualified."

A round of gasps circles the room. Predictably, many in the audience turn to James, who does an admirable job of appearing utterly stunned while standing behind his station.

"While I know this is shocking news, the show must go on. With only three contestants remaining, however, Mrs. Lee and I have agreed to make this bake the last of the competition."

"How's that going to work?" Edward asks with concern.

"We will use the technical challenge as our semifinal round. The top two bakers will then move on to the final highlight. Since this change is being made at the last minute, we will delay the start of the bake until two o'clock this afternoon. Take the extra time to prepare if you need, but don't forget to have a good lunch. Good luck."

No one moves at first. Then Jeannie urges Nathan to stand up and leave, which triggers a wave of activity toward the door. The family members file out first, since they're closest to the door, followed by the bakers. I suppress a smile when Edward grabs Sarah's hand in clear view of Mom. Once the room clears, Mrs. Lee is the first of the staff to leave, followed by Chef Anthony. Mom and I walk out last, arm in arm.

"Do you think it'll work?" she says under her breath.

"Definitely. He's plotting something."

"Is everything set up?"

"Yep. They're ready and waiting."

We head out to the parking lot. With Nathan standing nearby, Chef Anthony feigns forgetting to lock the front doors of the building. He waves goodbye and leaves, while the rest of us debate where to go for brunch. Nathan begs off with a sudden stomachache.

"Do you want me to drive you back to your Airbnb?" Jeannie offers.

"No, no," he groans, a hand on his stomach. "You go with your family. I can drive myself."

"Are you sure?"

"Positive. Go enjoy brunch for me."

We keep on our masks of sympathy until he's pulled out of the parking lot. James steps out of the building once we let him know it's safe. Ben and Grace then hop out of her car to join us.

"I've got the camera on record," Ben tells us. "We'll catch him if he tries anything."

"He will. There's no way he can resist," James answers.

"In the meantime, I'm starving," Dad blurts out. "How about we head to the restaurant and I'll cook?"

The suggestion earns him enthusiastic replies. Mom agrees to let me ride with Grace and the guys, but I try not to look too thrilled. I hop into the back, and James links our hands as soon as he gets in the car. He also leans in for a kiss, but I push him back over to his side.

"My mom's watching."

He pouts. "How do you know?"

"Trust me."

In that very moment, Dad drives by us. Mom stares directly into the car, her eagle eyes searching for inappropriate behavior.

I burst out laughing. "Told ya."

"Phew! That was close."

Once my parents are out of view, I slide across the seat and cup his cheeks, bringing our faces within inches of each other with a grin.

"Not as close as this."

Without warning, James closes the distance and presses his lips against mine. I don't resist when he kisses me a second time and giggle when he plants one on the tip of my nose as well. Ben groans loudly from the driver's seat.

"Can't you guys save it for later?"

We break apart and laugh. James makes a face at his cousin.

"Don't be jealous. You volunteered to drive."

"Speaking of which," Grace reminds us all, "we should get going before Nathan catches us in the parking lot."

The thought is sobering, and I scoot back to my side. Once we arrive at Yin and Yang, Ben gets out, his laptop tucked under one arm and Grace under the other. Jeannie opens the door so we can head inside and locks it behind us. Dad scurries through the curtains to start cooking. Meanwhile, Mom heads into the bakery kitchen but shoos me away when I come near.

"It's a surprise," she says.

My eyebrows shoot up, but I know better than to question her. Instead, I join everyone else at one of the round tables usually reserved for large parties.

Dad really outdoes himself, pulling together a four-course

brunch in less than thirty minutes. When the food is ready, Jeannie and I help carry out all the dishes. Then, we sit around the table to eat.

"This is delicious," Ben tells him a few bites later. "Better than my mom makes, but don't tell her."

James nods. "He's right. This three-cup chicken tastes exactly like the *sānbēijī* I ate during a trip to Taiwan. Maybe better."

Grace doesn't bother with words, her enthusiastic request for seconds a compliment in itself. Mom disappears about halfway through the meal, and within fifteen minutes, the aroma of freshly baked pastries wafts over to us.

"What did you make, Mrs. Yang?" Grace asks, her eyes lighting up. "Please tell me it's your custard buns."

Mom grins. "It's my custard buns."

"Yes!" Grace whoops.

Ben raises an eyebrow. "That good, huh?"

"Wait until you taste them. They're the best things *ever*."

Mom proves her right when she brings them out in baskets to share. I gently pull mine in half to release the steam and let it cool. Then I pop it in my mouth, savoring the softness of the white dough mixed with the lightly sweet yellow custard inside.

"Ugh," Ben groans after devouring what's left of his bun. "This *is* the best."

I peer over at James, curious how he'll judge them. His eyes close briefly as he chews. When he swallows, he tips his head toward me.

"Can you make these?"

"Of course I can. My mom taught me years ago."

He stares deep into my eyes. "Marry me."

Chopsticks clatter onto the table. I don't need to see who dropped them. Thankfully, Mom knows he's joking.

I slap James on the arm. "You keep that up, and she'll make sure you're stuck with me forever."

"I could live with that," he quips.

I feel my cheeks flush at his playful grin. Ben comes to my rescue, or at least, his laptop does. He set it up on the next table over, and it's going off, alerting us that the surveillance system has been triggered. All conversations cease as we huddle around to watch the feed. Nathan steps into view, clear as day, and heads straight for James's workstation. He sifts through the ingredients for the technical before removing several key ingredients and pocketing them. Then he covers everything back up with the cloth and sneaks out of the room.

Ben grins. "Bingo."

He saves the clip into a separate file and closes the laptop. Jeannie's face crumples, and she excuses herself quickly. I start to go after her, but Mom puts up a hand.

"I'll take care of her. You finish eating."

My nerves have returned, and they chase away my appetite. Nevertheless, I force the rest of my food down before helping Dad clear the table. Then we all head back to the culinary school. Chef Anthony is already on site, and we all step back inside.

When Mrs. Lee arrives in the break room, Mom pulls her aside to talk privately. As their hushed whispers give way to aggravated tones, it's clear whatever camaraderie they'd built over the past weeks is fading fast.

"Are you trying to get rid of your competition? Is that why you're doing this?" Mrs. Lee fumes. "Because I'll tell you now it's not going to work. Accusing my son of something like this is only going to earn you a lawsuit."

To Mom's credit, she remains calm. "Mrs. Lee, if that was my intention, don't you think I'd find a better way than sabotaging my own contest?"

"But you said this was Ben's doing!" Mrs. Lee jabs a finger in his direction. "You told everyone."

"Yes, I did, because it was the only way to confirm who the real culprit was," Mom replies. "We needed time to gather the evidence."

Mrs. Lee pales. "Evidence?"

Mom sighs and gestures for her to sit. "Let me show you."

Mrs. Lee sinks into the seat while Ben cues up the video. We stand behind her, clustered together, as she watches. When she sees Nathan grab the ingredients, Mrs. Lee gasps and clutches her chest, her face etched with shock.

"I can't believe it's really him. Please accept my apologies, Mrs. Yang. I don't know why Nathan did any of this, but if I had known, I would have stopped him. I hope you believe me."

Mom lays a hand on her shoulder. "I believe you. We're planning to confront him with the footage, Mrs. Lee. I'll understand if you'd rather not be here for it."

"No, I'll stay. He's my son, and my responsibility." Mrs. Lee turns to Chef Anthony. "Please send me the bill for everything he damaged. I'll take care of it."

He nods. With the first reveal out of the way, we take our places and brace for what's to come. Mom turns to Jeannie.

"Are you sure you can do this?"

"Yes. I need to make this right for Ben."

"Okay. We'll be here when you get back."

She leaves to find Nathan. A few minutes later, we hear them in the hall. Jeannie's voice is tinged with anxiety, but Nathan doesn't seem to notice. He's the first to walk into the room.

"What's so important I have to—"

His eyes land on Ben and James. He stiffens, his hands forming fists at his sides. When Mrs. Lee steps forward, however, the hard, angry look in his eyes softens into fear. Her normally polished demeanor has given way to fury, and she glowers at him with the death glare all Asian kids recognize.

"Nathan George Lee, what were you thinking?! Do you have any idea how ashamed I am of you right now?"

He backs against the wall. "Mom, they're lying! I didn't do anything!"

"Don't you dare try to deny it. I saw the video of you stealing ingredients off James's workstation."

To prove her point, she presses play on Ben's laptop. Nathan's face turns ashen as the proof of his guilt plays out in front of him.

"If you think I'm mad, wait until your dad finds out what you've been up to," Mrs. Lee threatens. "You can kiss your expense account goodbye."

"But this is *his* fault." He explodes, pointing at Ben, then James. "And his too."

"Stop blaming everyone else for your bad decisions, son. It's my fault. I've spoiled you for so long, but not anymore." Mrs. Lee crosses her arms over her chest. "This time, you risked our family's reputation. We could have had a lawsuit on our hands!"

Nathan balks. "What about Dad? What about him cheating on you with Ben's mom? If it wasn't for her, we'd still be a family!"

Mrs. Lee flushes, her eyes darting from face to face. Every major ad campaign for Mama Lee Bakeries has her loving husband standing by her side. I clued Mom and Dad in to the divorce already, so they don't react. To his credit, Chef Anthony manages to keep his expression blank.

Mrs. Lee glares at Nathan. "I don't know where you got that idea from, but that never happened. Your father and I decided to split up for other reasons—ones I will *not* discuss right now."

Nathan, getting no sympathy from his mother, grabs on to Jeannie for support.

"Babe, you have to believe me. They forced me to do this. It's their fault!"

She shrugs his hand off her arm and walks over to the door.

"Well, I'm not being forced to do this. Nathan, we're done," she says.

Jeannie gestures to the open doorway, but Nathan doesn't leave. Not yet. Blotches of red mar his even complexion as he lunges toward James. Ben steps between them at the last minute, giving Mrs. Lee a chance to clamp a hand on to her son's arm.

"You've embarrassed us enough already. Leave right now. I'll deal with you later."

"But, Mom—"

"Now!"

He rushes out of the room, humiliated. It's only then that Mrs. Lee slumps against the table and covers her face with her hands. Mom sits down beside her.

"Would you like me to push the baking to tomorrow?"

"No, thank you," Mrs. Lee replies after a pause. "Let's go ahead and finish."

After composing herself, she joins the rest of us in walking back to the bakeshop. Excitement and nervousness are palpable in the air as we enter. Chef Anthony steps forward, raking his eyes across the room.

"It's time."

# Chapter 26

There's less than a half hour left of our final technical challenge—dessert jelly. Inspired by the agar cake I made in New York, I created a recipe based off *yōkan*. In addition to the two different colored layers of jelly, it must be flavored with red bean and milk with chunks of strawberries mixed in. To make it even more difficult, the dessert needs to be light while still holding its shape.

Before we began, all of James's missing ingredients were replaced. Since Ben wanted to be in the audience to support him, he snuck in after time began and sat in the back row. I'm pretty sure some of the other mothers noticed him, but Grace glared at them until they went back to minding their own business.

I'm glad we're finally nearing the end of the bake because my patience is at its end as well. Mom grabs my knee to stop me from squirming in the chair for the hundredth time.

"Which two contestants do you think will pass your challenge?" she asks.

"James, definitely," I answer honestly. "It's a toss-up between the other two, but my money's on Sammy."

"You don't think Edward can do it?"

Despite giving James her approval, Mom apparently hasn't let go of the hope of matching me with a future doctor. Even the way he keeps smiling at Sarah hasn't been enough to deter her.

I shrug. "It's always possible. There is a science to getting the right consistency. If Edward times it right, he could win it."

Chef Anthony's voice rings out into the hallway a second later.

"Ten seconds left, contestants! You have ten seconds left!"

Mom and I stand just outside the door as our host counts down.

"Time, gentlemen! Move away from your jellies!"

Once the three plates are transferred to the table, we walk in and face the remaining contestants. Only one of the jellies is perfectly set. It's easy to assume it belongs to James, but I do my best not to jump to conclusions. After all, Sammy surprised us all last time. We start with the dish on the far right. It's held its shape, but tiny cracks in the jelly reveal that it was pushed out of the mold rather than carefully removed. When I press the fork into it, it bows ever so slightly.

"It's just a hair too soft for this type of yōkan," I conclude. "However, it looks pretty good, and the flavors are well balanced."

Mom nods in agreement, and we move on to the second jelly. Rather than a pert, bouncy dessert, the yōkan has spread across the plate like Jabba the Hutt. Mom pokes at what remains of the saggy jelly.

"This baker struggled a lot. It wasn't given enough time to set, which means the flavors have melded together. On the plus side, it does still taste like it should."

The last one is by far the best looking, with the right firmness and chew. The flavors are distinct in each layer but also come together beautifully.

"This is exactly how it should look and taste." I turn to Mom. "What do you think?"

"I agree. Whoever made this knew what they were doing."

The deliberation is pretty much already done, so we go ahead and rank the jellies. I'm glad we didn't bet on the winner because I would have lost. It's Sammy's jelly we loved the most, followed by James, and then Edward. I quirk an eyebrow at James, who grins sheepishly.

"I'm sorry, Edward," Mom says gently. "You had a great run, but unfortunately, you are eliminated from the finals. Congratulations, James and Sammy. You are our finalists."

Edward's face falls, but he puts a broad smile on and bows in our direction.

"Thank you all for the opportunity. I wish both James and Sammy good luck."

We give him a round of applause as he walks over to his mom in the audience. She gives him a comforting pat on the back as he plops into the seat next to her. Sarah surreptitiously slides onto the chair on Edward's other side, and he sneaks his hand into hers. She catches me looking at them and blushes. I guess it's official now.

Chef Anthony raises his hand to get everyone's attention.

"Let's take a quick break. Make sure you get back in time because the final is next!"

He ushers everyone out of the room quickly so we can get set up one last time. Gloria and the other students have the stations cleared off and cleaned within minutes. Mom and I then rearrange everything by going through the lists of ingredients Sammy and James gave us for their highlights. When we give Chef Anthony the signal, he escorts everyone back in. As soon as we're all in position, the final bake begins.

With Mom and Mrs. Lee set to judge like usual, I head over to sit with Grace and Jeannie along the wall. This puts Sarah directly behind me, and she taps me on the shoulder. I swivel halfway in my chair as she leans over.

"Is everything okay? I was really worried after you ran off the other day. I know you said you were busy with all this, but . . ."

With all the chaos surrounding the last few days, I'd completely forgotten to tell Sarah what happened. As if in sync, several people in the audience shift in their seats to listen in on our conversation.

"I'm sorry I haven't been in touch," I answer in a low voice. "We should get together after this and catch up. All of us."

Sarah smiles, leaning closer and dropping her voice down to a whisper.

"By the way, I wanted to tell you what Edward told me. He said he only joined the contest for his mom. He refused to date an Asian girl she picked for him, so she pressured him into competing."

Oh, the irony.

"Well, I'm glad he made his own decision this time," I remark after sneaking a peek at James.

"But what if his mom doesn't approve of me?" Sarah asks, eyes brimming with worry.

"Don't think like that. Remember, you're smart, kind, and amazing. That's why Edward likes you. You'll win her over. It just might take some time."

"Are you speaking from experience?"

My eyes drift over to Mom. She's strolling between James's and Sammy's stations with arms folded across her chest, watching them like a vulture.

I smile. "You could say that."

"Well, that answers one of my questions," Sarah answers, giggling.

I poke her on the arm. "Speaking of which, don't forget you can always ask me questions. Grace, too."

"I will. I promise. I really want to learn more about Asian culture." She pauses and shakes her head. "I mean, cultures. Plural."

"That's definitely a good start."

Sarah turns back to Edward when he taps her on the arm. Our eyes meet for a brief second, and he offers a faint smile. I grin before turning my attention back to the bakers.

James is all technique and precision with his coffee and cream jelly. He's bent over his station in fierce concentration, measuring and slicing each layer with knives and rulers. I bite back a sigh. Nothing makes my heart race like a guy who knows how to bake.

Except for maybe a really hot guy who knows how to bake.

As if to prove my point, James applies gentle pressure to the grid slicer to cut his finished jelly. A shiver runs down my back when the tool slides out without disturbing a single square. James meets my eye and winks before turning away to plate his highlight.

Boba tea sounds really good right now. With extra ice.

I force my gaze over to Sammy and his three-layer rainbow jelly cake. Dyes are spread all over his table, and his apron is covered in splashes of bright color. He pours the different combinations into his mold, eyeing his proportions rather than weighing it all out. His instinctual baking style is utterly entertaining, and I find myself cheering him on.

The two of them reach the end of the bake in what feels like minutes, instead of the three hours allotted for this final highlight. Both James and Sammy plate their jelly at the last minute possible to ensure a clean presentation. When Chef Anthony calls time, James walks over to Sammy, and they shake hands. Mom and Mrs. Lee step up to taste their final highlights. James is first.

"The layers are identical in shape and size," Mom observes in an awed voice. "It looks like it was cut and put together by a machine."

After tasting, Mrs. Lee is the first to offer her opinion. There isn't an ounce of disdain in her expression.

"I am a self-professed coffee snob, and this tastes just like the cakes from my favorite shop. You even managed to mimic the foam on top. Delicious. Great job, James."

He's clearly not expecting such praise from her, but he recovers and murmurs a thanks. James trades places with Sammy. He's carved his jelly cake in the shape of Texas, even marking Houston's location by hollowing out a star.

"You really pushed yourself on this highlight," Mrs. Lee comments. "I count . . . four, five, six distinct colors in your jellies?"

"Yes, and they're each a different flavor," Sammy replies, chest puffed out.

"Really? Well, let's dig in, then."

As they each take a bite, the two judges exchange identical looks of appreciation. Mom even goes back a second time before critiquing it.

"You've surprised me again, Sammy. I expected to be overwhelmed with too many flavors, but you managed to pick ones that blend beautifully together. And the extra effort in cutting it into the shape of Texas? Very nice!"

Sammy floats back to his station with a giant, toothy grin. With the judging complete, Chef Anthony addresses the room.

"Both our bakers delivered amazing pieces today, and I don't envy the judges for the job they have to do now. Mrs. Yang, Mrs. Lee, you may leave to deliberate."

Once they're gone, Ben turns to Grace and me with an anxious expression.

"Who do you think will win?"

I already know the answer but decide it's more fun to wait and see their reactions. Sammy moves over to chat with his family, and James strolls over to us. To avoid any accusations, he stands close to me but doesn't take my hand.

"Congratulations, James," Grace offers with a smile. "They really liked your cake. I hope you win."

James tugs at his collar and takes a deep breath. "Grace, you deserve an apology. What I did was wrong, and I know it really hurt you. I hope you'll forgive me."

"Has Ben forgiven you?"

Her question takes him off guard. James glances over at Ben before answering.

"Um, yes?"

"Then I forgive you too. But only if you promise to keep a certain person happy."

He's careful not to look my way, but he grins. "That's a promise I don't mind making."

The judges walk back into the room then, cutting off the rest of our conversation. James and Sammy position themselves at the front of the room, and Mrs. Lee and Mom stand on either side of them. Though I've already guessed who they've chosen, I'm still excited for it to be official.

"The judges have made their decision," Chef Anthony proclaims loudly. "And the winner of the Fifth Annual Yin and Yang Junior Baking Competition, the one who will receive the scholarship and private lessons at Yin and Yang Bakery and Restaurant, is . . ."

He pauses for effect. It's so quiet you can almost hear their hearts pounding, and the entire room leans in to hear the answer.

"Sammy Ma!"

Sammy's frozen in place as his family starts whistling and screaming. James gives him a clap on the back before stepping aside. Mom hands him the glass trophy, and Mrs. Lee steps up with an oversized novelty check.

"Sammy, in addition to your trophy and bragging rights, I'm delighted to give you this fifteen-thousand-dollar scholarship check to the college of your choosing. We see great things in your future."

Sammy beams through a series of photos with Mom, Mrs. Lee, and Chef Anthony. His family runs up to embrace him, crying and laughing at his win. It reminds me of how excited I was whenever I won a baking contest. Mom must be thinking along the same lines because our eyes meet across the room.

I smile.

She does too, and for once, there's only pride in her eyes.

● ● ● ● ●

After the celebrations are over, everyone convenes in the cafeteria, where Dad, Danny, and Tina have set up a little celebration to thank Chef Anthony and all the students who helped with this year's contest. Two rectangular tables have been pushed together, lined with catering trays brimming with Dad's most popular dishes. There are also gift bags containing an assortment of Mom's pastries on the far end.

As Mom and I are filling up our plates, Chef Anthony walks over and shakes Mom's hand.

"Mrs. Yang, it was quite the roller coaster this year, but it was a ton of fun too. I hope you'll come back and visit us next year."

"Thank you, for everything," she tells him. "We couldn't have pulled this off without you."

He smiles warmly at Mrs. Lee. "It was a pleasure meeting and getting to know you. I would love for you to consider mentoring some of my students."

"I'd be happy to," she answers, handing him a business card. "Contact my people, and we'll work something out."

He puts a hand on my shoulder and peers down at me. "Speaking of which, Liza, you really impressed me this year. If you ever decide you'd like to give culinary school a try, you've got a spot here."

My eyes fly immediately to Mom and Dad standing by the lockers. I'm happy neither of them is scowling, but I know better than to assume anything more.

"I'm so honored, Chef Anthony. Thank you so much for the offer."

"You're welcome. Now it's time for me to go check on my students."

He heads over to where they are sitting a few tables away. Mrs. Lee turns to Mom.

"I must admit, this was by far the most unpredictable competition I have ever judged. However, you handled it far better than most professionals I've worked with. Thank you for the opportunity . . . and for your discretion regarding my son's behavior."

"Children make mistakes. It's our job to guide them," says Mom graciously. "I hope you'll accept my invitation to judge again next year. I've learned a great deal from you."

"And I, you." She turns to Dad and me with a smile. "If you'll excuse me, I have a naughty child to punish."

Once Mom is satisfied we've left nothing behind, we head for the parking lot. Dad and Jeannie have gone to get the car, and Ben, Grace, and James are waiting for me off to the side. At the top of the stairs, Mom tugs on my elbow.

"Liza, I want to talk to you about something."

I tense instinctively. "What did I do this time?"

Confusion and then regret flits across Mom's features before a smile rises to her lips.

"I know I put a lot of pressure on you this year. And I admit I wasn't sure if you could handle it, but you proved me wrong. I'm really proud of you."

That's it? No "but this" or "you need to do that"? Warmth spreads through me like honey.

"Oh, one more thing. About Chef Anthony's offer."

My heart stutters, and I sigh. She could have given me a few more seconds to enjoy that moment.

"I know," I say, eyes dropping to the ground. "I need to go to college and choose a stable career. I got it."

"That's not quite what I was going to say."

Mom tips my chin up so I'll meet her eye. "Yes, Dad and I want you to go to college, but we understand how much you love baking now. We'll talk things over with Chef Anthony, but I can't make any promises, okay?"

I may or may not black out in that moment. Either way, Mom doesn't give me a chance to ask any questions, descending the stairs and getting into the car with Dad and Jeannie. Before they pull away, though, she pokes her head out the window.

"Don't be out too late, understand?"

I bob my head and continue to do so long after they're gone. Eventually, I give myself a shake and head down to meet up with the others. James throws an arm over my shoulders.

"You okay?"

"Um, yeah. I'm really good, actually."

We stand together in the near empty parking lot for a few seconds longer before I twist to look up at him.

"So," I say, "why'd you do it?"

He pulls back. "Do what?"

"You know what. Why'd you mess up your technical?"

"How do you know that's what I did?"

I scoff. "Come on. I've been watching you bake for weeks. If anything, you're too much of a perfectionist to make a mistake like that."

I stare him down until he relents with an easy smile.

"Sammy's a good guy. He wants to go to the University of Houston, but his parents don't have a lot of money."

"So you made sure he would win. Because that means he would get the scholarship."

James shakes his head. "Sammy made an amazing jelly. Between that and bread day, I'm pretty sure he would have won anyway."

Surprisingly, I agree. Mom's nothing if not a stickler for good bread, and it would have given Sammy the edge he needed in the end.

Ben suggests we head to the car, so the four of us make our way across the asphalt.

"Besides, I didn't need the money," James admits with a nonchalant shrug. "My parents can afford whichever school I choose."

"Have you decided where you're going, then?" I ask, voice wavering as we reach the car.

"Haven't you guessed?" He smiles down at me softly. "Rice, of course. Although I haven't told my dad I'm not declaring a major right away. I want to figure things out for myself . . . for once."

I throw myself into James's arms, catching him off guard as I kiss him hard. His eyes nearly bulge out of his head.

"What was that for?"

"For being you."

James gives me the special smile again, the one with his dimple. He tugs me in for another kiss before finally letting me go. Not wanting to be left out, Ben kisses Grace soundly before tipping his head to the side. Then he unlocks the doors, and we climb into the car.

He turns to look at each of us. "So, where to?"

We glance at one another. There's only one answer to that question.

"Boba Life!"

# Chapter 27

"Are you paying attention?"

I throw James an irritated glance. We're alone in the back kitchen of the bakery, something Mom only allowed because she needed to get set up for Eastern Sun Bank's charity festival tonight. James is supposed to be learning how to create flowers in a raindrop cake, but I've been talking to myself. Instead, he's been staring at his phone for the last twenty minutes. Judging by the way he's scrolling, he's online shopping.

I sigh and put the syringe of colored gelatin back into its cup. "James."

He doesn't hear me, engrossed in whatever item he's staring at. "James!"

His head snaps up this time, instantly contrite when he realizes what he's missed. James tucks the phone into his pocket and comes around the stainless steel table. When he reaches for me, I shake him off with narrowed eyes.

"You know, if you were going to play around during these private lessons, you shouldn't have accepted them from Sammy."

"That was nice of him to offer," James agrees, smirking. "Although I admit I might have said something to convince him."

"Then all the more reason to pay attention."

"I'm sorry, Bun. I didn't mean to ignore you."

James tries to dimple his way into convincing me to forgive him, but the smile has no luster for me today.

I cross my arms over my chest. "What can you possibly be looking at that's so interesting, anyway?"

He starts to answer but suddenly squints at me.

"You know," he replies, dragging out the words, "you kind of remind me of your mom right now."

I choke on the insult. "Get out."

"Oh, come on, Bun . . ."

*"Get out."*

He stares at me with puppy eyes until I waver a tiny bit, then swoops in and captures my lips in a kiss. We've shared so many over the last few months, but it always feels new. In fact, we're getting better at turning up the heat. My arms snake up his neck, fingers threading through his hair as he pulls me ever closer. I'm so focused on the way his hands roam down to my hips I nearly miss the buzzing oven timer.

"Oh! It's gonna burn!"

I throw on the mitts and run over to pop the doors open. A few minutes later, the tray has been safely transferred onto the cooling rack, and I breathe a sigh of a relief. I head back to the table, where both a batch of unfinished mango milk custard buns and my demo raindrop cake are sitting.

I'm not even trying to think about the fact that we're launching my baking recipe book tonight. Dad helped me self-publish it, and I was shocked when Mom ordered copies to sell at the bakery. I was even more surprised when Chef Anthony offered to keep some in the BCCI gift shop too. He even sponsored me for some of next year's summer courses. I couldn't wait to tell James.

That reminds me of what I'm juggling to give him these lessons. My annoyance returns.

"Let's just stop for today. You'd rather be on your phone, and I need to get these buns baked for Eastern Sun Bank's charity festival tonight."

He cocks an eyebrow. "What's the drive for again?"

"You should know," I chide him as I scoop custard into a pastry bag. "Your uncle's donating the proceeds to local elementary school libraries for books and author events."

"That's very noble of him."

"Yes, and I need to get these done in the next hour for our booth. So why don't you go meet up with Ben and Grace so I can finish?"

I turn my attention back to the baking. As I pick up a bun to fill, he sidles up next to me.

"How many of these do you have left to make?"

I stop and do a quick count. "This batch and one more."

"How about I help?"

I eye him up and down. "You'll get those nice clothes dirty."

"Hmm. I guess you're right."

I'm instantly suspicious of the mischievous smirk on his face. He tugs his shirt out of his pants and unbuttons it, shrugging it off and giving me an eyeful of his bare chest.

"You can't bake like that!" I sputter. "It's not . . . sanitary."

James feigns a sigh and grabs hold of a nearby apron. After securing it around his waist, he does a little twirl.

"Ta-da! Problem solved. Now tell me what I need to do."

The buns take twice as long as they should to make, mostly because I keep gawking at my boyfriend. He certainly doesn't help, spending a great deal of time flexing his muscles as he kneads the dough. By the time we're done, I'm wound tighter than the elastic band holding my hair back. The devilish glint in his brown eyes only infuriates me more.

Well, two can play at this game.

"Will you help me deliver these buns to the booth?" I ask casually. "Mom wanted to go make sure my book is displayed properly."

"Of course."

I wrap each bun carefully in cellophane and lay them in the largest paper box we have. I then tape the top and side flaps and send him on his way. The minute his car pulls out of the plaza, I jump into action. I grab the clothes I brought from home and change before putting the finishing touches on my face using the makeup bag Jeannie left for me. My hair is the last step, and once I'm finished, I take a look at my reflection.

While trees are changing color in other parts of the country, it still feels like summer in Houston. The skin at my waist peeks out from beneath my blush lace crop top, and I've paired it with a pleated black skirt and my favorite white sneakers. I've also left my hair down this time, with rose gold bobby pins glinting off my black locks. Another layer of lip gloss later, I'm done.

I dash back into the kitchen to wait for James to pick me up. While I'm there, my phone goes off. It's a text from Jeannie.

**Good luck tonight! I'm sorry I couldn't be there.**

I smile. When Jeannie went back to New York, she decided to quit modeling and finally declared a major—psychology. She said she was inspired by what I said to her about being such a good listener. Even though she was super nervous to tell our parents, they had nothing but encouraging things to say.

**Thanks, sis. Miss you.**

I snap a quick picture of my outfit and send it to her.

**Very nice!** she texts back. **Jeannie approved.**

**BTW, tell Brandon I said hi.**

Brandon's her new boyfriend. They met right after she moved into the new condo Ben's mom found her.

**Will do. Gotta run. Talk later!**

Another text pops up right before I lock my phone. This one's from Sarah.

**Get your butt over here! We're starving, and Edward's dying to try those buns!**

The bell over the front door jingles as James enters the shop. I send Sarah a quick reply and tuck my phone into my back pocket. Then I grab a cloth and pretend to clean.

"I'm back, L—"

He makes a choked sound. I glance up innocently, secretly reveling at the look on his face.

"Oh, good! I'm ready to go."

I brush past him, purposely trailing my fingers lightly up his arm as I make my way to the door. I'm barely through the curtain before he twirls me around and tugs me against him. I fight the urge to sink into him.

"We've gotta go, James. It's my big night, remember? Everyone's probably waiting."

"Liza."

I'm the one ignoring him this time, counting the steps to freedom.

"Liza."

I keep moving, even though the air crackles like the top of a bo luo bun. I reach for the door and dash out. His footsteps are no match for the pounding of my heart, but he catches up with me nonetheless. James doesn't let me escape this time, spinning me to face him as he backs me against the car. I giggle as he reaches up to twirl a lock of my hair around his finger.

"Are you punishing me for earlier?"

I bat my lashes as I play with one of the buttons on his shirt.

"Actually, I figured since you'd rather be dating your phone, I'd find myself a new boyfriend."

"*Liza.*"

James whispers my name and presses closer, the aroma of mangos and butter flooding my nostrils. I resist the temptation to inhale deeply.

"Do you know why I was on my phone today?"

I jut out my chin. "Do you know my knee is at the perfect angle to inflict bodily injury?"

James laughs and backs away, hands up in surrender.

"Okay, okay, fine, but before you do that . . ."

He unlocks the driver's side door and reaches down to retrieve a blue-and-white Tiffany box.

"I was on my phone because I was checking to make sure this was delivered to Ben's house."

"You're buying gifts for Ben now?"

He makes an exasperated sound. "Just open it."

I purposely drag things out for another minute before reaching into the felt pouch. I pull out a silver charm bracelet with a minia-ture cupcake charm and a small Tiffany's heart tag dangling from its links.

"Turn it around."

I gasp when I see our initials engraved on the back. He helps me put it on and then smiles sweetly at me.

"Happy sixth-month anniversary."

As touched as I am, I eye him suspiciously. "We've only officially been dating for five months."

"I know, but it's six months since I met you in the parking lot at Salvis. I knew that day I wanted to be with you."

"How did you know?"

"Because you didn't hide your feelings from me, even if it meant telling me I was a jerk. Almost everyone I've known has always agreed with everything I said and did. They didn't really care about me. They only cared about my family's money and the connections we had."

I stare deep into his eyes, marveling at the once-hidden depths within them. To think I was so determined to paint him a villain I nearly overlooked all the pieces that didn't fit.

Now, that would have been a recipe for disaster.

I shrug. "Well, I can't make any promises when it comes to my mom, but I'm not interested in those things."

"So you wouldn't dump me if all I could do was bake?"

I grab hold of his collar and yank his head down for a kiss.

"Just as long as you remember I like things hot."

As James's fingers graze the bare skin at my waist, he whispers his answer against my lips.

"Now, that I could never forget."

# *Acknowledgments*

This is it.

This is really happening.

Growing up, being published was a dream I held close to my heart, one I rarely ever spoke of. After all, there was no room in life for the uncertainty that came with writing. I was the oldest in my family—the one expected to set the example for my younger brother and become successful so the sacrifices my parents made would not be in vain. So I wrote stories in secret, something I shared only with the anonymous readers whose enthusiasm for them encouraged me to continue.

In the meantime, I studied hard and eventually fulfilled my father's dream of becoming a doctor. He was smart and dedicated enough, but like me, he was the oldest. His mother and brothers needed him, so he gave it up to start working to support them. I will never forget the pride in his eyes the day I walked the stage to receive my medical diploma. The smile on his face was the widest I'd ever seen.

Still, something was missing. I felt restless.

Then one day, a story idea burrowed into the crevices of my mind. I tried ignoring the whispers of characters begging for their stories to be told, turning a blind eye to the images of faraway worlds inviting me to visit. In the end, I couldn't resist. Soon, my fingers were flying across the keyboard, the words flowing as fast as I could put them down.

That was the beginning, and now here we are.

As many other authors have said before, the road to publishing is not an easy one. It can be lonely and isolating, but I've been fortunate enough to be surrounded by some of the most amazing people in the world.

First, to my parents: You've always wanted the best for me, even if sometimes we didn't agree on what that was. You taught me persistence, determination, and patience, but most of all, the importance of challenging yourself. 媽媽, 爸爸, 我非常感謝你們.

To Martin, Stephen, and Shetal. Your love and friendship helped me weather the worst of storms. You were the first to read my stories, and I started this journey because of you. I can't thank you enough.

*A Taste for Love* wouldn't exist if it weren't for my wonderful critique partners. Cass, Pri, Alisha, Tana, Sabina, and Francesca—you all left a little piece of yourself in *ATFL*, and it's so much better for it.

The MSS—a group of the most talented, passionate, and kind writer friends I could ever ask for. Your voices deserve to be heard, and the stories you tell will change the world. Let's continue reaching for the stars together.

Jessica Watterson, my phenomenal agent, cheerleader, and champion. You believed when I doubted, and shined a spotlight on me when I wanted to hide in the shadows. I am forever grateful Thao brought us together, and I can't wait for all the adventures we'll go on next!

To my fabulous editor, Jess Harriton. Thank you for loving this little boba book and giving me the chance to share it with the world. I promise to tempt you with more yummy goodies in the future.

Of course, it takes a whole team of dedicated people to put books on a shelf. Special thanks to Krista Ahlberg, Marinda Valenti, Vanessa DeJesus, Felicity Vallence, Dana Li, and Theresa Evangelista for all your hard work, especially during such a challenging year.

*A Taste for Love* is not just a romance; it's a love letter to a little Taiwanese girl who felt trapped between two worlds. It took a while, but she's finally found where she belongs.

To my readers, I hope Liza's story will inspire you. Life may give you a path to walk, but you can choose the destination. Dream big and believe in yourself. Be afraid, but do it anyway.

Last but not least, always make time for boba.

Courtesy of the author

**JENNIFER YEN** is a Taiwanese American author who lives with her adorable dog in Texas. She spends her days healing the hearts of others and her nights writing about love, family, and the power of acceptance. Jennifer believes in the magic of one's imagination and hopes her stories will bring joy and inspiration to readers. If you find her wandering around aimlessly, please return her to the nearest milk tea shop.

You can connect with her on Twitter and Instagram **@JenYenWrites**, or check out her website at **jenyenwrites.com**.